Zara's Dead

Sharon Butala

Zara's Dead

Coteau Books

© Sharon Butala, 2018

Edited by Lara Hinchberger
Book designed by Tania Craan
Typeset by Susan Buck
Printed and bound in Canada

Library and Archives Canada Cataloguing in Publication

Butala, Sharon, 1940-, author
Zara's dead / Sharon Butala.

Issued in print and electronic format.
ISBN 978-1-55050-947-2 (softcover).–ISBN 978-1-55050-924-3 (PDF).–ISBN 978-1-55050-925-0 (HTML).
–ISBN 978-1-55050-926-7 (Kindle)

I. Title. II. Title: Zara is dead.

PS8553.U6967Z37 2018   C813'.54   C2017-907475-X

2517 Victoria Avenue
Regina, Saskatchewan
Canada S4P 0T2
www.coteaubooks.com

Available in Canada from:
Publishers Group Canada
2440 Viking Way
Richmond, British Columbia
Canada V6V 1N2

10 9 8 7 6 5 4 3 2 1

Coteau Books gratefully acknowledges the financial support of its publishing program by: the Saskatchewan Arts Board, The Canada Council for the Arts, the Government of Saskatchewan through Creative Saskatchewan, the City of Regina. We further acknowledge the [financial] support of the Government of Canada. Nous reconnaissons l'appui [financier] du gouvernement du Canada.

To my Calgary friends

The dress, white with irregular red blossoms on it, lies crumpled on the floor as if torn off heedlessly in the heat of passion or after an exhausting night of dancing. We are in a bedroom; it must be in a basement because there is only one small window, high up to the right of the bed, near the ceiling. The grey morning light passes between a few stiffly bent weeds, illuminating nothing. The bed is torn apart, a quilt lying bunched and twisted on the floor at its foot. Those black shadows on the creased sheet, on the pillows shoved furiously against the wall, on closer examination are not shadows at all, but more of the same wide red flowers that stain the once beautiful silk of the dress that, were it not for its deep neckline, might be a wedding gown.

Chapter One

W hen she finally noticed the brown envelope lying on the sensible grey mat just inside her front door, she was startled, and stared, frozen, as it seemed to grow in size and give off a faint glow, and she looked away quickly, thinking *I need a new mat; I hate being reminded of where I came from.* She glanced back and saw that in the second's interval the envelope had subsided to a commonplace nine by eleven inches, and dulled to the flat ochre of all such envelopes. She slowly let air out through her nose – had she been holding her breath? – and took a tentative step toward it, before halting again, suddenly, thinking, but when did it come? How long had it been lying there?

She noticed she had begun to tremble.

Years she had been waiting for just this moment, maybe as long as a decade. Ever since that casual barbecue at which a nondescript middle-aged former civil servant had said, after hearing the story that, in those days, she couldn't seem to stop herself from telling over and over again, "So now you just have to wait for the brown envelope under your door."

She remembered thinking, *What? Is that how things are*

done? She had meant, *in this netherworld that I have, in perfect innocence and belief in truth and justice and the integrity of others, entered.* Every day that she had worked on what she called "Zara's death," but others called off-handedly "the case" or "the file" – how the latter infuriated and disgusted her – she had learned some new, terrible thing about how the world really worked.

And yet, hadn't she been the one to say to a particularly unhelpful police officer not long before she published her book and officially gave up the search, "So you're telling me that now all we can do is wait for the deathbed confession?" She hadn't even listened to his answer before she hung up the phone.

She was about to call, "Roman!" Then, remembering he was not here, not now, not ever again, she closed her mouth with a snap. Vonnie. She would call Vonnie. She backed away from the envelope, hurried to the phone and dialed the number she had memorized thirty or more years earlier, not forgetting that now it was a long distance call.

"Fiona! What's up?"

"How did you know it's me?" But what relieved pleasure flooded over her at the sound of her friend's voice.

"Your name came up on my phone," Vonnie told her. "Wake up, Fee, we're into the two thousands now. No more barbed-wire telephones," which made Fiona laugh, a gulping sound, her breath catching. She noticed that her hand holding the phone was still trembling, and sat down abruptly, as though someone had knocked the back of her knees. "Are you all right?"

"Of course, I'm fine, I'm okay. It's just – I just..." She took a deep breath, imagining Vonnie gazing out her kitchen window, catching a glimpse through the trees that bordered her farmyard of the blue roof of what had been Fiona's house, a mile away across the wheat fields. She felt a pang, pushing it down as fast as it came. "You won't believe what just happened."

"What?"

"Somebody just pushed an envelope under my door."

There was a silence, then Vonnie said, puzzled, "An envelope?"

"Remember? I told you – years ago – that man who said that all I had to do was wait for the brown envelope under my door, and how surprised I was because…" She was suddenly afraid.

"You're kidding!"

"I'm not. It's right over there," and she lifted herself up enough to see the envelope lying on the worn doormat. She noticed she wasn't trembling anymore.

"Are you telling me you haven't opened it yet?"

"Haven't even picked it up off the floor." They laughed together; Fiona in embarrassment, Vonnie in disbelief.

"Go get it right now," she said, as Fiona must have known she would.

"Okay, hold on." She pulled herself up out of the armchair, set down the phone and went with suddenly purposeful strides to the foyer. She picked up the envelope, surprised by how cool it felt in her fingers, then went back and sat again, letting the envelope lie on her lap. "I can't believe it," she said. "I mean, isn't this supposed to go under some big-wheel reporter's door? Or some private detective's? Or aren't I supposed to go into some big-city parkade and…umm…Jason Robards wearing a balaclava will hand it to me?"

"Quit stalling."

"Easy for you to be brave," Fiona answered. For once, Vonnie was silent. Fiona understood that Vonnie was giving her room, showing her a little respect in the face of her situation, which was that Roman had died nearly a year ago and she had sold the farmhouse they had shared for more than forty years of marriage and now lived alone in a big city condo. *That I've become a cliché.*

She could hear a rustling sound down the line: Vonnie rearranging herself, making a small cough, maybe to let Fiona know she was still there, waiting. Fiona wanted to speak, but she was struggling to make her tumbling emotions slide into place. She had thought this was over when her book was published; it had *seemed* over – where else was there to go? – and now, this.

"All I ever wanted to do was to tell people what happened to Zara that night. I was never trying to solve her murder, no matter what the police thought." The police, who in the midst of all this, would answer none of her questions and treated her as if she were their enemy, following her in a marked car so as to warn and/or frighten her off, or making apparently pointless slow drives past their farm with lights flashing to attract her and Roman's attention to their puzzling but also menacing presence.

"I know that, Fee," Vonnie told her. "And you did do what you said. You found out what happened, you told people that Zara Stanley was a decent young woman, not just a pretty face." She made that clicking sound with her tongue, a habit of hers when she was thinking hard. "It was a damn good book, Fee, never doubt that." Best friend stuff, Fiona thought, but was grateful.

She thought of how it had taken her years to write her book, and how during that time Zara's story went from an interesting incident in their mutual pasts to a tale that grew ever weightier and darker. Once in a long while, alone in her stylish Calgary condo, she would pause in whatever she was doing, and ask herself how she could live knowing what she now knew about evil.

She laughed, though, as she looked for the first time at the address on the envelope, one loud half-snort, half-peal.

Vonnie said, "What?"

"My name and address is made up of letters cut from newspapers. Can you believe it?"

"Somebody else who doesn't know what year it is," Vonnie answered in an amused tone. Then, impatiently, "For God sake Fiona, open the damn thing!"

Her heart was tapping at the bottom of her throat, but before Vonnie could insist again, she slid a finger under the gummed flap and tore through the heavy paper. As she shook the envelope a single sheet floated onto her lap, and she realized she'd been half-expecting a key to fall out, or a flash drive or a CD or a DVD, maybe even a chip. But no, only this single sheet of paper with nothing on it. *Oh, wait.*

"It's a number, Vonnie. That's all, just a number. A long one, with a capital 'F' at the beginning. And below it, in tiny letters, there's a name: Evan Kirby." Or was it Ewan? The print was so small she reached for her reading glasses on top of the novel she had set by the phone.

"I'd say this has to be from some old guy because a young one would have sent a computerized file," Vonnie said crisply, as if this were a normal everyday problem, such as who would take out the garbage or what she would cook for dinner.

"Or a woman? Why not?" Fiona answered. "It's the old women, the secretaries, the personal assistants, the clerks:

they're the ones who knew where the bodies were buried. There was nobody more loyal than those women." Fiona was aware that, once again, she was stalling.

"It's just embarrassing to think of it. Loyal for no rewards, either. Loyal because they were raised to be."

"So, maybe…," Fiona launched the idea slowly, "The cut-out letters and numbers are a joke, aimed at me. Just a sort of sly, in-joke. Della Street, Jane Moneypenny, and all that. Or a message in themselves! Couldn't they be?"

"Saying what?"

"Saying, look to the old guys!"

Again Vonnie was making the clicking sound with her tongue. Fiona went on. "But that's not worth a thing, because everybody who has ever been directly involved in the case is an old guy now." A pause. "Including you and me."

"All old *men*, not old women," Vonnie said. It was a conversation they had had a dozen times over the years: surely it was because only men had been involved in the investigation and in whatever actual formal processes – the coroner's inquest, for instance – had taken place that the case wasn't solved. And Zara's background weighed against her. She came from some backwater, her family were nobodies, the men in charge would have taken it for granted that she was going nowhere but to marriage and babies. Although Fiona had always suspected that some thought Zara had been headed for prostitution or maybe, given her beauty, to call girl status. It infuriated her to think of it. Men desired her; if they couldn't have her, they denigrated her. At least, the bad ones did.

"They probably thought she asked for what had happened to her!" Fiona hadn't meant to speak aloud.

"What?" Vonnie could put a thousand twists on that one

word. This time it was exasperated.

"Or are we being bitches?" Fiona asked. "Most men in Ripley thirty years ago felt as bad about what happened as we women did." She studied the number. "It could be a file number, maybe. But belonging to whom? The police? The Mounties? Some lawyer who'd been in business a long time? It's nearly ten units long.

"I think that somebody is telling me that, somewhere, there is a file with this man's name on it or in it, and that I should find it." Suddenly she could feel her so-called mind ratcheting into gear again, a good feeling that surprised her. "I think somebody is telling me that I should find it because it will finally show the way to the answers."

"Maybe it belongs to a government office: the justice department, for instance, or the attorney general's office; or even the Premier's office," Vonnie said.

Fiona's brain was whipping fast through a new set of ideas. She said, tentatively, "Could it be that somewhere in the bowels of the provincial legislative building there is a secret room full of secret files?"

"What?" Vonnie said; this time the tone was disbelief. "Why would anybody be dumb enough to keep files they never wanted anybody to see?"

"Or maybe over the years what had started as small deposit by some official who then left, or died, grew, and governments changed and changed again until the current government no longer knew it was there…" No, she thought. That theory is full of holes, and she would have bent her mind to making it work better but instead, drew back from her increasingly fantastical thoughts.

Vonnie said, "But what about that name? Say it again."

"Evan Kirby," she read aloud, carefully.

"Did we go to high school with somebody with that name? Or some name like it?"

"I don't recognize it," Fiona said. "It has a kind of lawyer sound to it, doesn't it?"

"These days everybody's a lawyer," Vonnie said, as if she were thinking of something else. "Even Rudy Kovalenko." They both made slight disparaging sounds. He hadn't been the greatest student when they were all kids together, and now he was this big legal success. Vonnie and Jack, when they were still a couple, occasionally ran into him at exclusive events in Ripley. *Remember him?* Vonnie had asked, sighing, and Fiona had answered, *who could forget him?* A dreamboat, whom they had both dated before Vonnie met the too-handsome Jack, and Rudy had dumped Fiona, politely, after a few pleasant enough dates, just not calling again. Ever.

But Vonnie was moving on, as if the mention of their old classmate was enough to shift her thinking.

"Just turn it over to the police, Fiona." A certain resignation in her voice.

"Never!" Fiona said. "So it can disappear forever? Not a chance." She took a deep breath. "I'll just hang onto it and see if I can come up with some clever idea. About what I should do, I mean."

"Look what happened before," Vonnie said, in a low voice. "Do you want to go through all that again? Being watched at every turn? Come on, Fee."

But she was roused again, as she had been when she set out to write her book and ran into opposition at every turn and, instead of drawing back, grew bolder. She said in a louder, firmer voice, "And anyway, who else will stand by Zara? Who else will be her advocate when she can't speak for herself? I have to follow this!"

She sat for a long time after they hung up, not looking at the sheet of paper resting on her lap, thinking of Zara. The high cheekbones, the perfect patrician nose neither too long nor too short, the light, almost transparent, blue of her eyes; how she'd made their teacher laugh in one of the classes they'd taken together, made the whole class laugh in fact, Fiona too, with some silly remark that took everybody off-guard. How, when Zara had heard the laughter, she had turned her head almost shyly, in surprise, and her eyes had met Fiona's, just two high school girls surviving another boring history lesson. It was the first time Fiona had realized that the prettiest girl in the school was a real person, maybe even a half-way nice one.

The poignancy of that moment shook her again as it had ever since Zara's terrible death only a couple of years later: savagely raped and bludgeoned nearly to death and then – oh, most horrifyingly banal detail of all – because she wouldn't die, smothered. Or smothered just to make absolutely sure she would never get up again.

"All I want," she said out loud for the thousandth time, "is justice for Zara." The words seemed to echo around the room.

Then she shook her head and set the paper aside. She would not think of it anymore, would go to bed instead, and get some sleep so she would be in shape to tackle things tomorrow.

But lying in bed, she found herself rehearsing it all again: her own efforts, forty years later, to dig out some truth from what material she could find: to identify the apparent mistakes in the newspaper coverage, to dissect as minutely as possible the statements of the ranking investigating officers, official or otherwise – in those days it seemed the higher-ups in the police force could be casual if they felt like it – looking for errors, misinformation, places where they disagreed with each other or with what was reported in the media. She thought of all the information she was refused. On one occasion even, two different people showed her what should have been identical copies of the same document and in a critical place it had said two different things. So somebody had been altering documents. Not that she could prove it.

For the millionth time she repeated to herself: it was either a murderous drifter who had then moved on as anonymously as he had arrived – that was why he was impossible to catch – or else it was somebody Zara knew, most likely one of the many men who, mesmerized by her beauty, chased her so relentlessly.

But who was Evan Kirby? She could recall no one by that name, although it might have been one of the seemingly endless number of people she'd interviewed over the years, those who had known Zara as a friend, or dated her, or known someone who knew her, or knew about the case. Maybe he was one of those. He wasn't a police officer – that she would have remembered. Could he be a government official? Some lowly clerk who knew a few secrets and could no longer live with them?

She might have gone on this way all night, but the phone suddenly pealed, startling her out of the reverie. Both exasperated and slightly afraid – she could see by her bedside clock that it was 2:00 a.m. – she fumbled for the phone, dropping it as a voice mumbled against the bedclothes, finally getting the receiver lopsidedly against her ear. It took her a second to recognize her brother-in-law's voice.

"Please, Fiona, you have to come right away."

Chapter Two

The sign next to the door of the ICU read "Ring Bell to Enter," but just as she was about to push the button, one of the double doors swung open and Arnie emerged. Pale, with his thinning brown hair dishevelled and exposing a small bald spot, his shirt looking as though he'd slept in it, mis-buttoned striped cardigan revealing the beginnings of a pot belly on a physique that still suggested more retired football player than retired accountant. Her heart contracted when she saw him – this wasn't some terrible mistake after all – and she put her arms around him, saying his name, "Arnie," then releasing him quickly. "How is she?"

"Fee. I knew you'd come as soon as you could." She could see his confusion, his effort to concentrate on her, and stepped away from him, lowering her head, sniffing. He took her arm and steered her to the waiting area across from the double doors, easing her into a seat beside him.

"We have to wait," he told her, when she looked questioningly at him. "Her kidneys…" he swallowed, "they've shut down. They're setting her up on dialysis. They wanted me out of the way while they do that." He blinked rapidly and she took his near hand in hers. "They might be doing something else, too; I don't know."

"Have they…do they know what happened?" He

shook his head, no, and took back his hand, patting hers absently, so she wouldn't be offended.

"They put in some…" he hesitated, apparently unable to think of the word, "stents, to keep the clogged arteries open. They think it's congestive heart failure. A nurse will come and tell us when we can go back in," he said. "The kids are on their way, but it takes a while from London, and I don't know if Greg is that keen to come right now, and Angie is so hard to reach in Bolivia, I can't be sure she even knows." Greg the banker; Angela the human rights worker. Or something. Always off somewhere daunting, if not impossible, with an NGO.

For the first time, he raised his eyes to her face and studied it, lifted a hand in sympathy to touch her formerly vibrant red-blonde hair, now a beauty-parlour pale blonde. He had admired her deep blue eyes, once, "Just like Marian's," as if that were somehow odd and wonderful. Arnie and Marian had come to Roman's funeral, even stayed on a couple of days, but her memory of that time was vague at best, and she saw him now as if it had been years since they last met in person.

"Once we get things sorted out, I want you to go home and get some sleep. I'll stay with her." Roman's death struggle would never leave her, the rising up of his chest, the contortion of his face with his pain, his hands reaching for something, not her. That, as it happened, she could only watch in helpless horror.

"She's not going to die," Arnie said, his voice having changed to a deep growl from his usual light even one. Fiona was startled, but let her head fall back against the hospital green wall above the chair's back and closed her eyes. They sat together in silence.

"Mr. McMaster? You can go in now." A nurse stood in front of them; Arnie was already rising unsteadily to his feet.

While Fiona had had her eyes closed, someone else had come to sit in the waiting area with them, a young, frightened-looking woman in faded torn jeans and stained 'Star Wars' t-shirt. Black eyeliner ran down the curved flesh of her cheeks as she cried silently, oblivious to anyone else.

"We've had to ventilate her," the nurse told them as they crossed the hall. By the quiet way she said this, Fiona understood that there had been a further deterioration in her sister's condition. The nurse was speaking again as she held back one of the doors so she and Arnie could pass into the inner sanctum. "We'll know the extent of the damage by morning, I think. The tests should be back by then."

It was a vast ICU: staff in faded greens or shapeless white smocks pushed stainless steel machines from which knobs and plastic tubing protruded, or walked briskly about, while all the while a steady beeping sounded, interrupted by a buzz or two, and once, briefly, an alarm. The voices of all these people talking to each other quietly, a laugh, quickly modulated, and then a nurse calling a patient's name over and over again, assailed Fiona, confusing her. Marian was on the left near the door. Staff still milled about her bed, but when the nurse guided Fiona and Arnie into the area, they melted away.

Her sister lay with a sheet carefully covering her, tubing emerging from under it in various places along her anatomy. Fiona identified her only by her cap of now paled and thinned red-blonde hair with its new streak of dead white at one temple. Her face was swollen and mostly hidden by the thick plastic tubing in her mouth, held in place with clear plastic tape. Arnie found Marian's hand beneath the sheet and held it gently, gazing down at his wife of forty years, murmuring something softly to her that Fiona couldn't make out over the muted racket in the long room. She sought Marian's other hand. It was cool to touch, too cool, and now that Arnie had stopped murmuring, she put her face close to her sister's to kiss her forehead, telling her she had come and that Marian should get better quickly so they could have a good chat. Telling her she would take care of Arnie, too, then thinking that perhaps it had been a mistake to say that.

In the lull that followed, for no reason she could identify, she remembered the envelope. She had thrown it into her carry-on bag at the last second, and then just as quickly taken it out. She had gone into the space she had given over to her office, not that she had any work to do, and photocopied the page inside it, then replaced the original in its envelope. She had put the copy – neatly folded into a smaller rectangle – into her handbag and tried frantically to think of a clever place to hide the envelope in her condo, but had given up. The futility of trying to hide anything in such a small space was obvious, all clever potential hiding places having been revealed by Hollywood scriptwriters. And anyway, it was ridiculous to be worried about secrecy, for, after all, who would know she'd received it but Vonnie? And the person who had delivered it, of course.

Abruptly, she straightened "I could have left it with Carla!" she said aloud, but in the muted cacophony Arnie seemed not to have heard her. On her way to the taxi, she had stopped at the condo next to her's, where Carla, a young imaging technician, lived, just to let somebody know she had been called to Vancouver on an emergency, and would Carla please keep an eye on her place for a few days. But, too late now. And how would I have explained leaving her an envelope anyway?

A doctor and Arnie were having a brief, low-voiced conversation at the foot of the bed, but she didn't try to overhear it. She bent again and studied Marian's face. It was flushed an unnatural colour, as if she were wearing stage makeup, and so swollen that it was hard to see the girl she'd grown up with. Yet here Fiona was, tears trickling, nose running; she fumbled for and found a tissue. She thought of Marian crying because her older sister had a new mauve formal dress and would be a bridesmaid at their cousin's wedding and she would not; Marian on her wedding day in a champagne satin suit and a beaded, sparkling pillbox hat instead of a veil. She'd always had a sense of style that Fiona lacked; the triumph in her eyes because she was married and Fiona, although older, wasn't; her rage when, years later, she'd found Arnie and Fiona in an embrace in the front hall of their North Van house. The arguments, the tears, Marian finally only partially mollified by both Arnie and Fiona's protests that it had been innocent, just a moment when they'd laughed together about some old family thing, and had hugged spontaneously, just as Marian had opened the door.

In fact, it *had* been innocent, just as they said it was, Fiona insisting, "Marian, I *love* Roman. How can you think such a thing?" as if Marian were the one at fault. Even if she didn't see her sister for years at a time, and usually quarrelled with her when she did, Fiona loved Marian, knew she could not have a normal life without her alive on the planet. Not with Roman gone too.

Later, in the hospital cafeteria, Arnie seemed more exhausted than worried.

"After we've eaten," she told him, "I want you to go home and sleep for a few hours. You can't do her any good if you make yourself sick." He nodded, whether in agreement or mere acknowledgement, she couldn't tell. He had given up even trying to eat his sandwich, and while she chewed and he stared into space, the contents of the envelope rose to her mind again. After a moment she said, "Arnie, do you remember anybody named Evan Kirby?"

"From where?" he asked.

"Maybe from our high school or in a college class?"

"I do not," he responded, dropping his half-eaten sandwich onto his tray. "Marian is better at remembering names than I am."

"When she wakes up," Fiona said firmly, as if the fact that she *would* wake up were a foregone conclusion, "I'll be sure to ask her."

In the end, Arnie got a room at the hotel across the street rather than making the trek through heavy Vancouver traffic across the bridge and up the mountainside to his and Marian's house. He told Fiona he'd rest better if he knew he could be back with Marian in moments. Fiona took his place by Marian's side, rising and moving out of the way whenever the staff came to check gauges, dials and tubes, and then sitting again.

She began going over in her mind every interview she'd done over the nearly ten-year period she investigated Zara's death, trying to recall if Evan Kirby had been one of them. No, she was sure she had never interviewed anyone by that name, not even over the phone. And yet, it had begun to sound familiar. She wished she had a copy of her book, un-memorably named *The Death of Zara Stanley*, so she could check the index.

Three years her book had been out there in the world, but after its publication she'd been deluged by people with information to give her about the case, or stories to tell her, and she couldn't help but think, *Where the hell were all of you when I needed to know what you know?* Which, of course, wasn't fair because they couldn't have known she was writing the book.

In the end, none of their revelations or theories had made any difference. In the end, her book had, if not exactly fallen flat, certainly not propelled her into stardom, or solved the murder. It had stirred up excitement in Ripley, and that was about it. Well, and hostility from certain quarters, some of them surprising. She shuddered, forcing her mind away from that subject.

Back in the waiting room where the nurses had sent her while they did something or other to Marian, the young woman in the soiled t-shirt was gone, replaced by a beefy man in his early twenties wearing what she had learned at the newspaper where she'd worked for years to call "leathers." She could see a tattoo on the side of his neck just below the collar of the black leather jacket that squeaked every time he moved. He looked so ordinary, like an actor still in costume taking a break, and the freckles across his nose spoke of a rural childhood, a farm, maybe horses. He didn't so much as glance her way. A nurse was supposed to come and get her when they were finished 'the procedure,' but it was taking a long time, and her mind repeatedly skittered away from Marian's condition. Thinking she might catch a few minutes' sleep, she let her head roll back against the wall and closed her eyes.

Immediately the envelope rose up before her, the letter "F" and the numbers floating unsteadily in front of it, and again, the name, "Evan Kirby," in tiny letters. She tried to shake the picture, to interpose Marian's face in front of it, but what she saw instead was a bloody bed, shadowed, in Zara's bedroom in the shabby apartment she and a friend had rented. The bed was empty, because her body had been taken away, and hard to see clearly because it was the photo that had been in the newspaper, a photo from a film camera, not a digital, which hadn't been invented then.

She became aware that someone else had entered the room and stopped near her. She opened her eyes. Arnie said, bending to kiss her cheek, "Here's the room key. You go get some rest now. I'll phone you if anything changes." He glanced around at the man in the motorcycle gear, but the young man was motionless, staring at his thick hands folded on his lap. Fiona remembered that a few years ago she would have wondered if he was an undercover cop, or an informant. She would have laughed aloud at her old paranoia, but the shiver creeping down her spine made it impossible, even now, to be amused. "I stopped to ask what's going on with Marian before I came here. No change, they say." He rubbed his chin as if checking to see if he needed to shave or not, and blinked several times, his eyes fixed on the wall above her. Reluctantly, she accepted the key card and rose, touching his shoulder lightly with her palm, in commiseration or encouragement, before turning to the door.

"Oh, by the way, I remembered who Evan Kirby is."

"What?" she said, faltering, turning back to him.

"Evan Kirby. He went to our high school: Small guy, skinny. Pale hair and light-skinned, freckles. Smart, but the kind you never even notice. Didn't take part in sports or go to school dances or even hang out in the cafés with the rest of us, that I can remember. But then, he was ahead of me in school." She stood, half-turned toward him, her head down, frowning, struggling to remember.

"I'll have to find a yearbook, I guess," she said in a vague tone, as if this was of no importance to her.

"I think he's a lawyer," Arnie said. "Disappeared into the civil service, I think."

Fiona was pounding on a high glass door, made nearly opaque by etchings of swirling designs that looked like galaxies, the glass so thick that she couldn't break it. She was trying to get into the room behind it where many voices, all male, could be heard rising and falling in somber tones. The voices faded as she rose out of sleep back into the drab hotel room, thinking even as she recognized where she was, oh no, not that old dream again.

It had begun years earlier when she'd been a reporter, then a columnist for the Ripley newspaper where she was known as "FLL" for Fiona Leith Lychenko and was the only female columnist (other than the woman who solved household cleaning problems). The paper had needed somebody to write a column about farming, the small city itself being so full of part-time farmers, farmers living in town for the winter, retired farmers, ersatz farmers, and would-be farmers; "FLL" because she was a woman and in those days, what farmer (read "male farmer") would read a column about farming if he knew it was written by a woman? Even a woman who had spent as many years on a farm as Fiona had.

The dream always left her feeling hot and angry in that old way that she never did rid herself of after her firing. Yes, FLL, she reminded herself bitterly, as she lay awake in the gloomy hotel bedroom listening to the ceaseless drone of the city, you were fired. Don't ever forget that: fired. Because of one column I wrote that was true and everybody knew it but nobody talked about: "Farm Women are Still Second Class Citizens." Because my editor had the flu that week and it got through by mistake.

"I don't care," she told herself out loud, then snorted. Sometimes she suspected there was nothing in her entire life she cared more about than her ignominious firing over a column. I wouldn't have survived that crisis without Vonnie, she remembered.

"We didn't have kids," she had told Vonnie. "What was I supposed to do with myself when Roman was away all the time?" As if Vonnie ever needed her to defend herself. "How was I to know that Roman was more interested in working his way up through the farm organizations than he was in actually farming? An office job in the city, maybe even Ottawa – that was what he really wanted." Had she cried telling Vonnie? Yes, probably. It was all so embarrassing to remember, relying on Vonnie that way when Vonnie never relied on her for anything, not even to babysit her three daughters.

Eventually, Roman had gotten himself named to an agricultural delegation heading to China. "You have to go with him." How many times had Vonnie told her that, and she had resisted, saying, "Roman doesn't care if I come or not. He says I'd just be bored stiff. He says China is cold and strange and that I'd have to go on endless tours of grain-handling facilities and sit through dozens of speeches in Chinese. He says no other wives are going. A whole month, Vonnie. That's a long time. I'd rather stay home with a good book. Anyway, I have a column to write." She remembered turning away from Vonnie, getting her coat, at the door adding, "Somebody has to stay on the farm and look after things," at which Vonnie hadn't stopped herself from contradicting Fiona, by stating the obvious, "Look after what? You don't even have any cattle!"

How odd, it suddenly occurred to her, that Roman did everything he could to persuade me not to go with him. Ever since, now and then, she would wonder if she'd missed an important opportunity; sometimes also if Roman's advising her to stay home was something she should have asked him about. But enough of this, she had to get back to Marian.

Still, she thought, *If only he were here*, as she made her way down long, nearly empty corridors and up elevators to her sister's ward. Roman, who hadn't been much good to her in so many day-to-day ways, yet who always showed up when it mattered. Always running off to meetings, gone all day, or half the night or at conferences for long, three-day weekends, while she sat at home and read or wrote, or worked in her garden, or helped Vonnie with Arts Council work or, occasionally, went shopping with her in the city.

As the elevator opened, she remembered the time Al Gagnon had phoned to ask where the heck Roman was – he was supposed to be at a meeting in Hart City – and she had said, surprised, Why as far as I know he should be there by now. Then, worried that he had had an accident, she called Roman on his cell, only to find that he'd confused his schedule, and had thought he was supposed to be in Riverbend, in fact, was just arriving at the city limits. I'll call Big Al, he told her, and I'll turn the car around right now. She smiled to herself. For such an organized man, and an organizer, he had a way of mixing up the simplest things. Too much on his mind, she repeated what she had always told herself, then realized that her lips were pursed and she was frowning.

Arnold was stretched out on one of the thinly-padded, imitation-leather couches with the shiny aluminum trim, sound asleep. Suddenly he opened his eyes, pushed himself into a sitting position and in one movement swung his legs around so that he sat, his feet in their worn brown loafers flat on the floor, his fists on the leather on each side of his thighs, ready to push himself upright, but his head down, staring at the floor. She gave him a couple of seconds, then said, softly, "Arnie? Are you okay?"

He looked up at her, his eyes cleared, and he laughed quickly, embarrassed.

"I couldn't remember where the heck I was," he told her. "I know: hospital, Marian. Is there any word?"

"I just got here," she said. "I haven't phoned in to ask."

"Never mind," he said. "If there is anything, they'd send somebody out to tell me." He checked his watch, then tried to flatten his hair with both hands. "Last I heard there was no change," he told her. "About 3:00 a.m., that was." She was about to speak, but he said, "They took her off the dialysis machine last night. Said her kidney function seemed to be returning. Now that was good news."

"A hopeful sign," Fiona agreed, as if they were speaking about somebody else's only sister. "Do you think I should go in?" She felt ashamed that she couldn't seem to care more about Marian's plight. Yet, it was as if a hard glass wall existed between her heart and her mind, and it was her heart that, since Roman's death, she couldn't access. No, it had begun before that. It had begun during all those days and nights she'd spent alone on the farm waiting for him to come back from a conference or a meeting; it had begun when the newspaper had fired her, and she couldn't seem to get over it, until she'd gotten the idea of writing a book about Zara and her murder.

"Up to you," he said.

"Go to the hotel, Arnie, get some good sleep," she said, handing him the key card and putting her other hand on his shoulder. He stood slowly, so that, because of his height, she had to remove it. "I'll call the moment I hear anything new."

"Okay," he said. "Or the hospital will. I gave them the number." He gave her a wavering smile, and walked away.

She rang the bell for entry and was told that the nurses were busy with Marian at the moment and that they would come and get her in a few minutes. Fiona sat, alone, in the waiting room. She thought about how bitterly she and her little sister had fought as teenagers, how much they had disliked each other to such an extent that they had persuaded their parents to let them go to different high schools. Marian always jealous of Fiona's every tiny success, refusing ever to congratulate her, always pretending she hadn't heard or wasn't interested in whatever success Fiona had had. And they were tiny, Fiona reminded herself, thinking of an essay prize in grade eleven, becoming class president in grade twelve – which was really nothing if you weren't elected to the student council, and she hadn't been. What a humiliation that had been. And yet, hadn't Marian been genuinely sad at that? Genuinely supportive as only a sister can sometimes, surprisingly, be?

She blinked, not wanting to cry, wanting Roman again.

And hadn't Fiona been a good sister to Marian, at least sometimes? That time Marian got dumped by that boy, what was his name? Chuck. Hadn't they even hugged that night when he failed to show and Marian had stood in her going-to-the-movies-on-a-date best skirt and sweater in a corner of the hall, crying softly to herself?

"He's just a jerk, Marian. If he'd do something this awful, what would you want him for?" Marian had smiled even as her eyes had filled with tears, so that Fiona had lost her temper and berated her, because she didn't seem to know what was good for her. Now, she shuddered. No wonder she hated me.

She got up and went back into the hall just as the door buzzed open for her.

It was as she entered a somewhat quieter ICU and began the short walk to her sister's bedside that something, some trace of memory, entered her brain and she saw a face, hazily. It belonged to a skinny boy with pale red-blond hair close to the colour of her own. Wearing a plaid shirt buttoned neatly to his throat – yes! She did remember Evan Kirby from high school, if only vaguely. Always had this super-clean look – hair slicked down, face scrubbed to a shine, pants so carefully pressed you could cut your finger on the creases. There was something weird, not quite right, about those obsessively pressed pants. People said he was smart as a whip. He was older than she was by what? Two or was it three years? A little rush of excitement whipped through her.

Marian's face was still without colour, the ventilator tubing still taped to her mouth, her eyes closed as if sealed.

Fiona found her hand under the sheet and was surprised that it was warm, when yesterday it had felt cold. Surely a good sign? A nurse was tapping one of the collection points on the tubing apparently making sure the clear fluid inside was flowing properly.

"She's warm today," Fiona said. "That's good, isn't it?"

"She's much the same," the nurse said.

"Do you know what's going on with her?" Fiona asked, meaning, a prognosis.

"What relation are you?" the nurse inquired.

"I'm her only sister. Our parents are dead."

"I'm sorry, but I can't give you that information," the nurse said. "You should talk to her husband." She walked away.

Fiona leaned over Marian, "Hi, Sweetie, good morning, how are you this morning? It's me, Fiona. I'm here to make sure you're okay." Abruptly, feeling foolish as well as overcome with love, she ran out of words and sat down with a thump, still gazing at that swollen, half-hidden, unrecognizable face she knew to be her suddenly beloved little sister. But here, inside the ICU, there was no such thing as weather; no such thing as family, either; no such thing as hope. Tears filled her eyes, trickled down her cheeks before she could stop them.

She rose again, holding a tissue to her face, and made her way quickly out the double doors to the waiting room. It had filled while she was inside the ICU, so she backed away, turned and went through another pair of doors that led to a deserted, glass-covered walkway between two wings of the hospital. She stood there in the chill and the dull light while rain trickled down the window panes behind her, and cried until her tears dried of their own accord and calm returned.

She understood that she cried not just for Marian: she cried for Roman and the possibility that he had not always been honest with her. She cried for Zara Stanley and for her own failure; she cried too because a brown envelope had been shoved under her door and all of it was going to start again – being followed, somebody, surely the police, tapping her phone with old-fashioned technology so she would know she was being listened to, the threats about what would happen to her if she didn't stop asking questions. She cried because now she would have to find Evan Kirby and she didn't want to.

Chapter Three

On the morning of the fourth day, just as she and Arnie were about to buzz to get into the ICU, Marian's cardiologist stepped out of the door, nearly colliding with them.

"Well," he said, grinning at them. "Here you are! I have good news. Today we're removing her ventilator; her lungs are working on their own." Arnie started to cry, while Fiona gasped some words of surprise and delight that she would never be able to recall. The doctor went on a bit, about what she wasn't sure, details about Marian's condition, then said, "So, well, then," cleared his throat, and marched briskly away. Arnie slumped against the wall and put his hands over his face, and Fiona stepped forward, put her arms around him, holding him as close as his bent arms allowed. After a moment he lifted his head, put his arms down – his tears were gone – and kissed Fiona lightly, absently, on her cheek. He stepped past her, straightened his shoulders and took a deep breath.

"I'll go back home today," he announced, not really to her. "Marian will kill me if I let her plants die, and there's a stray cat that comes to the door in the evenings for some supper. There'll be dust all over everything too and you know Marian, a demon housekeeper."

She said, "I suppose I should book a flight out, too."

"Wait one more day," he said. "Greg arrives today. You should see your nephew before you go." They began walking side by side down the hall, away from the Intensive Care Unit, to breakfast in the cavernous hospital cafeteria.

"I can't believe it!" Arnie said. "I thought I'd lost her forever." She glanced up at him as he walked briskly down the hall beside her, alert and with the quickness returned to his steps. All because Marian would be coming back home to him. No, Roman didn't ever love me like this. Why did I never see that? *Maybe I did.*

She blinked rapidly, drew in a deep breath through her nose, and refrained from speaking until they had filled their trays, were seated and eating; Arnie as if he hadn't eaten in a week. Which in fact he mostly hadn't.

"What civil service did he 'disappear' into, the federal or the provincial?" she asked.

Arnie was finishing up the last of his bacon and eggs, while Fiona had toyed with brown toast, thinking of her cholesterol count, and sipping her third cup of coffee.

"Who?" He looked bewildered.

"Evan Kirby." His eyes finally focused on her face.

"Why do you care where he is?" he asked, wiping his mouth with a stained paper napkin. She shrugged, sliding her coffee cup back and forth, considering what she might say.

"I just think…I wonder if…"

"Oh, no," Arnie said. "You're not going to start all that again. You published your book; you did what you set out to do. Let it go, Fiona."

"Let it go to do what?" she asked, the anger in her voice surprising her.

"Start another book!" he answered, exasperated. He

shoved his plate away, leaned back, then sighed as if giving in. "The last I heard, provincial. He was a deputy minister, I think. As high as you can go. He's got to be retired by now. Maybe he's dead."

"Hmmm," she said, wondering if she should tell him about the envelope, what was in it, seek his advice.

"You really are going after that case again?" he asked. It seemed to her better to simply smile enigmatically and look at her coffee instead of him.

She wondered suddenly if it could have been Evan Kirby himself who'd pushed the note under her door. Who else might have been in a position to know things the public didn't? Then she remembered that one of the girls they'd gone to high school with had become the secretary to a couple of highly-placed civil servants. She'd been so good at her work that she had gone on to a job in Ottawa with a federal Minister, although Fiona couldn't remember which one.

Emily Zhao was her name – no, Zhang – and already in high school she could speak something like four languages beside her native Chinese, whichever one that had been – Cantonese or Mandarin, or maybe something else. What a smart girl she had been! She had kept to herself, been a pillar of reserve compared to everybody else's shrieky, giggling, blushing, either babbling or tongue-tied silliness. Especially me, Fiona recalled, and barely stopped herself from gagging out loud at the thought of her teenage self.

How would she ever find Emily Zhang? Especially if she had gone on to live in Ottawa. What was her married name? Hadn't she been one of the girls who had married right out of high school? Fiona's locker had been next to Emily's in grade twelve so they were inadvertently together

a half-dozen times a day. But despite the constant proxim-
ity they had never become close friends, especially with
Emily being such a loner. Or forced into being alone
because she was one of the maybe three or four Asian kids
in a school of 1,500, two of whom had been her younger
sisters, hadn't they? And why would she look for her? To
try to get a handle on what was in the envelope, that's why.

"Zara Stanley won some beauty contests, didn't she?"
Arnie remarked, as if now that Marian was going to be
okay, he could rejoin the world. "Looked a bit like Grace
Kelly, didn't she? Or am I remembering wrong?"

"Everybody said that," Fiona answered. "Kelly was taller
though, and her hair was a paler blonde. Not to mention
that she came from a rich family and the Stanleys were as
poor as church mice."

"Backwoods people, were even said to live off wild meat.
And her brothers – wasn't there something about her
brothers? Jail, I mean?" Fiona shrugged. "I remember: she
was 'Miss Ripley,' and then queen of…something. The big
summer exhibition, I think." His voice was admiring.

"It wasn't just her beauty she was famous for – or maybe
it was that you couldn't separate anything else she was from
that face…" She would like to have pursued this idea, but
Arnie had clearly stopped listening.

But the fact was that Zara had also been famous because
of an ambition that she didn't even try to hide. *She* would
amount to something; *she* was going places, specifically to
Hollywood where, she was confident, she would become a
movie star. The other girls laughed at her for this, of course,
but the laughter and snideness were hesitant, a bit uncertain, because Zara in some lights was even better looking
than the great Grace Kelly. And what else, in those days,

Fiona thought with a hint of bitterness, was a girl to aim for with a face like that?

In the early afternoon she drove with Arnie to the airport to pick up Greg. There wasn't much traffic for a change, and the sky was beginning to lighten in the far west where the mountains in their mauve and blue splendor emerged through the dissipating clouds.

"I'll take Greg to see his mother first. Then maybe back home so he can get some sleep. Would you stay with Marian while I'm gone?"

"You know I will," Fiona told him, thoughts of her empty condo half-beckoning, half-repelling her.

"Not a word from Angie," he said. "That daughter of mine…" He wouldn't say, *I don't know what's wrong with her,* although it hung in the air between them. Nobody knew what was wrong with her, but she seemed to be always on the run from her family, preferring the most dangerous, remote countries possible.

While they waited for Greg to get through Customs, Fiona said, "I have to make a phone call," really wanting only to leave the two of them alone for a moment, it having been nearly two years since father and son had seen each other. But when she went off to a quiet corner as if to use her cell phone, she couldn't think of anybody to phone. Her next-door neighbour, Carla? *I could just ask her if everything's okay and tell her I'll be back maybe tomorrow?* But that seemed too much trouble and she didn't have Carla's phone number anyway. Instead, she dialed Vonnie's, only to hear the phone ring and ring until a voice came on saying "the mailbox is full."

She looked back and saw that the first passengers from the London flight were coming down the hallway toward the baggage carousels and that Arnie was waiting expectantly as close to the open glass doors as he could get.

She thought suddenly that she could check to see if there was an Evan Kirby anywhere in Vancouver, then thought, it's such an ordinary name, there could be ten of them in a city this size. But her excitement at the idea was enough that she borrowed an actual phone book from a car rental cubicle, to find that the only Kirbys spelled with an 'i' rather than an 'e' did not have the first initial 'E.'

She was about to shut the giant book, when she remembered trying to find Emily Zhang before, when she'd been in the throes of her first investigation, choosing Emily out of the other girls in their class only because she had heard she and Zara had lived near each other and sometimes walked to school together. She had thought Emily might know something about Zara's boyfriends. Why hadn't she pursued that further? I suppose because I thought I could find out about Zara's boyfriends from a number of other people. And I never gave a thought to what she might have found out about the murder as a private secretary – now called *Executive Assistant* – in a government office. Why would I?

She handed the massive book back to the attendant, and when she turned again, found herself wrapped in a hug by her nephew while Arnie beamed like a kid on Christmas morning.

"I hear mom's on the mend," Greg said, grinning too. "I'm glad I came anyway. It's been too long and I'd planned to come this summer. This has just speeded it up a bit." He was built like his father, but without his father's good looks, although the attentive friendliness in his face made up for the lack of evenness in his features. Fiona had known for a long time that Greg, now in his late thirties, was gay, but she wasn't sure that Arnie knew, and Marian definitely didn't, because she kept saying how she wished he'd hurry up and get married so that she could finally have some grandchildren.

"No use counting on Angela," she would say, her lips tightening.

Not wanting to intrude on their family time, however fraught it might be, considering that Marian was still unconscious, Fiona went back to the hotel room where she stretched out on her bed and read for a while, or tried to. It occurred to her then that she might use the hotel computer to see if she could track Kirby down. That way there would be no record on her own computer that she'd been looking for him.

That was the sort of thing that, in her absolute naiveté when she had first set out to find out what had happened to Zara Stanley, hadn't occurred to her, until one day a woman she didn't know called her out of the blue to make a lunch date in order to help her, she said. And to offer her advice gleaned from her years in a profession of helping people out of scrapes with authorities – scrapes they hadn't even realized they were in, or certainly had never meant to get into and that people in her line of work regarded as unjust. They met in an out-of-the-way café between lunch and afternoon coffee-hour, and Fiona had a hard time taking the meeting or the woman's advice seriously. The woman – Gail was her name – said she was a lawyer and a former worker for various human rights causes, mostly in the U.S.

"Get on Gmail at once," she said. "Don't use the province's email server. They can get into that."

"Really?" Fiona had said, staring at her as if she were from Mars.

"Yes, really," the woman repeated. "Don't be a fool." Fiona had been faintly offended, but in the end, she had done so, although who "they" were hadn't been specified. The police? The Justice Department? The killer or killers? Or some unspecified, maybe hired, bad guys?

Fiona thought to ask the woman how she even knew about Fiona's "investigation," and the woman had said, "Don't you realize everybody in law enforcement and justice in the province is interested in it?" When Fiona had asked why, the woman had stared at her as if she were an idiot, then, turning her face away with a grim expression, merely shrugged.

Fiona was anxious to avoid alerting anyone that she was on the trail again, if anyone continued to watch her, which she doubted.

Oh, that's ridiculous!

This isn't Raymond Chandler country, and I'm no jaded but fearless private eye. But her phone had been tapped; no question about that, although only briefly and using clunky old equipment that she could actually hear being activated on the line. That, of course, she finally realized, had been more designed to scare her than to steal information. There was no information – she took a deep breath. Getting angry all over again wouldn't help.

She was in the hotel lobby, just shutting down the computer with an air of triumph, having located an Evan Kirby in, of all places, back in Ripley, when her cell rang. It was Arnie, calling to ask her to come back to the hospital so that he and Greg could go up the mountainside to the house for some real food and a brief rest.

"Take all the time you need, Arnie," she told him, although she couldn't wait to get on a plane and return to Calgary where she could get in her car and drive to see Kirby. "I'll stay at the hospital until you get back." And then she would try to find out who Emily Zhang married, and where she lived, and give her a call. *Pretend I'm just calling to say hello, or something,* though that might not work because they had never really been friends, just kids thrown together by circumstance.

She thought suddenly, my God, I really am back into it, but instead of the horror and the fear that had assailed her at the sight of the brown envelope, she felt a return of the old excitement, the thought that maybe this time she would succeed. She hadn't liked failing, especially hadn't liked being beaten, or being, as she suspected, an object of derision to those men who had succeeded in stopping her from finding the answer to the puzzle.

Which reminded her of the big puzzle that nobody official had seemed willing to address, that Fiona had been led to believe was only a rumour. And yet, for Fiona anyway, had always had a strong hint of it being the truth.

The rumour was that Zara (who had gone on into secretarial school while Fiona had enrolled in the local university) had been buying some expensive formal dresses in the weeks before her murder. Fiona had found this out fairly early after her decision to write her book, but when she asked around – the unasked question was 'where would she get the money?' – nobody she asked had actually seen the dresses or even claimed to have been shopping with her. Fiona would have gone to the two best dress stores in Ripley to ask them if Zara had shopped there, but both stores had closed years ago. The police certainly weren't talking, nor was her only roommate, herself a pretty girl – though hardly in Zara's class – and who apparently, even though she lived with her, had had no idea what was going on in Zara's life, and refused to answer Fiona's question about Zara buying new dresses. She also would not answer when Fiona had asked her what had become of the dresses, had only shrugged and turned her head away. Hmm, Fiona had thought, so there were dresses? Or there weren't. If there were, doubtless they were forever lost in the maw of police headquarters. Or taken by the roommate?

Fiona had always doubted that the roommate, Delphine, didn't know anything about her roommate's life, but in the one short interview she had managed to wangle with her, Delphine had answered her questions in monosyllables, no matter how straightforward and non-threatening Fiona had tried to be, and either stared off into the distance or fixed Fiona with a look of such cold disdain that she had given up. Was she always like this, Fiona had wondered? Or had the police warned her not to talk to anybody about what she knew? Or was it her lawyer? Why would she need a lawyer? Nobody was accusing Delphine of anything. No, she surmised: it had to be the police who told her to keep quiet. That is, assuming she did know something about Zara's life that nobody else knew.

She tried to remember where the box containing all the files and records of her ten years of question-asking were. Downstairs in her storage unit, she supposed. She wondered if she could find it when she got back. She felt a strong need to familiarize herself with the details of the coroner's report and the inquest. And it wouldn't hurt to go through the Delphine interview again to see if she could pull out even the tiniest inconsistency. As if she hadn't already done all that a thousand times when she was writing her book.

She had done the same with accounts of the murder itself. Not so unusual in the details the coroner provided to the inquest: certain wounds to the face and skull from being bludgeoned with some blunt object; raped, although it was never revealed whether by one or by more than one man, at least in part because DNA technology as applied to criminal cases had not yet been invented. And then, possibly or not (that was never clear either) dying from her wounds, she had been smothered either with a pillow or with bedclothes while she still breathed and her heart still beat, and her blood still flowed through her veins.

Or, more coldly: the coroner determined that she had died from suffocation, telling the inquest jury that the pinpoint hemorrhages in her eyes proved this. Fiona thought that surely the pillow cover would have saliva and maybe blood on it, but no mention was made of this at the inquest, or anywhere else that she knew of. Nor had the object she'd been clubbed with, as far as Fiona knew, ever been identified. Now why was that? Maybe the murderer had taken his weapon away with him. That would make sense, she thought.

And again her mind wandered to the worst question of all: would Zara have survived her wounds and rape, had she not been smothered? Maybe there would have been brain damage, maybe plastic surgeons would have been unable to return the smashed face to its former beauty, but

Zara would be alive today, probably married and with a family, probably having the middle class life they had all aspired to. All dreams of fame and glory gone with the destruction of that exquisite face.

When she returned to the ICU, Fiona was surprised to find Marian twitching her hands and occasionally moving her mouth. She called her nurse over.

"Oh, yes," the nurse said. "Now that the ventilator is gone and all her major organs seem to be working again on their own, we've decided to wake her up so that we can do some tests to see how she is faring." She was cheerful enough, but not about to give any real details to Fiona.

"And we'll be moving her out of here, probably later today or maybe during the night. Once we're sure she's still doing all right." Fiona wanted to ask, and she will be fine again? She will be quarrelsome, envious Marian again? She'll be able to go back to being Arnie's wife, in their beautiful house across the water? But she didn't bother because she knew that the nurse would not tell her. Also, although Arnie hadn't mentioned it, she knew that the possibility of brain damage was very real. First things first, she thought, and now that Greg had arrived, Fiona decided to leave in the morning.

er condo was bright in the clear autumn sun when she unlocked the door and stepped inside, so bright that she felt at once that some of the gloom under which she'd been labouring had been caused by the Vancouver weather. Feeling better than she'd felt for days, her sister on the mend, she hung her raincoat in the closet, kicked off her shoes, and did a quick inspection. She made herself a cup of her favourite dark-roast coffee, and allowed herself a few moments of rest and readjustment. Marian would live and prosper; she, Fiona, was back in the business of Zara's murder. She had a half-dozen leads to get to work on at once, the most pressing being to find and talk to this Evan Kirby.

She had no sooner seated herself in her favourite armchair, her legs stretched out on the footstool before her, her coffee on the table beside her, when the phone rang.

"Fiona Leith! Have I found you at last? This is Marigold Martin. You once knew me as Marjory, Marjory Popowich. Or Margie Popowich." She said it with a hard 'g.' "I'm still Margie, of course, although I prefer Marigold."

Fiona was tempted to simply hang up as she remembered Marjory all too well. Another pretty girl, also a blonde (although not a natural one), who, despite being three years younger, had been excessively jealous of Zara, and more or less led the pack of those girls who were always criticizing her. From the moment Marjory had stepped in the door of their high school, a fourteen year old who could have passed for eighteen, she had presented herself as an important person, and acted as if she were one of the envied seniors, so that people forgot she was just another 'freshie,' as they said in those days, and the older kids, including Zara Stanley, had let her hang around with them. Marjory had been one of those hinting at dark secrets, which only meant that she wanted people to believe that Zara had slept with all her boyfriends, the worst kind of calumny back in the days before the so-called sexual revolution.

"Yes," she said, injecting no friendliness into her voice. "You have the right Fiona, although my last name has been Lychenko for forty years. I remember you very well."

Marjory laughed, the sound false, although not uncertain. "Maybe you know what I'm doing now?"

"Yes, you work in television. That's right, isn't it?"

"And you know," Marjory went on as if Fiona hadn't spoken, "I just thought my real name needed a little tweaking so it would sound better on TV. And I always loved the name Marigold. Don't you?"

"A very pretty name," she agreed, although 'tweaking' was an understatement.

"You always used 'FLL' in your columns, instead of your real name," Marigold/Marjory pointed out. "I made it my business to find out who FLL was. I'm sorry you lost that job," she added, but her tone was smug.

"I was rather sorry myself," Fiona said, making her voice as wry as she could. "Why are you calling, Marg–Marigold?"

"Oh, you know," Marigold answered. "I've done rather well in television. I have my own interview show now – it's being syndicated by the way – and I've been casting about for new challenges." She said "new challenges" as if she were a Nobel laureate looking for a new research project. Fiona had caught Marigold's show once by accident when she was flipping through channels, and almost at once recognized the Botoxed, face-lifted countenance. At the time, Roman being still very much alive, she had thought she would never stoop so low, but lately she'd been wondering if she should look into what might be done for her own aging face and body. Doubtless Marigold knocked ten years off her age, too, or how would she even be allowed on television so filled with young, pretty women. Maybe that was why she was looking for "new challenges."

"Oh?" she said, not trying to sound interested, waiting patiently for the reason for Marigold's call.

"I've decided to go into made-for-television movies, or MOWs as we say in the business. That stands for 'movie of the week.'" Fiona chose not to say that she knew this. "And I read your book. The one about Zara Stanley's murder? I thought it would make a great film so as soon as I finished it, I started work right away on a screenplay. Now, before you say anything," Fiona could feel heat rising from her chest up her neck and into her face, and it was all she could do to keep from shouting an outraged 'What?' at her caller. "Before you say anything," here Marigold laughed gaily, "the story belongs to everyone, you know, not just to…" she hesitated, "the person who wrote a book about it."

"I know that, Marjory," Fiona said.

"Marigold. And finally, we're about ready to start shooting. In fact, the first day of the principal shoot is tomorrow. I just couldn't wait to tell you! I knew you'd be thrilled!"

"Why would I be thrilled?" she asked, although even as she said it, it dawned on her why Marigold was phoning her. To crow. No other reason. Just to crow about having one-upped her. She gritted her teeth.

"Oh, come on, Fiona," Marjory said. "When I told people I thought I knew you, and phoned around a bit to find out just who you were in school, I discovered that nobody could remember you."

Fiona was at a loss as to how to return the insult. "Well, it is so kind of you to call and let me know about your film. I do appreciate it. Best of luck" Marigold interrupted, saying rapidly, "And I thought you'd want to know that I think I've solved it. I know who did it."

For a second, she couldn't get her breath. She managed to say, "Tell me then, who was it?" although she doubted she could hear an answer over the loud whooshing in her ears. Still, how many times had she heard that from one person or another? And hadn't they all been wrong? Suddenly, she remembered Emily, saw her chance, and instantly, her annoyance vanished.

"Do you remember who Emily Zhang married?"

Marjory/Marigold, sounding a bit disconcerted, replied, "Well, wasn't it Lawrence Cheng? You remember him. Incredibly good-looking, for a…I mean just really handsome. He was way older than me, but you couldn't miss him in the halls."

"Right out of high school?"

"Heavens, no. It was maybe ten years later."

"Oh right. I think maybe I heard that somewhere."

There was a pause, and then Marigold asked: "Don't you want to know who I think did it?" Fiona almost said, did what?

"Well, sure," she said, easily, as if she found Marigold amusing.

"You'll have to wait for that," Marigold said. Fiona took a deep breath and expelled it into Marigold's ear. "You'll have to wait just like everybody else. Oh, and it wasn't who you think it was, either, not who you pointed to in your… book," the last word said with a hint of disdain.

"I pointed to no one in the book," Fiona said, suddenly furious, but Marigold apparently anticipating Fiona was about to hang up, said hastily, "and I know something else."

"Something?" Fiona prompted her.

"Something about the case."

"Yes? What?"

"Do you remember Troy Venables? He went into law enforcement."

"Vaguely," Fiona answered, her irritation rising again. "Very big kid, wasn't he? Towered over everybody in the halls. What about him?"

"I started to date him – later, out of school, after our divorces. He was on the Ripley Police Force then."

"I never even knew you'd been married!" but it seemed this wasn't what Marigold wanted to tell her.

"He was involved in the investigation, back in the beginning. The *real* one, you know." Fiona held her tongue. "He told me something nobody else knows."

"There are a heckuva lot of things about that case that nobody knows," Fiona said, doing her best to sound as if she were simply bored.

"Not this one," Marigold said. "This one is the clincher."

"Okay, Marjory – er, Margie," Fiona said, impatient again. "What is it? Is there a witness nobody knew about? Is there a confession? Was it Jack the Ripper?" She was getting angrier as she spoke.

"The murderer took a souvenir," Marjory spoke very slowly, leaving spaces between her words. "Nobody knows that, but Troy said, find the souvenir, and you've got the killer." There was a long silence, triumphant on Marjory's part; deeply thoughtful on Fiona's.

"But you're not going to tell me what the souvenir was."

"You'll have to wait for my film." A tinkle of false laughter, and she hung up with a gentle click.

Gotcha!

"What a stupid bitch you are," Fiona said out loud to the absent Marigold. Ah, she thought, Marigold doesn't know what the souvenir – more likely a trophy, she thought suddenly – is either. Troy Venables was big, but he was as dumb as a post, and he would have been only a constable then. How would he have known anything at all important about the case? Probably he had just made it up to get into Marjory's pants. And besides, isn't that standard police procedure in a murder? To hold back some detail only the killer would know?

Upset as she was, her face still hot, her palms sweaty, still fuming, Fiona was already beginning to forget the conversation because she recalled now that she had seen Emily and Lawrence's wedding notice in the paper, indeed about ten years after she had left high school. The wedding had been in Hart City, where Larry had run a lucrative if small chain of men's clothing stores. More than once, Roman, in Hart City on business, had brought home a new suit or shirts from the flagship location there. When he had brought home that elegant grey silk suit sometime after the trip to China – for Ottawa meetings, he said – she remembered mentioning to him that she'd known Larry Cheng in high school. Maybe she'd even told him that she'd been in the same class as his wife, Emily. Some years after that she had heard that Larry's business had gone into bankruptcy. Too bad. If it was even true.

She turned away from the phone, gazing down at her cooling cup of coffee, puzzling over her own brain's peculiar behaviour. She'd known all along that Emily Zhang had married Lawrence Cheng. So why hadn't that information floated to the surface at once?

Because, she thought, even though there is nothing that I want to do more, I also dread the prospect of trying to find Emily, of trying to get her to talk to me. I dread the thought of getting into all that *stuff* again: people hanging up on me, people refusing to talk to me, or talking to me so stiffly and rudely that I have no choice but to give up. Being followed by the police again as soon as they figure out that I'm back asking questions. Or having my phone tapped again just to scare me.

But how would they know I'm involved again? Her mind scrabbled backward to the evening the envelope had appeared in her foyer. Whoever had brought her that envelope; if they knew who that person was because they were watching him or her. Not me. That person. And not for the first time in the ten or so years since she'd been involved in Zara Stanley's story, she wondered if just maybe Zara was a restless ghost who kept dropping bits of tantalizing information into her lap, was the one who would not let her quit.

She would spend the rest of the day gathering her thoughts, remembering details from her earlier researches, searching for that set of mind that made it possible for her to keep going in the face of setback after setback. Being hung up on, being followed, being yelled at. *Nothing,* she told herself, *compared to what happened to Zara.*

Chapter Five

Once in bed, though, she couldn't go to sleep. A city bus went by and stopped outside her building with a pneumatic sigh; in the distance a police siren burped once, twice, then began to wail, stopping as abruptly as it had begun. Yet she preferred this to the rural hush that had begun to say to her, over and over again, you are alone now in the world, the *void* not even a half-step away, a terrifying, endless black depth. Every day since Roman's death, she had felt herself inching closer and closer, so that sometimes, out of nowhere, sweat would break out all over her body, even while chills raced up and down her spine. She knew somewhere in her brain that the *void* was a breakdown, maybe even the temptation to suicide. But she refused to go to a counsellor, wasn't about to find herself drugged on top of everything else she was suffering: grief, loss, emptiness, at its worst, this nameless, faceless terror.

No, starting a new book was her only hope. I've been trying for years to save Zara, maybe now she will save me.

She put on the light, sat up against her pillows and stared across the room at the blank space just above where she had hung a row of pictures, pastoral scenes, prints not originals, that she and Roman had bought at an art show in the village near their farm, because Vonnie, the convener of the show, had cajoled them.

She made a disgusted sound, pushed back the covers, crossed the room, and took down all four of them, and one by one, carefully, she leaned them, faces to the wall, below where they had hung. Satisfied out of all proportion to the act itself, she retreated back to bed. Vonnie wouldn't care, or, if she did, Fiona would simply say that she had liked them when she bought them but was now indifferent to them and wanted to find something to hang that truly appealed to her. Come to think of it, there was a good chance that Vonnie wouldn't even remember she had bought them.

This was in the nature of a revelation: it was true; she knew it; she always took her relationships with people more seriously than they did! It occurred to her to wonder, given how satisfying taking them down had felt, if maybe she had just taken her first step toward a new life. Don't be silly, she told herself, but she couldn't stop a small smile.

She got up then, made herself a cup of tea, found the novel she'd been reading when – it seemed months ago although it was only days – Arnie had phoned her about Marian, took it to her favourite armchair, tossed the afghan over her feet and legs, and began to read.

She woke to the ringing of the phone. Sunlight streamed in her east-facing windows, her back hurt, and she knew she must have been snoring because her mouth was open and her lips so dry they were stuck to her teeth. Bewildered, struggling to untangle herself from the afghan, she managed to find the phone before it switched to voice mail. Had she been dreaming? Must have been, because unidentifiable voices were still echoing in her head, and pictures that made no sense began to fade and recede.

"This is your dearest friend and former neighbour Veronica Sorrel," Vonnie said, sounding as if she were holding the phone too close. Through her kitchen window Fiona could see gangs of kids making their way toward the school across the way from her building, and thought to glance at the clock to find it was eight in the morning.

"Where the hell are you, Veronica Sorrel?" she demanded, pushing her hair back out of her eyes.

"Home," Vonnie said. "I got back late last night. I think you've got the right idea about giving up this blasted country living. It rained and I had two miles of muddy road to negotiate at 1:00 a.m. It wasn't any fun, I'll tell you. My new car is cute as can be, but it hasn't got more than an inch of clearance."

"And no handy male to rescue you," Fiona said, then quickly. "Which is why I left the farm. What are you doing home so soon? I thought you were staying in Toronto until Christmas at least."

"Was," Vonnie said, "But something happened. That's why I'm phoning."

"What?" Fiona asked, suddenly breathless. In her recent experience all news was bad.

"Nothing bad," Vonnie said, "just that I've gotten notice that I'm going to receive a provincial honour as a volunteer and…" she stopped talking, apparently waiting for Fiona to say something before she went on.

"And what?" Fiona demanded. "Vonnie that's great!"

"Isn't it? I'm totally thrilled, as the kids say. Will you be my date?"

"I don't get it, why me?" Fiona was glad Vonnie, who was always perfectly groomed and coiffed, couldn't see her, her hair standing on end and still in her, it must be admitted, close-to-ragged nightgown at such an hour. And yet, with Vonnie on the phone, and the sun lighting her whole condo as if it were spring instead of early fall, the *void* had retreated to a small black dot somewhere near the front door.

"It's simple," Vonnie told her. "You may have noticed that I no longer have a husband to be my escort; that my brothers all live in Ontario, and I have three daughters and no sons, and even the girls are nowhere very close by."

"Couldn't you find some man in all those committees you're on? There must be one who isn't attached."

"If there is, I don't know who, and anyway, the divorce isn't final yet. I don't like the idea of showing up with an escort for everybody to speculate about. I want you to come with me, be my guest of honour. It'll give you a chance to dress up, get your hair done, find something fabulous to wear. Like we were girls getting ready for the big dance."

"When is it?"

"Two weeks," Vonnie said. "Quit stalling. Just say yes."

"Yes," Fiona said, making her voice cheerful, "Okay, you bet."

"Good. I knew you wouldn't let me down. I'll be in touch about details, and in the meantime, Fee, you go shopping, get yourself a stunner of a dress. And don't tell me you can't afford it. I know Roman didn't leave you poor."

"Bossy as ever," Fiona told her before saying good-bye. She could imagine that there would be nothing but beige lace mother-of-the-bride dresses that would fit her, and she'd stay home before she'd dress that badly. But two weeks wouldn't leave her enough time to lose weight. She could imagine Vonnie in some chic number she'd picked up in Montreal or maybe in Ottawa when she was at one of her meetings there. Even now Vonnie was probably enjoying a cup of coffee in her green-flowered breakfast nook, wearing a quilted satin dressing gown with matching slippers. The image made her laugh – it was so fifties, and so true. She wondered again how much longer Vonnie would last on the farm by herself. Doubtless the divorce would force her and Jack into selling.

Before she could stop herself, riding on the wave of good feeling Vonnie's phone call had brought her, she found the Kirby phone number that she'd written down in Vancouver, and, trying not to even think of what she would say, or what it was she wanted from him, she was punching his number.

"Kirby residence," a woman answered. His wife then.

"Hello, this is Fiona Lychenko calling. May I speak with Mr. Kirby?"

"I'm sorry, but Mr. Kirby isn't available."

"When will he be available?" She had decided to do her best to maintain a Vonnie-voice as self-assured, undismissible, as her own voice, at least these days when she had to stop and think most of the time before she could say her own name, was not.

"May I inquire as to why you would like to speak with him?"

"Am I speaking to Mrs. Kirby?"

"I am Mr. Kirby's housekeeper, Mrs. Edel." Fiona felt herself faltering, couldn't think what to say next. Into the silence Mrs. Edel, hesitating herself, said, "Mr. Kirby resides in an elder-care home now."

"Perhaps you could give me the name of his home?" Fiona felt she was starting to fail in this encounter as, shocked by the news of the elder-care home, she had lost that Vonnie-voice. "He and I went to high school together. We were good friends once, and..." improvising now, "he was once close to my sister. I thought he would like to know that she has been seriously ill." It amazed Fiona to hear herself lie, wasn't sure why she had, suspected that she didn't need to. Still, there would be only this one chance, and she wouldn't give up without a fight.

"He resides at the Willow Bend Home in the southern part of the city," Mrs. Edel told her.

"We're talking about Hart City, are we?" Fiona asked briskly, success causing her to recover some assurance.

"Heaven's no," Mrs. Edel said. "We are talking about here in Ripley where he lived." Ah, Fiona thought, I have to go there right away, and while I'm at it, I'll drive on to Hart City and find Emily Cheng. I've got to shower...

Her hand was still on the phone when it rang again, startling her.

"Fiona." She recognized Arnie's voice at once. "Marian's awake now. Not talking because her throat is too sore, but I told her you'd been here with her, and she smiled, so I thought I'd phone and let you know."

"Is she...umm...okay?" Fiona asked, not sure herself what she meant by this.

"She'll have to learn to walk again, even to feed herself

because her throat is a mess from the intubations, but," here he heaved a sigh, "here is the best news: her mental faculties are pretty much intact. Who would have thought it?"

"It's truly wonderful," Fiona agreed, although it hadn't quite registered that even if she lived, Marian might not be her normal self ever again. "I'm so very glad."

She could feel her face heating and knew it was because she was ashamed of only now allowing herself to realize how desperate Marian's condition had been, and, in fact, still was, and that she was not a proper sister, but a selfish, unloving one. She also knew if she said this, Arnie would deny it, whether he thought it was true or not. She asked herself, not for the first or the last time, *What the heck is the matter with me?*

"Fiona?"

She said, "Who will help her learn to walk and so on?" She had to pause mid-sentence to clear her throat.

"She's going into a rehabilitation facility for a couple of weeks before she comes home. Then I'll take over." There was another long pause. "Honestly," he said, "I have to tell you – I never realized how much I love that little sister of yours." She could hear him swallow and knew he would be wiping away his tears. "And you and Roman…"

"Roman and I did just fine," she told him, although with the passing of the weeks since his death, and her becoming accustomed to his absence, she had begun to think more and more often of this and that, episodes, conversations they'd had, and she was surprised at how much resentment she was uncovering, not just on her part, but on his too. Do all widows go through this? A lot of widows seem to go through a process that transforms their husbands into saints, and their marriages into paradise. She had never been in any danger of that.

For some reason, she thought again of that long trip he had taken to China without her. She was beginning to think that she wouldn't be able to put it aside until she did some serious sleuthing about it. If she could remember who else had gone. But Arnie had moved on in the conversation.

"I finally found Angela. Can you believe it? She says she can't come right now."

"What does go on in that girl's head," Fiona said, her mind already on hanging up so she could bathe, dress and get into the car to drive to Ripley.

"I know," Arnie said, his voice positively gay. "Well, must go. Lots to do, bills to pay, housework, quick visit to the hospital."

It was a six hour drive to Ripley, lots of time for thinking, although usually thinking was the one thing she didn't want to do. There had been too much thinking after Roman died and she had to make major decision after major decision: whether to sell the farm or not; how to handle the money Roman had invested, not to mention a startlingly large amount of cash she had found in his safe deposit box. And then, when she'd gone through his boxes of papers, she'd found by accident another large amount she had known nothing about, in a trust account in Edmonton. One that didn't have her name on it; in fact, he had somehow gotten away without naming a beneficiary.

That particular piece of business really puzzled her – as if the cash in the safety deposit box wasn't strange enough – because although Roman had managed their finances he had always kept her informed. And why Edmonton? She still hadn't figured that one out. It was almost as if he were hiding it, a thought she erased at once. Probably that trust had been offering better rates. Or the deposit there had to do with diversifying for safety. Still…why hadn't he told her? Or put her name as beneficiary? Not that it mattered, as she was sole inheritor of everything.

Of course, she'd wondered too why he had been stowing money away in his safe deposit box instead of investing it, or even putting it into a savings account so it could be earning for them. The bank manager had been as startled as she was when they'd opened the box, had sat motionless for a second seeming to be thinking, then composed himself, and let it pass. It had occurred to her that Roman might have been trying to escape some taxes, although he'd never been one to complain unduly about taxes as some of their farmer friends did. Or maybe he was saving it for some purpose, or just hadn't gotten around to investing it when he fell sick and never recovered. How unimportant that money must have seemed to him when he was inches from oblivion. Whatever. Now it was hers, what was left after the taxes, even though she hadn't much idea what to do with it, and didn't want the responsibility of managing it. Just another of the endless widow-things she had to deal with.

The road between Calgary and the small city of Ripley was so familiar to her that for once she could relax and drive without strain. Some of the fall colours were still out, the fields on each side of the road mostly harvested, and many of them full of wild ducks and geese starting their migration south. As she drove past one field a host of snow geese rose as one and circled the field, rising higher and higher until the leaders began to head east, the great mass of birds becoming a wide, lifting spiral following them. The burning blue of the sky was blotted out by hundreds and hundreds of wheeling, calling birds.

Tears had smeared her view and soaked her cheeks without Fiona being fully aware of it. This is what she had lost by Roman's death, because she had sold the farm, never questioning whether this was necessary or not, and, in what she now suspected was a mistaken belief that she could have a whole new life, had gone to live in a strange city. Because, she was admitting now, it had been lonely enough with Roman gone all the time; she couldn't imagine a life completely alone on the farm. They had set themselves apart from the rest of the community: Roman, through his appointments to government commissions and committees, thus getting his name in the paper a lot; she, a woman, by writing a newspaper column about, of all things, agriculture and then by writing a book that, if it wasn't exactly a national bestseller, was definitely a *cause célèbre* in Ripley, had gotten her on the local TV talk shows.

Driving with one hand, she wiped her eyes. The view out her windshield was once again ninety percent sky, and she drove slowly, leaning forward over the wheel so that she could see it all. She even rolled down a window so that she could fill her lungs with the delicious prairie air tinted with the smell of damp stalks and wheat chaff lying in the fields, hinting at the wild. Instead of making her feel worse at what she had lost, she found herself soothed, and soon her thoughts had moved elsewhere, to the object of her journey. Next time, she thought, echoes of her old caution returning, maybe she should rent a car rather than driving her own.

But nobody knows I received that envelope – do they?

When she drove into Ripley she could see the spreading blue and white of the extended care home she was heading for on a hill to the northeast and she turned her car in that direction. Just as she was about to pull into the parking lot, though, she had a second thought and drove on by. Four blocks down the road, she knew, there was a small shopping mall anchored by a large chain grocery store where she had sometimes shopped when she came into town from the farm. She parked in the busy lot by the grocery store, took out her handbag, got out and, locking the door behind her, walked toward the elder-care home where Evan Kirby now lived.

She had to remember that she'd lied to Mrs. Edel about Kirby's having dated Marian. She would have to refer to it with Kirby, but then explain that she must have confused him with someone else. Marian was too young to have dated Kirby even if she had known him, which Fiona was sure Marian hadn't. Besides that, they'd gone to different high schools so chances of them meeting each other were slim to zero.

She had put on shoes with medium high heels because he was a man after all, and then because she looked such a nonentity in her serviceable grey pant suit, had tucked a patterned red, black and white scarf in the neck of her white blouse. As she strolled, she tried out different scenarios for the interview with Kirby, but soon gave that up, remembering that she had to first find out his room number which would mean talking to a nurse or an attendant in the reception area, to whom she would also have to lie. Any fool could tell when Fiona lied. In person that is; evidently she could get away with it over the phone. Maybe if I just pretend I'm Vonnie – stride in with a big smile and act as if nobody could ever refuse me anything.

From the hilltop the sky again took up most of the view, the city small and pale, its furthest boundaries easily seen, its downtown mostly lowrise, and, in the afternoon light, shining white and pale blue with abundant, half-leafless trees lining the avenues. A pretty city, if small, an easy place to live, as Calgary was not. She supposed it never would be, for her anyway, as an aging woman – why can't I say *old*? she asked herself angrily. *I am an old woman.* Hardly noticing, she had crossed the busy parking lot, gone in the big front doors, and was looking about for someone to ask about visiting Mr. Kirby.

The inevitable question came from a stout, middle-aged woman in street clothes who stood behind the desk holding a pair of scissors, with bits of coloured paper strewn around where she stood: "Are you a relative?"

"I am an old friend, or rather, the sister of an old friend who is too ill now to visit herself. Fiona Leith Lychenko."

"Here," the woman said, sliding a notepad and a pen across the desk toward her with a free hand. Fiona must have looked puzzled. "Your name," the woman said. Fiona printed it carefully and pushed it back to the receptionist.

"Lychenko?" Fiona nodded. "I'll ask Mr. Kirby if he'll see you." Taking the paper with her, she went away down one of the halls radiating from the busy central area, where people in wheelchairs sat watching television or playing board games or cards, and women wearing brightly-coloured smocks pushed carts with glasses of fruit juice and plates of cookies on them, or piles of magazines, or paperback books. Nervously, Fiona tried to see which room the receptionist had gone into, but could only determine that it was somewhere in the middle of the long, bright hallway with the shiny floor and sunlight pouring in through skylights. She was back at once.

"That way, third door down on your left." Fiona thanked her with a bright smile which the woman ignored, and went at a steady stride in the direction she was pointed, trying to keep her head up, her back straight, as if to say that she was fully in charge. She knocked lightly on the open door and entered.

Two of the walls were covered with bookshelves bowing under the weight of many leather-covered books. The one long window was opened to a smooth lawn and past that, to the main road beyond. Pink and mauve gladioli interspersed with wilting white daisies sat in a tall vase on a table by the window, to the left of which a hospital bed stood; on the wall above its foot, a television set hung on the wall. Evan Kirby, presumably, sat in a leather easy chair with an extended foot support. She recognized him, but barely. He was bald now, and wore glasses, and she noticed at once how pale he was and how his hands, resting on the arms of his chair shook steadily, the left more than the right. Under the green and brown plaid afghan that covered him from his waist to his feet she saw a frame wasted to almost nothing. The paper with her name printed on it lay on his lap. He lifted his head shakily from the headrest as she came forward.

"Hello, Mr. Kirby. What a pleasant room," she said, smiling in a formal way at him, not quite daring to pretend friendliness.

"I recall your name," he told her, his voice quavering as though he could no longer control it. "But I can't remember our acquaintanceship." The last word had descended to a throaty whisper.

"I believe you knew my sister," Fiona told him. "Marian was her name. Marian Leith."

He appeared to ponder. "I think not. You may have confused me with someone else. She's ill, you say?"

"I'm so sorry," Fiona said. "Maybe I have made a mistake, but I thought…" She did her best to mimic puzzlement. "Marian has had a heart attack. A very serious one. She's in Vancouver General. And as I would be in Ripley, I thought I should find her old friends, her close ones I mean, and let them know so that if they wanted to, they could maybe…see her." He motioned with a shaking arm and hand that she should sit. She sat in a straight-backed chair across from him that she hadn't noticed until he indicated it, wondering how to proceed. "You and I were in the same high school," she began.

"I know you from somewhere else," he interrupted. She was unnerved by his gaze, so direct, so piercing in so frail a body, as if he might see right through her, and she was stricken with something like pity and looked down at her knees. "Oh, of course. You wrote that book. I have it here somewhere."

"I'm flattered," she said, offering him her most pleasant smile which he seemed to be trying to return. "I'm afraid it was all a bit of a bust in the end." He laughed, swallowed, coughed, then regained his breath.

"Did you think you could solve a case the entire police force couldn't?" he asked her. "Or the Justice department?

The Attorney General's office?" But now he was frankly smiling in a wry way. How many times had she answered this question, even if it was only implied. *I wasn't trying to solve it; I was just trying to put pressure toward getting it solved; I just wanted to stop the ugly rumors about Zara. I was just trying to find something interesting to do with my life.* This last she had never said aloud to anybody.

"I'm not aware that the latter two were involved," she told him mildly, still smiling. "Weren't you a Deputy Minister in one of those offices?" Maybe that was too direct.

"Have we established that I do not and never did know your sister...did you say Marian?"

"My memory was that you dated during your last high school year and that you were informally engaged. But... it must have been somebody else, although I can't think who. I am sorry to have bothered you."

"I am glad enough for a new visitor now and then," he replied. He lifted one hand to do something with his glasses, straighten them perhaps, but couldn't seem to grasp them, and finally gave up, lowered his hand to his lap where it fell against the piece of paper with her name on it.

"Can I help you?" she offered, uncertainly. He didn't reply. She thought, what the hell, and asked in a rush, "Do you remember Zara Stanley?"

"I am a male," he replied. "I could hardly forget her." He laughed, soundlessly this time. "It is such a shame what happened to her."

"Just terrible," Fiona said, "and that her killer or killers weren't caught somehow makes it worse."

"I absolutely agree," he told her, turning his head

toward the window through which the sun shone softly, and having trouble with the word 'absolutely.' Fiona hesitated, moved by his emotion, or what she thought was his emotion, at the mention of Zara's death.

"But you know," she said, lowering her voice as if she were merely ruminating, "to this day I wonder why the investigation failed. I mean, despite what a few people claim about the police not bothering much about her murder, that sort of thing. My impression when I was doing the research was of an earnest and intelligent effort on their part. But…"

"But what?" he asked. It came out in several syllables: Bu…u…t. His left hand was joggling more intensely now, and he lifted his right from the paper to push the left down between the armrest and his body, which stilled it. Fiona kept her eyes on his face.

"But they all know they failed, and they all feel terrible about it. And besides that," she went on, warming to her subject. "It seemed to me that there was a lot of buried anger about what happened then – I mean, in the police force. As if they thought they were on the track, and then, just like that, something happened. And then the whole investigation went off the rails. I've wondered and wondered about that. What happened, I mean."

When she glanced up again from her soliloquy she was disconcerted by the expression on his face, one of something close to dislike, unless it was his illness – Parkinson's, she supposed – that forced his face into grimaces he didn't intend to make. The intensity in his eyes was equally disturbing. And yet, why had she come? *Evan Kirby*, the paper had said, and it was as good as saying, *Evan Kirby knows.* What could she do but ask him what he knew?

What would a private detective do? A police detective? A real investigative journalist? But she had no idea.

"This is an intuition on your part?" His expression had softened. "You have guessed that, and now you have turned it into an article of faith, and are pursuing it as if you knew it for a fact." She would have answered sharply, but held back because she would want to see him again, or so she thought.

"Maybe you're right," she said. "Although it seems self-evident to me." There was a long pause. "But tell me, what do you think about it? Who do you think killed Zara? And why do you think the police failed?" He sighed, let his head fall back against the headrest.

"I have no idea. I was in government then, living in Hart City. I'd just married my second wife, we were expecting a child. I hardly noticed the case."

"I suppose that would be true of a lot of people at the time," she said. "You were in government a long time, I'm told, and at a very senior position. You must know all kinds of things. Didn't you ever hear anything about this case in all those years?"

"So this is why you've come." He made a strange noise; a laugh, she realized. "You made up the sister story to get in! Well," he went on, "I did read your book and I must say, nobody could ever say you're stupid." He was still laughing, although soundlessly. She laughed with him, her voice sounding forced even to her own ears.

"I'm sorry," she said. "I just…"

"Can't let things go," he finished for her. She didn't know how to answer this.

"I guess I should," she said, finally, but his eyes were closed; he seemed to have fallen asleep. She waited a minute, but when he didn't open them and she saw that his hands were both stilled, she rose hesitantly, and quietly left the room.

As she was about to exit through the main doors, coming through them was a handsome, smartly-dressed elderly woman, her smooth white hair pulled back in a chignon, carrying a large bouquet composed of the same flowers she'd seen in Kirby's room. This had to be Mrs. Edel. She turned to watch the woman's progress down the hall, and indeed, it appeared to her that she had gone into Kirby's room.

I learned nothing, she told herself in dismay as she hiked back toward the shopping mall and her car. I doubt he'll see me again when I finally have a real question. Stupid. I shouldn't have gone without preparation. But what could I have done? Proper research about his career, I suppose; I could have tried to find out about his life, who he worked with, what departments he had been in, for how long, and when. Then I would have had something to talk to him about. I could have pretended I was going to do a profile on him – but everybody in Ripely knows I don't work for the paper anymore. Everybody knows I got fired.

She sat in her car for a minute before starting it, trying to decide whether to get a hotel room for the night or to go on to Hart City, which she could easily reach before nightfall. Stay there overnight, track down Emily Cheng, go to see her before she drove back to Calgary. She felt exhausted, the long drive to Hart City more than she could manage, and Vonnie was only fifty miles away. Why not call her? See if she could spend the night with her?

But when she dialed her number, the voice mail came

on. Fiona debated, then hung up without leaving a message. Since Jack's perfidy had come to light and he had moved out, Vonnie was at home as little as possible, had told Fiona that was her plan, her way of keeping away the blues, as Fiona's had been to move to a strange city. On the run, both of them. On the run from their own newly unbearable lives.

Sitting there in the grocery store parking lot she could have wept right then for all she had lost. It was all too hard; it was pointless. Yet, at seventy, how much time had she left anyway? What a relief to let all this go, to be free of this constant grief, this sense of floundering, of her own uselessness. If they had had kids – but they hadn't had kids. There were no children to busy herself with, no beloved grandchildren to babysit.

As always happened when she hit these low points, a physical pain would start, sometimes in her chest, sometimes in a hip, or unaccountably racing down an arm as if she were having a heart attack. Angered by the pain, furious at herself over the failed interview with Evan Kirby, she opened the car door, got out, and right there in the parking lot with people walking by did some stretches she'd learned in an abortive attempt to do Tai Chi. Abortive because she could only remember a few moves at a time, and her balance wasn't sure enough anymore. Finished, shaking out her shoulders, she found the pain had retreated, as had also any nearby shoppers. She got back in the car, put it in gear, and pointed it to Hart City and Emily Zhang Cheng.

iona hadn't attended Zara's inquest – she was a student at the time and such a thing wouldn't have occurred to her – nor had anyone else she knew. She had seen the jury list though, comprised entirely of men, as were all the presiding dignitaries. But in her research for her book she had gotten a copy of the transcript of the inquest and had gone over it with the proverbial fine-tooth comb, over and over again, in fact, looking for discrepancies, new information, places where she might intuitively find something unexpected or inadvertent on the part of a witness to pursue. She was particularly careful about the testimony of Zara's roommate, then called Delphine Chartrand. If anybody knew what was going on in Zara's life, Delphine would have been the one.

Delphine had testified that she had been away visiting her parents in Winnipeg for a week, the night Zara died. She found Zara's body a full day after she had been killed. Zara was in her own bedroom, half on her bed and half off, the sheets and pillows soaked in blood, her face and the back of her skull smashed so that the body was recognizable only because of its location, the flowered nightgown twisted up around her waist, the length of her slender legs, and the blondeness of her blood-spattered long hair. Delphine told the jury quite matter-of-factly (although several times she had to be asked to speak up) about her reaction on finding her roommate's battered, bloodied body.

"I vomited," she told the coroner's jury and the lawyer who questioned her. "I screamed, I think; then I vomited. I dragged myself to the living room, and called my mother at home in Winnipeg and she called the Ripley police. They came at once. After that, I wasn't allowed anywhere near Zara's room and in fact (how cool she was, Fiona thought), they made me sit in a police car outside." She seemed to be particularly resentful about this small fact.

To questions about Zara's schedule and her plans during the weeks leading up to her death, Delphine could only say that she didn't know, that Zara might have had a boyfriend, but she didn't know that either because Zara was out of the apartment they shared more than she was in it, and as Zara had a job as a clerk in an insurance company, and Delphine was a typist on the opposite side of downtown – she was saving money to go to teacher's college – they didn't see that much of each other. The prosecutor then asked her, "You didn't see anything new in her room, did you?" Delphine had looked baffled for a second and then, keeping her eyes tightly on the prosecutor's face, mutely shook her head, no. "New clothes, maybe, or anything like that?" Again, Delphine shook her head, no. "I hear roommates sometimes share their clothing. Did you and Miss Stanley do that?" the prosecutor asked her.

"Zara was taller than me, and slimmer," Delphine had pointed out. "Her clothes wouldn't fit me." Fiona remembered that Delphine was a short girl with a Sophia Loren kind of figure.

"Where did you go after that?"

"I moved into my boyfriend's apartment for a couple of nights – he slept on the couch," she hastened to tell the all-male jury. "Then I moved over to another girl's place. She'd lost her roommate and couldn't pay the rent. That's where I am now." Before the prosecutor could speak again, she said – and Fiona could practically hear the smug tone in her voice – "My boyfriend and I are getting married next month."

Forty-some years later Fiona had had a devil of a time tracking down Delphine Chartrand who had become Delphine Roy as planned, then, some years after that, Delphine Jellinek. By the time Fiona found Delphine living in a small community in the north where she had been a school teacher for years before retiring, Mr. Jellinek seemed to have gone the way of Mr. Roy. Or maybe he had died. Darned if she could remember what had happened to Mr. Jellinek, not that it mattered. Maybe she hadn't asked Delphine.

And Delphine had answered her questions in monosyllables, as if she were angry at Fiona's having found her and especially that she had dared to telephone her and bring up "that old business again."

"But the case was never solved," Fiona had said in surprise. "Don't you care? I mean, she was your friend…"

"I barely knew her," Delphine insisted, "And I'm not going through this again," and had hung up.

Fiona remembered wondering, is there something wrong with me that I still care? After all, I barely knew her too. Or is it that this is what journalists do? They try to find things out, they lift the rocks and see what scuttles out; they shine the light on all the old obfuscations and dig out and reveal the lies.

Because no society can function without someone willing to do this work. Not even a democratic society. Because people are still people and the ones who put themselves and their interests first, no matter what they say out loud, are still around in democracies.

Fiona hadn't bothered with the by-then elderly widow whose flat was on the main floor between Zara and Delphine's in the basement and the one on the top floor; she'd been away on a cruise when Zara was killed, and the upper apartment had been empty. There had been no one in the house to hear Zara's screams. She hadn't even tried to interview the neighbours. If any of them had heard anything, she had thought, they might well have been ordered not to tell anyone, and besides, since the murder those houses had been torn down, their previous owners moved who knew where, or dead. She had settled in her book for quoting the newspaper reports, which consisted mostly of the neighbours saying, one by one, that he or she had heard nothing that night.

She was passing one of those deserted hamlets that had died when the new highway had bypassed it. The few derelict buildings in the middle of a stubble field reminded her of her farm, caused her to wonder how this year's harvest had been, which brought her back to thinking of Roman's trip to China thirty-five or more years earlier. Out loud – too loud – she said, "I am not leaving Hart City until I go to the Prairie Farmers' Commission office and find out who was on that delegation. Maybe Roman was lying about that, too."

In the far distance the high rises of Hart City were

gleaming in the late afternoon sun, bronze, gold and rose, as if it were a great metropolis. Somewhere in that city of civil servants and politicians lay the answers she sought, she was sure of it; they lay hidden in vaults, warehouses, archives, and protected files, and in the minds of some still living. The closer she drew, the more rapidly the gold and bronze turned into dull greys and beiges, and her apprehension of the mythic, ignited briefly by the sight of the sun on the city, faded along with the colour. She thought how glamourless murder turned out to be in reality; how very mundane and stupid.

At roughly the time Zara had been killed, as nearly as Fiona could tell, she herself had been stretched out full length on her bed, still wearing her best date dress, sobbing, because she had just been dumped by her boyfriend. She'd been in love with Keith and every single thing about him, was set to spend the rest of her life with him and when he had taken both her hands in his and looked into her eyes, she had thought he was going to propose. When he proceeded instead to break off their year-long relationship, she had drawn back her hands as if they were being scalded, and stared at him, gasping for breath at the suddenness of the blow, reeling, she thought now, more from the humiliation than from the pain of his loss. Now that she was fully grown up (or almost, she often told herself), she could gaze not without fondness on that young woman, twenty years old, seeing life unfold before her as she'd been led to believe it should, and then, bang, her world view being given its first, radical readjustment.

Between Keith and Roman, Fiona had dated but no

relationship ever worked out. Then Roman had come along and she'd been enamoured at once, had felt a certain rightness in their being together. She could tell that Roman felt it too, although he fought it to such an extent that it was another five years before they married, when she was twenty-seven and he was thirty. Over the years she'd figured out that he'd been checking out his options, not wanting to commit himself too soon – there was a certain hard-headedness to Roman that Fiona had kept her distance from – and had settled on Fiona only when he'd been sure she was the right woman, or, Fiona now was beginning to suspect, when he was sure there were no better options.

But on the night Zara was being murdered Fiona was in her bedroom, the house empty because their parents had gone off on a week's holiday to the mountains, and Marian was out on a date, so that she had let the outraged tears pour from her eyes, smear her face, drip off her cheeks until even her hands and her dress front were wet too. Such excessive crying; it was ridiculous. It had always shamed her that she had given herself over utterly to self-pity at the same moment as someone, some devil, or several of them, were only a mile or so away beating, raping, smothering her school friend.

Two or three mornings later, Zara's murder, along with grainy photos of her wrecked bed, were all over the news, the police asking anyone who knew anything about her whereabouts that night or who she might have been with to come forward at once. A crackling tension saturated the city; Zara's death was the only subject of conversation on the city buses, the coffee shops, department stores, classrooms, offices, kitchens and sidewalks. For a while, everyone listened avidly to the radio and read the city page in the newspaper to find out how the investigation was going, everyone muttering to everyone else that it was surely so-and-so who lived across the back alley from her apartment and had just gotten out of prison, or a certain boy she'd dated in high school who wouldn't leave her alone, or that weird guy who might have been stalking her, but interest eventually dropped off, replaced by the rounds of constantly-modifying gossip, with new elements being introduced along with sudden shifts in the old gossips-versions.

As she approached the outskirts of Hart City, slowing and letting some clearly hyperactive drivers pass her, Fiona wondered how healthy is it to be so immersed in those high school years that ended more than fifty years ago? Not healthy, she concluded, and would have pushed those long-ago years out of her head, but, she asked herself, how else to figure out who had been a part of Zara's life?

No, that's the wrong tack, she decided, so surprised at herself she slowed further only to be honked at long and loudly: not Zara's life, not the old high school crowd, not the details of what is known about the murder, about Zara's movements that night or the nights before, not who trailed her or dated her, or who didn't. But, instead, *who put that envelope under my door?* And, backtracking to her first, even more important question, *why, in the first place, had the case not been solved?* The whole business had just trailed away into nothing, taking about a year to do so. And nobody ever said, *we are immeasurably sorry to have to tell you that we have failed, that Zara Stanley's barbaric, meaningless death will not be avenged.* That was what so enraged Fiona; that was what made her want to never, never give up.

Although she had given up, she supposed, when the book had been published, and no hint had reached her, despite all those who phoned, emailed, wrote her letters about what they knew about Zara's life and/or death, of why the investigation had come to a halt. Although, perhaps the very thing that stopped her from getting answers was the repeated declaration by the police that homicide cases remained open until they were solved – even fifty years later – and that no information could be given to journalists or the public as long as a case was open. According to them, the investigation hadn't ever come to a halt.

Settled at last, after stopping for a lunch in a nearby café, into a decent room in an upscale hotel, she searched and found Lawrence Cheng's name in the phone book, an address beside it. This was way too easy, Fiona thought, but then, Larry hadn't had anything to do with any of this and had no reason to hide. And his business made him a public person whether he liked it or not. She put the receiver to her ear, and dialed the Cheng number.

"Cheng residence." Using her best Vonnie-voice, although more dignified and less brightly assertive than before, Fiona asked, "May I speak with Emily, please," not really asking.

"Who shall I tell her is calling?" Good heavens, Fiona thought, who have those kids I went to school with turned into? She half-wondered if the woman answering the phone was playing a prank by pretending to be a servant or a housekeeper.

"Fiona Leith Lychenko," Fiona told her. "We were chums in high school." She stopped herself from going on about being in town, and blagh, blagh, blagh. Or should she have gone on?

"One moment please." She could hear the phone being put down and the murmur of female voices somewhere too far away for her to decipher what was being said.

"Fiona!" a voice was saying that she recognized as Emily's before she had properly prepared herself. "It's so nice to hear from you. It's been years! Are you nearby?"

"I'm in a downtown hotel, just for the night. I'm passing through, and I suddenly thought – I guess I'm getting nostalgic in my old age." She laughed, sounding lame even to her own ears, but Emily didn't miss a beat.

"Can you come over? We aren't too far away. It would be such fun to see you again."

"Of course I can," Fiona told her. "Just give me some directions. We have a lot of catching up to do."

Going down to get her car Fiona made an effort to plan her encounter with her old school friend as she had failed to plan the one with Evan Kirby. In her purse she carried the copy of the note she'd received under her door; she supposed that would be where Emily's usefulness would come in: Emily would probably be able to recognize the number as belonging to a government file, if it did, or to the…She hesitated. Could it be a provincial archives file? And if so, perfectly available to the public. No subterfuge required. Unless, it occurred to her, it had some proviso attached to it such as, *Not to be opened for fifty years*, or something.

Soon she was pulling up in front of an up-dated, substantial, wine-coloured, brick house with shiny black shutters on the white-trimmed windows, and a wide, well-tended lawn bordered by trees and flowerbeds. A man who must be Larry Cheng was raking the last of the fallen leaves, their colours dulled now, and piling them in the centre of the lawn.

When he saw her car pull up, he waved, set down his rake and came through the gate to the sidewalk where she stood uncertainly. She remembered now that Lawrence Cheng was a math whizz, had been a nice kid who had helped Fiona once when she'd been doing homework in the library and found herself baffled by a math drill. Still fabulously good-looking although with graying hair.

"Fiona," he said, extending his hand and then pulling it back, apologizing. "I am covered in dirt. Forgive me."

"Imagine us being in the same school, seeing each other in the halls every single day, and then not ever seeing each other again." She said this meditatively, overcome by the sight of what had become of the tall but slight boy she had known: now a sturdy man, broad-shouldered, with big hands. He looked like somebody who knew how to fix things; he looked a lot like Roman had, and for an instant, she almost forgot her errand. As if he could read her thoughts, he said, "I'm so sorry about your husband. I knew Roman a little; he sometimes shopped in our store. It happened so fast, I thought."

"It seemed as though one day he was well and we were talking about going to Europe for six weeks and the next day he was gone forever." She had said more than she meant to. As they spoke, still not having touched, they were walking up the stone pathway to the white-painted front door with the shiny brass doorknocker and matching mailbox to one side and Fiona had time to wonder how Larry had managed to keep this beautiful house if his business had gone bad. Then the door opened and Emily stood, smiling widely, her arms out to enfold Fiona. Before she bent to accept the embrace Fiona saw a woman as slender as she'd been in high school, and as tiny as ever, barely making Fiona's shoulder, wearing a slim-fitting, taupe-coloured dress, and matching high-heeled shoes. Very high-heeled shoes. The enveloping hug she had expected turned into one of such a light touch that it hardly happened at all.

Emily stepped back and led her into the front room where the white marble fireplace faced artfully-arranged pale sofas, big lamps whose lavish tasseled lampshades called attention to themselves, and large, vague landscapes in ornate gold frames hung on the walls. Larry vanished back to the lawn and the leaves, and Fiona and Emily sat across from each other in sudden silence.

"You look wonderful," they said at once, and both laughed. Fiona said, "I think it's obvious you're the more wonderful looking. I'm a bit…battered."

"I've followed your career," Emily said. "I loved your column. What a shame your editor was so gutless." Her word choice surprised Fiona; surely Emily was too elegant for such language? And further, was it *that* common knowledge she had been fired? She hadn't expected even people in Hart City to know. Or did Emily know because she had connections? But Emily was going on. "And I'm also so sorry about your husband. I never met him, but Larry thought a lot of him and that's good enough for me. Cancer is a plague." She sighed, not looking at Fiona, then lifted her head. "How are you managing? Are your children near?"

Used to this last question, Fiona answered, still smiling, "Roman and I had no children. What about you?"

"Two," Emily said, apparently choosing to ignore or simply accept Fiona's remark rather than commiserate with her or show any sign of embarrassment because she didn't know how to respond. "Serena, the youngest, is a microbiologist married to a biologist. They live up in Yellowknife. Jonathan is an accountant, married with children. He lives in Winnipeg."

They went on in this way for some time, idle chat, laughing a bit and exchanging memories. There seemed to be no one else around, and Fiona wondered who had answered the phone and if maybe the voices she'd heard had been on television. But surely Emily didn't dress that way just to hang around this spotless house by herself.

"Have I interrupted something?" she asked. "I hope I haven't interfered with your plans for the evening."

"Not at all," Emily said. "When you called a couple of my neighbours had dropped in and we were sitting in the kitchen chatting. They both went back home, that's all." She had crossed her slender legs, and swung one foot rhythmically, the shiny taupe shoe falling to hang from her toes. With her fashionable haircut and her exquisitely slim body, it was hard to locate the nondescript Emily Zhang she'd been, vaguely, friends with through high school.

"You went to a great job out of high school, I heard," Fiona said. "Personal assistant to various ministers…"

"Mostly deputy ministers," Emily said. "You graduated with a degree, I think. I've always envied that, but I had that great job, and after eight years at it, Larry and I got married and decided to start a family. I took time off with each child, but I couldn't manage the job and the children and a university degree too. I suppose I could have gone during these last years, but really…" she turned her head to gaze out into the shadowed hall, "I had somehow lost the enthusiasm." There was a note in her voice that for the first time touched Fiona.

"You have a stunning house," she remarked. "Larry is probably the only reason I got my grade twelve, helping me with algebra assignments I didn't have a clue about." She paused, tried to remember her agenda. "Did you like your job?"

"Loved it," Emily said, instantly. "It was exciting to be so close to real power in this province, exciting to see cabinet members every day…" Her voice trailed away.

"Did you know Evan Kirby?"

"I started out working for him," Emily said, her voice easy, but a certain tension appearing around her mouth, as if she had tasted something sour. "He kept getting married and divorced. Funny he should turn out to be a ladies' man. He was never much to look at." She said this idly, straightening a few magazines that sat carefully arranged on the shining glass coffee table between them. Fiona realized that she hadn't been offered a glass of wine or tea or anything at all. Was Emily waiting for Larry to come in, or was this visit actually unwelcome and she was trying to get it over with as fast as possible? Anyway, she had spent so many hours in the car today that her back had begun to ache – cutting it short would be fine with her. She made an effort to imitate Emily's mockery as if this was all so much fun.

"I remember him as this skinny guy, big ears, a shiny small nose. And freckles. A ladies' man? Never. Although now that I think of it, he did have a certain…" She felt herself frowning, trying to name that quality of his, as if he were actually removed from everything around him. Not really there. There was a silence. Emily, who appeared to have lost interest, abruptly lifted her head.

"That book you wrote, about Zara's murder – I forgot to say that I read it. It really brought back a lot of stuff I'd almost rather forget."

"Wouldn't we all," Fiona said.

"I don't know why your question about Evan made me think of Zara. I guess I just remembered that you'd written the book. That must have been a lot of work."

"It was," Fiona answered, shrugging. "For all the good it did."

"You kept people from forgetting what happened," Emily said. "Zara deserves at least that."

"That's what I thought," Fiona told her. She would have gone on, but Emily said, abruptly,

"Kirby made a pass or two at me. I rejected him very firmly. Pointed out that he was married." Fiona couldn't help but notice that Emily's hands were moving over her silken lap, that her jaw had tightened. "Give a man a little power and he thinks he can have any woman he wants. Not long after that he divorced his first wife, poor girl. I guess he thought he could do better. It was pretty clear she didn't have what it took to be any help to him. Career-wise, I mean." She smiled faintly. "After that I got myself transferred to George McKenzie's office. He was assistant to the deputy minister then. It was a good job too."

"What department?" Fiona asked, as if she were not

very interested, not even looking at Emily. Later, it would occur to Fiona that Emily had reacted pretty strongly over "a pass or two" that had happened forty-five or more years earlier.

"Attorney General's," Emily said, swinging her foot faster and looking at the magazines rather than at Fiona.

"And that is where you ended your career? I mean, in that same department, or did you move around? You went on to Ottawa, didn't you?"

"I only lasted a year there. Larry and I were involved then, so I came back."

"How long were you in McKenzie's office?"

"Oh, a couple of years, I guess. It was an interesting place. Would you like a drink? A glass of wine?" Were they running out of conversation already? Fiona bestirred herself.

"Funny Evan Kirby's name should come up. I saw him today," she told Emily. Emily stopped swinging her ankle, reached down and pushed her shoe back securely onto her foot, uncrossed her legs, placing her knees and ankles carefully together. Her eyes had turned watchful, the friendliness gone. Somewhere at the back of the house a door closed, followed by muffled thumping. Larry, she supposed, finished with the lawn. It was dusk outside now, nearly nightfall.

"He's in a nursing home in Ripley and my guess is that he has Parkinson's. He couldn't stop shaking. But he seemed mentally sound still."

"Why did you see him?" Emily asked. She turned her head away from Fiona as she spoke, a movement that alerted Fiona, once a reporter, to Emily's particular interest in Fiona's answer.

"I don't know. It just came to me that maybe he would have information about Zara's case, or know where there was information to be found that I didn't know about."

"You're still on that?" Her voice was sharp; she went on, less stridently, "And did he?" Emily was still not looking at her.

"He would barely speak to me."

"So you came here." Quietly, all warmth gone from her voice.

"I have what I think is a file number. I hoped you'd recognize it and could tell me where to find the file." Emily held out her hand, her lips pressed tightly together.

Fiona picked up her purse from the floor, extracted the small square of paper where she had copied the number and handed it to Emily.

"You knew Zara too, maybe better than I did," she said, matching Emily's steady, impersonal manner. She meant, how can you not help? How can you keep silent about whatever you know? Then thought that the threat of being sued, of going to jail for revealing government secrets could still be in effect, in fact, probably were. She'd once met a woman on a beach in Hawaii when she and Roman were on one of their rare holidays, who had been a high level consultant to an American governor. The woman, relaxed by a Mai Tai and Fiona's obvious unimportance, had said, *The things I know, that I can never tell anyone.* Now she bestirred herself to persuade Emily. "We can't let the killers get away with this. It isn't right. Zara deserves better." At which point Emily's eyes flickered toward her, quickly, then went down to the paper.

"It looks familiar," she said. She had crossed her legs again, and again was letting her foot swing. Fiona waited.

"Could be from anywhere. I don't know what department. I've long since forgotten the filing system. And it's sure to have changed anyway. Everything would have been computerized long ago." She continued to stare at the paper for another few seconds, her foot stilled. "This could be a file going back to the sixties. It probably has a new number by now. If it exists at all. Where did you get this?"

"I can't say," Fiona said, meaning *I don't know who gave it to me,* but then decided to say no more. Make it sound as if she knew something more than she actually did.

"Evan Kirby," Emily said, not asking a question.

"No."

"Did you have this when you were researching your book?" Again, Fiona chose not to reply. Seeing this, Emily went on.

"Why didn't you come to me when you were researching your book? I wondered then."

"It didn't occur to me. I thought we were talking about some standard street criminals."

"And you don't now?"

"Now I think..." she hesitated, annoyed that she'd implied her real thoughts without meaning to. "I think the same way; I just think that the sources I went after were only part of the story. And look – that got me nowhere. Since then I've begun to think in wider ways: that the justice department must have a file on the case, one that we both know they would never let me see. I remembered you had worked in that office at some point. Then, or a few years later. I thought this time I'd start at the top and find out what people like you knew at the time."

"Nothing," Emily snapped. "It never crossed my desk." Fiona thought, the civil servants standard denial, but tried not to show her exasperation. Larry appeared in the doorway.

"How about I mix some drinks?"

Fiona said, quickly, "I really should be going, it's been an awfully long day." She rose. "It's been great seeing you both again. What a lovely house you have." Larry looked surprised, but Emily rose too, not demurring, clearly wanting Fiona gone.

"I'm so happy to have seen you again, Fiona. Drop in again the next time you're in town."

"Well, that hardly ever happens," Fiona said. They were in the foyer now, Larry standing back in the wide doorway between the living room and the hall, looking puzzled.

"Where are you staying?" he asked.

She named her hotel. "But I'll be gone in the morning. Things to do back in Calgary." She opened the outer door and turned to say good-bye to Emily, to find her sunk in reverie, then rousing herself to ask Fiona, "Did you say the Hart City Hotel?"

"Yes," Fiona said, waiting for whatever it was Emily was about to suggest, but Emily said nothing more, except a gracious, letter-perfect farewell.

Fiona stepped outside, the door closing behind her before she had gone down the three wide, curved steps onto the paved walkway.

Although her car was, if anything, a little too warm, she found herself shivering.

Chapter Seven

Lying in the wide, comfortable hotel bed, she puzzled over Emily's behaviour. She's sworn to secrecy, fair enough, some sort of oath of office. But what was that in her eyes? One minute friendly as can be, as if they'd once been best of friends, which they definitely never had been, a reunion to tug at the heartstrings, and then, bang: the curtains went down, the blinds closed; she turned into steel. She has to know something; I'm sure she recognized that file. I bet you anything she's going to get in touch with…somebody to warn them that I might be on the trail. Otherwise, wouldn't she have told me what she knew? All these years later? Surely if she knew, for Zara's sake if not for mine, she could have broken her oath or whatever. Could have at least given me a hint. Or was she just mad because she realized I had gotten her invitation to her house under false pretences. No, definitely not the latter.

She berated herself for being stupid enough to just hand over the file number like that, and began to toss in bed, re-arranging her pillows, then arranging them once more. At last facing the fact that sleep would be impossible for a while, she pushed them up behind her and sat up in bed. A, she told herself, Emily would only act that way if she did know something. B, there had to be something about Zara's case that created a file. But – *a government file?* She had begun to shake again. Hadn't Roman told her that even in the grain commission work for farmers there was sometimes dirty work? But no, that couldn't be relevant. What's the matter with me? she asked herself, probing her shakiness, trying to figure out where it came from. From the fact that I've stumbled on something important, something that somebody doesn't want revealed. And Emily knows that, and she knows who it is, and why. This is *fear*.

She put her face in her hands, pushed her fingers hard up into her hair, then let her arms fall to the cool duvet. Remembering being followed by the police, she half-wondered if she should get out of bed and leave the hotel at once, go to another, or even drive west to a hotel in the next town. But she told herself not to be silly, not to overreact. I could be imagining this whole thing. And things don't happen that fast anyway, even if eventually they do happen, although she was less certain that things couldn't happen that fast; maybe they could. Besides, she reminded herself determinedly, I'm going to the Prairie Farmers' Commission archives in the morning. If I don't find out who it was precisely Roman went to China with years ago, I'll be furious with myself as soon as I get back to Calgary. She pushed the duvet back with her feet, got out of bed and padded to the window where she pulled the curtains tight so no crack of light could get in, went back to bed, shoved her pillows flat, and tried to sleep.

She finally fell asleep, only to dream that she was being chased and couldn't find a place to hide, and when that dream woke her, and eventually she fell back to sleep again, she dreamt that she entered a luxurious room, and there was Arnie, wearing the dark blue pullover sweater that Fiona had given him for Christmas, with his arms wrapped around Emily Cheng, kissing her passionately. Fiona woke again, sweating this time, filled with unease, and something she eventually identified as pure dismay.

Which brought Marian and her condition to mind. She really must phone Arnie in the morning to see how her sister was doing. This time she lay awake for an hour, not putting on the light, nor opening the curtains. It was so late by now that even the city seemed to have gone to sleep. Hardly a sound came up from the street below, and the hotel was equally silent.

She realized she still had to buy a new dress for Vonnie's big night, and that she hadn't much time in which to do it. Should she look for one in Hart City in the morning, before she left for home? Then she remembered something she had completely forgotten: she had been intending to go with Roman to an event in Ripley one night, something to do with Vonnie's arts involvement, but on the day of the event Fiona had come down with flu and had to cancel. But Roman would go by himself, just to make an appearance to show Vonnie they supported her work. Days later, wondering why neither Vonnie nor Roman had mentioned the evening to her, she had asked Vonnie casually whether Roman had managed to speak to her that night. Vonnie had replied in surprise that Roman wasn't there.

"Of course he was," Fiona said. "He was going to represent us."

"I looked all over for him," Vonnie said, "So did Jack. He wasn't there, I'm sure of it." Vonnie had gone on to point out that the show and sale hadn't been very well attended, when she had hoped and prayed for, indeed, expected, a big crowd. Fiona didn't pursue this, choosing to let the subject drop, so sure was she that Roman would have been there, and that Vonnie and Jack had somehow missed him.

Now she thought, I must have been out of my mind. If Vonnie said he wasn't there, he wasn't there. And if he wasn't there, where was he? And why didn't he tell me that he hadn't gone? She'd been asleep when he got back from the city, and the next morning he'd rushed out on his way to Hart City for yet another meeting, and by the time he got back a couple of days later, she had forgotten the whole thing. Or was it, she wondered now, that she didn't want to know?

For a long time she lay on her back, motionless, thinking about this. Her mind ranged to the puzzling details about the money in his safe deposit box and the investment in Edmonton. Why?

Now she wondered if Vonnie knew something and just didn't want to tell her. But she'd never seen any sign in her friend of the slightest attempt to hide anything from her. And what could there have been to hide? Roman had probably gone to a bar, or stopped in at a commission crony's house, or…Before she knew it, she was crying, for what exactly, she couldn't have said. That it was the middle of the night and she was all alone in a city she didn't know, that she had no purchase on life anymore. But it didn't last long. It was too childish. She fumbled in the darkness for a tissue on the night stand, wiped her eyes, and blew her nose.

By four she was thinking about Marigold Martin,

otherwise known as Marjory Popowich, who had taken Fiona's book, her mountains of research, her best ideas, and was turning them into a movie of the week for which she would be sure to get full credit, and all the money if there was any. She focused hard on Marigold-Marjory's face as she last saw it on television and sent her a ton of bad vibes. May your face peel of its own accord, she told her; may your eyelashes fall out; may your neck wrinkle. May people find out how old you really are.

She found the woman's silly claim that no one she talked to could remember Fiona from high school hurt her more than it should have. I should have told her that unfortunately, *everybody* remembered her, Marjory. But she suspected that even if she'd thought of it, her good manners wouldn't have let her say such a thing.

When morning finally came, she had slept maybe two hours. But she felt, if anything, hyper-alert. She skipped coffee and breakfast, showered, changed into the brown slacks and brown sweater set that was her other regular costume, choosing low heels this morning as she didn't think she would be needing to impress anyone, checked out, and left the hotel before eight. She was trying to get a head start on anybody Emily Cheng might have set on her, but not trying hard enough, she told herself. I should have checked out last night. Or else I have lost my mind and nothing is going to happen because this whole business is a figment of my imagination.

She drove to the Farmers' Commission building, parking at least two blocks away, walked to it, and went into the lobby, stopping at the information desk to ask the elderly commissionaire the way to the archives.

The woman who managed the archives told her briskly,

as if she had had to say this too many times already, that all the material had been digitized from twenty years earlier to within about a year of the present. If she wanted anything older than that the old system would apply, and she would have to dig in the files themselves.

"About thirty years ago or so, maybe only twenty-five, my husband went on trip to China with a large group of grain commission members and a few government officials. I'm trying to write a family memoir and I'm wondering if I can find out who was on the trip, what the purpose was, what cities they stopped in. That sort of thing." Fiona was amazed at how smoothly the lie came out, how believable it was.

"Who was your husband? What was his name?" the woman asked. She was small with thin, faded brown hair, maybe fifty years old, and with a pronounced limp. Two young women sat at desks by the long wall of windows, files open on them, typing on computer keyboards. Neither looked up when Fiona entered. Fiona told her Roman's full name and the approximate year of the China trip. She wondered what would have happened if she'd said to the clerk instead that she suspected her husband might have been having an affair with somebody on the trip, and wanted to see who had been available.

"First, let's try the material that has been digitized." The archivist, M. Sorenson according to her name tag, immediately began typing into the computer, its monitor facing away from Fiona. She paused to read a page on the screen, then began typing again. Another pause, more typing, a pause while she scanned the screen quickly, then more typing.

"I can find his name several times as on this committee

or that one," she told Fiona, her gazed fixed on the screen. "But he isn't on the trips I would have expected, so..." More clicking of the keys, then a final clack, as if to shut down the program, a sigh, and she looked up at Fiona through her stylish eyeglasses. "Do you want copies of the material I've found on him? I can print them for you." Fiona almost refused before she realized that would look strange so instead she said, "Oh would you, please?"

"While you search for the ones that aren't yet digitized, I'll get copies for you of everything. This is the number of the file about that delegation the government sent to China." She handed Fiona a filing card with a number neatly printed on it. It didn't resemble the file number that had come in the brown envelope, not that there was any reason why it should.

The archivist led Fiona into a medium-sized room full of identical cardboard boxes placed evenly on metal shelving, each box with a hyphenated number written on it.

"These are for the early years," Ms. Sorenson explained. "The seventies would be over there. There should be a list of contents inside each box. It shouldn't be hard to find what you're looking for, once you find the right box. I'll just be next door." She turned and left Fiona alone in the spotlessly clean windowless room, the lights too bright.

She began at the box marked 1972–19 (the rest of the number was missing) and went forward. The records of the trip were in the third box she tried. She pulled out the relevant file, looked about for a place to sit, and found in the far corner a small table and two chairs. She pulled out a chair, her stomach suddenly feeling unsettled, and was dismayed at her own uneasiness, as if an unadmitted part of herself knew very well she wasn't going to like what she found, sat down, and opened the file.

Official transcripts of meetings with Chinese officials, an itinerary apparently thrust in as an afterthought and out of order – this she extracted and set on the table beside the file – more pieces of paper, some in Chinese characters, some photos. Here she paused, slipped the few pages from their paper clip, pushed back the file, and spread the pages onto the table in front of her. They were old photos, of course, mostly black and white, some of two or three individuals holding shovels with a scrawny tree in front of them that they must have just planted, several of many people at long tables having dinner, one of a head table at which sat many officials, nearly all Asian, and the others unidentifiable, at least by Fiona. Finally, one photo of the Canadian delegation. A fine mist of sweat spread itself across her forehead, at her hairline, and her fingers were trembling, just a little, again.

She set the photo on the table in front of her and studied it carefully, forcing herself to go methodically from face to face. Roman was in the second row from the front on the left, the men who flanked him with faces familiar to Fiona, even though she could no longer put names to them. One of them in particular was familiar. She was surprised to find that they weren't all men in their fifties and sixties, but that there was a good age range, mostly in their forties, she thought, one of them appearing to be (although the photo was crackled on that side so that she couldn't make out his features), somewhat younger than the others. One of the men had white hair and looked more like seventy than fifty.

To the right stood two women, one of them middle-aged, tall, and bordering on fat, the other shorter, and judging by the way her coat was tied so snugly at the waist, slender, with exquisitely fine ankles and, letting her eyes slide up the image, Fiona noted a full, painted mouth, large dark eyes, neatly-coiffed dark hair. All in all, a beautiful woman. Was she a wife? Or a secretary? That she might have been a government translator crossed her mind, but she dismissed it at once as unlikely, as she seemed to be Caucasian. She scanned the photo again.

One face tugged at her memory: What was it about it that looked familiar? But the closer she looked the grainier the photo became and the more the features dissolved into shadows. Satisfied that she saw no one else she knew, she was about to go back to the file, when it occurred to her to look on the back of the picture. There she found a neatly typed piece of paper attached to it with the names of everyone in the picture, in order by row.

She read it rapidly: Roman Lychenko, check; the familiar male face belonging to Blair Fever, then the scion of the richest family in the province and a football hero, although retired from the sport, currently the head of the family's business empire. Not someone she'd ever known, or even met. Then, Evan Kirby. What? She looked again: Yes, that was Evan Kirby. But what would he be doing on such a trip? He was a lawyer, wasn't he? Wouldn't he be in Justice or the Attorney General's office or something? But then, he might have been working his way up the ranks and at that time still junior enough to be slotted into Agriculture; he was, after all, a career civil servant.

She thought to look at the women's names. The plainer woman's meant nothing to her, and she had a stern, forbidding look to her; the very pretty, considerably younger, shorter one was Livana Kirby. She had to be Kirby's second wife. There were no other women in the picture. Had she been wrong about Roman? Yet how beautiful Livana was, possibly as beautiful in her darker, smaller way as Zara had been, but safely married. No one would murder her.

She held the photo balanced on her left hand as if weighing it to assess the truths it contained. All men who had the slightest sense of self-worth felt a burning need to possess the most beautiful of women; married or not, they were not off-limits. And peering more closely at the face in the photo she thought she saw – or somehow picked up – a haunted look in the large, dark eyes, in the set of the richly-curved mouth. Disturbed by this, she set the photo down again on the file, face down so that she did not have to look at it again.

It was on the way back to Calgary that Fiona began to wonder why she hadn't seen these people when she'd been researching her book. Because when I started, I knew only what had been in the papers, all those names; those were the leads I followed. Sometimes one of them would tell me about another person who had been involved, and if I could find him or her, I would interview that person. Or people I'd never heard of phoned me on their own, ordinary people: a young newspaper reporter, a guy who ran a carwash, a retired telephone linesman, a couple of citizens who hated the Ripley police for reasons having nothing to do with Zara, and who wanted to catch them in negligence or corruption.

It had taken her quite a while to figure out that if she stuck rigidly to the line that the initial inquiry had laid out, and that the rumours were related to, she could only reach as dead an end as the police had. She had discounted any pieces of information that led in other, unlikely she thought, directions, and in the end, she *had* reached a dead end. Now, *somebody* was pointing her in another direction entirely.

She grasped the steering wheel more tightly, drawing in her breath and holding it. Was this, finally, the right one? She still had only a file number and Evan Kirby's name, but neither of these had surfaced at all during the years she had been asking questions the first, unsuccessful time. Why hadn't they? Was it only that this time the stars were in a better alignment?

But why hadn't that somebody given the information to the police? Wouldn't that make more sense? Or to a lawyer. Or to the newspaper. Why not tell what he knew fifty years ago when the whole city was in turmoil. Things change, the world shifts, people change their minds. The deathbed confession and all that. *The brown envelope.*

She glanced into the rearview mirror to see that while she had been mulling this over she had slowed, and with so much oncoming traffic had forced a line of vehicles to collect behind her, unable to pass. She braked, pulled over onto the paved shoulder, and put on her flashers. Car after SUV after half-ton truck swished past, until the last one, a nondescript blue, four-door sedan, pulled up parallel to her car, while the man in the passenger seat lowered his window.

"Need some help?"

Fiona collected her thoughts enough to smile and say, "No, everything's fine. Thanks." But the stranger continued to stare at her as if he were trying to memorize her face, a long, steady look that moved from her forehead to her chin. Then, as if satisfied that she was who he thought she was, his expression changed slowly, settled, became one of pure threat. He said nothing, just looked at her, his eyes flinty and hard, his mouth a thin, tight line, his jaw thrust toward her. He had placed one hand on the lower frame of the window as if he were using the other to open the door – in fact, the door was opening.

Frightened, she raised her window tightly, thinking, if he gets out, I'm going to lean on the horn, where's my cell phone, and with her right hand fumbled in her bag. As if he could read her mind, the car beside her hesitated a second longer, the door slammed shut, then the car pulled hard out into the traffic, in only a few yards moving to the fast lane. All she could think was *it has started again.*

What if it was because she had been to see Evan Kirby or Emily Cheng? Had she stumbled on some kind of a conspiracy? She felt at once wary; others, even Roman, had told her she was joining the ranks of *"Those conspiracy wackos,"* giving her a look she couldn't read. Sweat had broken out on her temples, and although she gripped the steering wheel tightly, a trembling was slowly spreading into her chest and downward into her gut so that she was for a second afraid she might throw up. Maybe he was angry because I was slowing down traffic. It was possible – lots of men especially hated women drivers. That was probably all it was.

She was trying to be more attentive to the traffic as she drove, not letting it pile up behind her, and now she seized the opportunity to pass a slow farm truck, and then an old sedan that seemed to be packed with children. Ahead of her the road opened out smoothly, the next cars more than a mile ahead of her. She was thinking, when she wasn't remembering that threatening look that had pierced right through her, I need somebody to talk to. Who can I talk to? And thought, of course, Vonnie. But she couldn't phone her, somebody might be listening on her phone again, this time with new, undetectable technology so she wouldn't know (that is, this time to find out what she was up to, unlike before, when the phone-tapping was designed merely to scare her) and she couldn't drive to her house because Vonnie was away, who knew where. And there was no one else. Not any more.

"Suck it up, Fiona," she told herself out loud, and the very firmness in her own voice heartened her.

She thought again of how it had begun to seem to her, when she was finally writing the book, that the investigation had gone on more or less openly and in what seemed to be a standard way: investigators sent off in all directions, according to the newspapers, but their specific intentions never revealed, and their results, if there were any, never reported. Could it be no men had ever been sent off around the continent? Could it be that the police department had given out this information for the sole purpose of convincing the people of Ripley that the investigation was being vigorously pursued when in fact it had ground to a halt?

All she knew for sure was that after the initial flurry of news, there was never again a single word in the newspaper to indicate any police progress at all in the case. After, she estimated, maybe a year, there wasn't another word at all about Zara's murder in the newspaper. Nothing.

Man, she thought, I was way too stupid, no, too naive to be trying to sort that mess out. I noticed that fact; over and over again I noticed it, but I always ignored it, because the fact was the police didn't solve the crime, and what else would you expect when leads ran out; every clue fruitlessly investigated.

Fiona was sweating again, holding the wheel so tightly her hands hurt. She had to force herself to loosen her grip. Could it be that it had ground to a halt because the police – not "the police" but somebody very high in the force, maybe even the police chief himself – had realized where their investigation was leading, and had decided to stop it before whatever it was he didn't want revealed was discovered? Could it have been who the killer – or killers – of Zara Stanley were?

Her head felt as if it might come apart. She wanted to pull over, but saw no approaches into fields, was still too frightened by what had happened when she had stopped on the shoulder a few miles back, and too upset by her own thoughts to concentrate on doing so anyway.

But why would he, whoever "he" was, do it? Because the man who had killed Zara was, say, just for instance, maybe a police officer, and his identification would cast a shadow over the senior officer's life's work?

Suddenly it was two o'clock in the morning and she was sitting up in bed beside Roman, the phone now giving out only a dial tone as she clutched it in her sweat-slippery hand, both shivering from the chilly air in the bedroom and sweating along her hairline and down her spine.

Roman, wakened by the phone, had not spoken as she lifted the receiver, and said, a tentative, "Hello?"

"Is this Fiona Lychenko?" It was a richly masculine

voice, neither young, nor old, a man in his fully-ripe male-ness; just the sound of it had reassured her, even given her a bit of a thrill, despite the fact she didn't think she had ever heard the voice before.

"Yes, this is she."

"I have something to tell you." He paused. Her breath caught, she became aware she was holding the phone too tightly. Was this it, the answer, finally? As far as she could remember, when the call came she had been nearly finished the first draft of her book and was struggling with the problem of making the work consequential when, in fact, she had no more answers about the killing as she came to the end of her investigations than she had had when she began. Was she at last going to find out the truth? Her heart began to go *pat-pat-pat* rapidly, in her throat and wrists.

"Yes?" she said, whispering now, swallowing hard. He chuckled – chuckled!

"Don't you get it yet, girlie?" Fiona wanted to laugh, who talks like that? This sounded like something out of a forties thriller – or something – yet at the same time it was almost too ominous.

"Get what." Not a question, exactly.

"They were all in on it! Lots of young police officers were called in for questioning! That's why you're getting frozen out!" It seemed to Fiona, even as she listened to the breathing of the man on the line, that the very air in the bedroom was newly fraught with tension, that Roman was listening hard, as if he knew too, even though he couldn't possibly have heard what the man was saying. I must have been giving off fumes or vibes or something, and would have laughed but the memory was pulling so hard at her that she was gone into it again.

"How do you know this?" finally, she thought to ask him, although she wasn't sure what "this" meant, if it meant anything. It occurred to her now that when it came to wrestling with a powerful opponent, the littlest thing meant more – much, much more – than it seemed to, and the problem was she had never been able to figure out what that "much, much more" actually was.

"I have connections," he said. "I can't tell you more. I have to protect myself. You have to trust that I know what I'm talking about."

"Journalists can't take things on trust," she told him, although she felt that this time maybe she ought to. And really, she wasn't actually a true journalist, but a poseur, a wanna-be, never the real thing. And she was clearly in way over her head.

He went on, briefly, telling her things about her own city and the dynamics of behind-the-scenes power that frightened her, that she could never again – absolutely never in her life – remember, they were just too shocking. I had just sunk them into the deepest depth of my psyche and I had not, not even once, been able to pull up the slightest hint of what else he said. And at this moment, hurtling down the highway in her car, she was baffled at herself, and profoundly disappointed.

At last he had hung up and she had sat there with the receiver humming away in her dampened hand until Roman sat up, took it from her, and put it back on its cradle. She told him what the man had said. He had studied her in a way she found peculiar, quite new, as if he didn't quite know her and was assessing her to get a grip on her capabilities – on who she was.

"I think I know who that was," he said finally.

"What? How?"

"You know I hear things," he said, and trustingly, mutely, she nodded. "Once you got to work on this book, and word got out that you were, after you started phoning higher ups to get interviews, you and your intentions just got to be scuttlebutt around the province. You know everybody still wants to know who killed that girl. Zara." He had looked at her questioningly. Again, she had nodded.

"There's this fella who gets in on all the investigations about murders, or scandals of one kind or another. Pretends to know things he couldn't possibly know. You wouldn't be the first journalist to fall for his nonsense." She waited, shivering. "Apparently police departments know all about him. It's a wonder nobody warned you you'd probably be getting a call from him." She slid down under the covers, pulling them up to her chin. "Fiona, he's crazy. Don't pay any attention to him."

In the lamplight his features were half in shadow, half brightly lit, as if he were two men. It was an image she had not forgotten; she thought now she never would.

And she had believed him. She had occasionally thought about that phone call, but she never received another from the man with the wonderful voice, had never found out his name, and had never seen one single item that made her wonder if he had indeed been telling her the truth. What he had said lingered in the back of her mind, but it never amounted to anything more than an unaccountable and frightening blip in her life.

But still, sometimes she thought about the police chief at the time, a man who seemed to think himself above even the mayor in his importance, and how, if there had been any truth to the allegations of the caller which there weren't – would have nearly destroyed him, so vain was he. Or proud.

She thought now that he might well have chosen to fail at catching Zara's killer, believing that if he dragged his feet, in time people would forget about her death, and the whole nasty business would just go away. Which it seemed to do.

He could have dismissed or fired the young police officers; he would have slowly destroyed any documents related to their interrogations. It would have been easy for him to do. Any incriminating records in the Ripley police files would have been long gone. Or files could have been altered. What was left would be only the – what did the police call it on television? – the material evidence: the torn nightgown, the bedding, whatever else that the public didn't know about, such as that item Marigold claimed they had held back information about. If – a very big if, one she had long ago discounted – what she had been told that night had even a grain of truth in it.

More likely it was a handful of "important men," all scratching each other's backs.

A loud roar filled the car; Fiona's heart nearly stopped, until she realized she had only strayed onto the rumble strip. She jerked the wheel back, thinking I need to stop somewhere before I have an accident or cause one. But the next village was twenty miles ahead, and she was afraid to stop anywhere but in a public place. She chose instead to slow down and let everybody pass her while she collected herself. Anyway, I'm just going in circles; I've been through all this before a hundred times. It is pointless to do it again.

In fact, she went so far as to forbid herself to think about the case, but instead, forced herself to gaze around at the scenery – colourless now that fall was almost over, and more flat than rolling – through which she was passing, to look up at the sky, and into the rearview mirror to see what traffic was behind her, and ahead to any that approached. She rolled the window down in an effort to clear her head, then rolled it up again. But her mind, no matter how she tried to divert it, reverted back to the puzzle she had set herself.

Some big thing, an idea, a cloud of an idea, she recognized finally was gathering far back behind her determination not to think. It made her shift the position of her legs, to fiddle with the buttons of the electric seat to raise it a little, then lower it, and to change the slant of the seatback. In this state of unease and confusion, she drove on toward Calgary.

Chapter Eight

When she finally got back to her condo in the early evening, too tired to think anymore, she found a voice mail from Vonnie.

"I made a reservation for both of us at the Panorama Inn. That's where the investiture and dinner will be. I got us a small suite so we can have some time together, too, to catch up." She paused, then asked, "Have you found a dress yet? Mine is a sort of gold-tan colour, just so you know." Which meant, do not buy a gold-tan-coloured dress. Buy something to complement it, preferably not as fancy or eye-catching as mine.

Much as Fiona loved Vonnie, the friendship had always required, on Fiona's part, willingness to play second fiddle when they were out in public. Come to think of it, it had been the same with Roman, although, she would remind herself, she was, after all, only a wife. Had even accepted her role as necessary and inevitable, tried to play it with dignity and even a certain queenliness, so that nobody would think of her as just "the little woman." She had thought that that was why she had made no friends among the wives and girlfriends of Roman's colleagues. Now she wondered if maybe the other wives had known things about Roman that she didn't, and that was why they kept their distance from her. And why was I always so acquiescent? She felt a surge of anger at herself, instantly suppressed.

There was a message from Arnold too: "Call me, Fee," and nothing more. She had dropped her overnight bag at the door, thrown her coat over a chair, and kicked off her shoes, wanting nothing so much as a long, hot bath. Now, without so much as pulling down a blind, she picked up the phone and dialed Arnold and Marian's number. Her nephew Greg answered.

"No, I'm staying another week at least," he told her. "Mom will be that long before she makes it into a rehab facility. I'll get dad for you."

Arnie came on the phone, calling something to Greg who replied, sounding by his voice to be moving away. Fiona could imagine him taking the three steps up out of the dated sunken living room, going on down the carpeted hall toward his bedroom, or the other way, to the kitchen.

"How is she?" Fiona asked, before Arnie could speak.

"Much, much better. She's awake now all the time, sitting up, not attached to any machinery, and she's been moved out of intensive care. She goes to the rehab ward as soon as they can get a bed for her."

"I bet she doesn't even know I was there."

"She knows. I told her how you flew out the minute you heard and stayed by her bedside and didn't leave until we knew she'd be all right. She smiled when I told her that. You can phone her now, if you want." But there had been a catch in his voice, as if he was remembering something about Marian's condition that belied the confidence he was projecting.

"I will, I will, just give me the number." She found she didn't want to talk about Marian, much less to her. She wanted some word from Arnold that he remembered who she, Fiona, was, and that he cared about her. She knew she was being childish to need to be told she was cared for; she'd never needed such a thing before Roman's death; she'd had Roman for that after all, even if he was poor at it, and away most of the time. She sighed into the phone without noticing she had.

"Hey, Fee, are you crying?" Arnie asked. "I know it has been an awful time for us both, but really, the worst is over. Marian is going to be fine."

"No, of course not, I'm just really tired, and – sometimes I miss Roman." She found she wasn't sure if she was telling the truth. She knew she couldn't tell Arnie the real reason: that she had just been threatened, that she was afraid again, because he would tell her to drop her question-asking at once. He would tell her not to be stupid, that it wasn't up to her to find Zara Stanley's killer. And, as Roman had done, that she was once again imagining things.

She would not let anybody ever again tell her that she was imagining things.

'I know it," Arnie said, that old rumble returning to his voice that said he was finally remembering who he was talking to, that they were family, that they cared for each other. "But Fee, you aren't alone. You've got us. You'll always have us." She wanted to tell him that "us" was not what she wanted, that "us" couldn't begin to touch what was ailing her.

"Of course, you're right, Arnie," she told him, lifting her voice into cheeriness, "Do you think I should come back to Vancouver again? Or should I wait a while?"

"I'd wait. They're still restricting visitors and with Greg here for another week and Angie finally on her way, maybe later would be better."

When she hung up, she stood for a few moments looking out her living room window across the rooftops of the housing development across the way. The streetlights were on, and each one cast a pool of streaked orange-gold light over the shingled slopes, many of them partially obscured by the bare branches of deciduous trees, or by large spruces and pines, their upper branches hung with clusters of cones so big that she knew from the ground the upper part of the trees look as if they had a rust disease.

The city was still; no cars rushed down the street below the building, no sirens wailed, no children's voices carried upward to her ears. Not for the first time she wondered what had ever possessed her to choose this city of all that were available to her. Like Ripley, for example.

She had told Vonnie "Because I want to try a new life; because I believe that I can make a new life for myself. Because I need to be away from familiar things so that I won't be seduced into remaining my old, boring self – just Roman's widow for the years I have left. So that life will again be full of interesting things to see and do."

Vonnie had looked dubious, but said only, "Well, it's not as if you can't come back to Ripley if it doesn't work out." Fiona couldn't deny that she still didn't feel at home in Calgary, but it wasn't Ripley calling to her; it was the farm that she had sold and that was gone forever from her life.

She found a half-empty bottle of white wine – she preferred red which was why she'd bought white as a guarantee she wouldn't drink too much – that she'd forgotten about in the fridge, poured herself a glass, and took it to the sofa where she turned on the television in hopes of finding something interesting to watch.

Then she remembered that she'd left that piece of paper with the file number on it in Emily's hand. Hadn't she? Why would it matter if she left it with Emily? If I find Livana Kirby would it be to see if she knows about the case, if Evan had ever told her anything, or would it really be to try to find out if maybe Roman had an affair with her? Both, she decided, and as for leaving behind the file number at Emily's, that wouldn't prevent her from asking Livana the same question.

The wine was making her sleepy. Now all she wanted was her bed, her exhaustion a bone-deep fatigue, and where it had come from, what it was about, she did not care to probe.

It was early afternoon before she left her condo and drove to the biggest shopping mall in the city, where she knew she would find two or even three quality dress stores among the dozens of ones that sold cheaper clothes for the hordes of young women with limited funds. She had taken the time in the morning to search for Livana Kirby's name and address to no avail. Not knowing her maiden name, nor if she had married again after her divorce, nor where she had come from in the first place, the task was hopeless, and before too long she had given it up. She was looking for a place to park when it occurred to her that if she could find a record of Livana's marriage, she would find her maiden name, and maybe even some other details. First, she should do an obituary search, she told herself. How do I know the woman is even alive?

Once inside the mall she put aside all such thoughts, intent on finding a dress that would cover all her faults –

her crepey upper arms, her stomach that no amount of dieting seemed to flatten – and yet make the most of what was left of her youthful attractiveness: her dark blue eyes, her slender hips and legs. A dress that would go with gold-tan. Black, she decided.

"I'm looking for a formal black dress," Fiona told the clerk, once again using Vonnie's manner, the one that said she knew what she was doing, that she wouldn't be put off or pushed around.

Immediately the clerk found three gowns, laid them out over her arm, then held them up one at a time, discussing each as she did so.

"This one looks lovely on; if you have a slender waist, it will show it off." She spoke gutturally, as if English wasn't her first language. A Slav obviously, Polish or Russian, or maybe not; maybe a Romanian.

"No," Fiona said, briskly, with reference to the first dress with its full skirt. "Too high school."

"This one," the clerk said, smiling coldly, holding up a draped, long-sleeved model. "See how these folds cover any problem areas?"

"I'll try it," Fiona agreed.

"And the last. It is (she said 'eez') a little pricey, but such style!" Fiona caught a glimpse of sequins or beads that caught the light and glittered. Something rosé up in her, some memory of being twenty or so, and buying a dress for a special date to go to a university formal, how the very glimmer of her dress made her feel beautiful, less afraid to flirt with her date, an engineering student whose college's dance it was. And yet, hadn't the evening ended in a wrestling match in the front seat of the car, hadn't she slammed out of it, running through the snow in her high heels for the house, and he had never called her again? Suddenly, she could have wept for that young girl, or was it for herself, now a date-less widow, second fiddle to Vonnie Sorrel?

"That one, too," she said weakly, and thought of Vonnie again, who called this "shopping therapy."

Once in the dressing room she discovered that the draped dress widened her hips, so that she couldn't possibly wear it. The second dress – she gasped when she looked at the price tag – was perfect: long, narrow sleeves, gracefully loose at the waist, but with a textured, glittery panel set on an angle so as to screen the new outward curve of her abdomen that even holding her breath could barely control, and a skirt that fell straight from the hips and flared subtly from below the knees to her ankles. The light-catching items, she discovered, were black glass beads fastened randomly in the folds of the skirt so that when she moved they winked, tiny pinpoints of light.

"Is magnificent," the clerk – more like a duchess masquerading as a clerk, Fiona thought – told Fiona in her rich accent, her voice deepening with admiration that Fiona suspected might be genuine. "Perfect on you, no?"

"It will do," Fiona said, grinning like a teenager. She was elated, thinking, hang the price, hang Vonnie's vanity; I will have this dress. And shoes to match. And earrings? Maybe. Probably.

She kept on shopping: As well as the shoes and earrings, a new sweater, new slacks. She felt, if not exactly liberated, a kind of giving up of something, although just what it was, she was having trouble identifying. After about an hour, though, she was tiring, the crowds in the wide concourses were annoying, and carrying her shopping bags with labels from the best stores embarrassed and in a wry way amused her. I have made myself into a caricature, she told herself, and grimaced.

She had found a coffee shop, gotten herself a mug of strong black coffee and was seated in a leather armchair, her boldly-lettered shopping bags stuffed down between her chair and the next one so their labels couldn't be read. She was alone in a buzzing space, people everywhere, turning pages of newspapers, leaning close to be heard as they chatted, others lined up by the counter, and the background hiss of the coffee machines making lattes and chai teas. She found it ridiculous that now, it seemed, one had to say "tea tea" if one didn't want some exotic variation.

A man sat down in the leather armchair next to hers, putting his coffee mug heavily on the low table between them. She glanced at him: around her age, once handsome, wavy grey hair combed back from his face, glasses. He didn't so much as look in her direction, and she guessed that while she'd been musing, not noticing him approaching, he had already labelled her "old" and dismissed her, even though he was as old as she. He was examining an extra-tall blonde in the line, very high heels, tight skirt, long, gleaming hair spread out over her shoulders. About thirty-five, no, on closer look, I'll bet she's forty. This reminded her of Zara, who had been far more beautiful than the blonde in the line, and hadn't needed to dye her hair or put on four inch heels and a too-short skirt to attract male attention. But at forty, would she have had to?

In a flash, she saw a fist shooting out with all the masculine power behind it to smash in Zara's face, to destroy that extraordinary beauty that men and women alike, no matter what else they might have felt, had enjoyed the sight of. Why had it been done to her? Because she had refused a man? And he had felt he was so little, despite his no-doubt greater size and wealth and whatever else his attributes had been, that it was unbearable to him to be rejected by this mere girl who had come out of poverty and ignorance, and still dared to think she was better than him? Had dared to reject him?

That was where the murder had come from, or so Fiona had always thought, investigating no further: the rape, and then the murder. The rape, of course, the age-old way bad men had of conquering the most recalcitrant woman. But then, why murder? Had she ever wondered that, exactly, before? Why did he go on to kill her? He could have given her anything she wanted to keep her quiet; he could have maybe bought her a role in a Hollywood film, or…or…? She gave up. If one came from an important enough family, maybe such a man could feel the right to kill her. Tie up the loose ends. She's nobody; she's dead; that's the end of that. No, she told herself, everybody thought, including me, that that was what her murder was about, and look where that got us. Nowhere. So, maybe it was over something else. But what?

Suppose it had been over something Zara knew about this man, or these men, and she had perhaps screamed that she would tell everyone, so that he had to stop her. What if…what if he had promised to take her into his world of rich and powerful people? Maybe she'd been a virgin, in spite of the rumours girls like Margie/Marigold spread, and he had come along and promised her marriage so that she would sleep with him. Maybe she had believed that he would come forward soon, make it all public, they would set the date for the wedding, but he disappeared, and so finally she called him. He would have told her not to, but she would do it anyway, because hadn't he said he loved her, and wooed her, and offered her marriage, and she'd slept with him because of that, even bought beautiful dresses she couldn't afford in preparation for her new life with him, and where was he now?

Then, when he put her off, she had grown angry. Men had never spurned her, she was the beautiful Zara Stanley after all. Maybe she had threatened to tell everyone, to tell his parents, to…Fiona found she couldn't imagine what else Zara might threaten.

Maybe it was all about telling his father – men and their fathers, after all. So he had made a date with her, promising to come to her again, he'd just been busy with his companies, had been out of the country on business, but he would be there and…Fiona had been about to think that he would say, *put on your best dress and we'll go out to dinner*, but of course, if his plan was to kill her, he would hardly want to be seen with her the same night. On the other hand, maybe he had told her that to calm any anxiety she might have had.

Or maybe when he set out to meet her, he hadn't planned to kill her. Maybe the fact that he would have to do so would come later. He would smash in her face, to show her that her beauty was nothing. Maybe to subdue her, to shut her up, and he had raped her because he could, and to teach her a lesson, and then…Then what? Then he would be planning to leave her there, but his blood was up, and…he feared that he hadn't been careful enough, that somebody would know of his promises, even though he'd made her swear she wouldn't tell anyone, not a soul, until the time was right. And hadn't she sworn this very night that no one knew about their affair or his promises to marry her? Had he come into her apartment alone and wheedling, or alone and belligerent? Did he have his friends wait on the stairs in case he needed them? Was there anyone there but him?

No, he had no choice, he would say to himself, and he would grab the pillow and press it down over her face and hold it there, even in her semi-conscious state from the blows to her head she would have struggled. Or did he hit her then, to get her to stop struggling? He would have held the pillow down until she stopped struggling, and then longer than that, just to be sure. Cleaned up his fingerprints, probably, Fiona thought. No DNA evidence fifty years ago, but the art of identifying fingerprints was very old even then. And if there were more than one man there, they would have helped hold her down, because they too had raped her – of course they had – and she would accuse them, get them into a courtroom, might even succeed in ruining their marriages, their businesses, maybe even their lives.

The apartment had been wrecked, the two kitchen chairs turned over, as was the small table, and dishes had been smashed on the floor. The police chief told the handful of reporters who had attended his first press conference on the crime that Zara had fought hard, said he knew this because of the disarray of the bed, because of the fact that both her dresser and her bed table were lying on their sides on the floor, contents spilled everywhere, and the small glass bed lamp smashed, its shade flattened and kicked into the corner of the room. Zara's body was also covered in bruises, so she had been beaten before she was raped. She must have screamed and screamed, Fiona thought; how could it be that no one heard her? Because there was no one else in the whole house, she supposed, although she couldn't explain why the neighbours had claimed not to have heard a sound either.

She stood up so abruptly that the man sitting beside her glanced up, and then quickly away again. She picked up her bags noisily without noticing she had, and strode briskly from the café, and down the mall's wide concourse as if she were the only one on it, people peeling aside to let her pass.

She would track down Livana Kirby if she had to hire a private detective. Now it was clear to her that the results of those many leads she had followed in the past, put all together, didn't amount to a hill of beans.

She supposed she ought to head to Ripley, or Hart City, immediately and start a computer/old-newspaper-and-archive search to find Livana Kirby, but there was still a week to go before the dinner in Hart City, and having just returned from there, she didn't want to make yet another trip, nor did the idea of going early to do the research hold any appeal for her. No more chasing the ne'er-do-wells, that creepy housepainter, the besotted clerks at the insurance company where Zara worked, the electrician who had fixed the wiring in the house in which she and Delphine lived. Suspicion deliberately thrown on them, she suspected, when all the while, she was growing ever more certain that it was someone wealthy and powerful behind the whole thing.

Chapter Nine

Driving home through heavy traffic, after a near miss at an intersection – her fault because she wasn't paying attention until the loud honk had made her slam on her brakes – she began to think that she had to stop this obsessive, continual thinking about the crime and who had done it and why. She was losing her mind, she was going crazy; she had better get out and, as the kids liked to say, get a life. After all, there was more to her life than Zara's murder, and now that she was a widow and in a strange city – had that move been a dumb mistake or not? – she needed friends and other interesting things to do or she would indeed go mad. People did, she told herself; widows did. She would not be one of them.

But by the time she had cooked herself a meal, eaten it and cleaned the kitchen area, she was in such a state of focusless agitation that she couldn't concentrate on reading, or think of anything else to do to fill up what was left of the evening, absolutely refusing to let herself think about who had killed Zara or why. She gave up and turned on the television. When she felt she could finally go to bed she found she had watched – my God, was it really? – three hours of television, none of which she could recall. She vowed that she would not waste the next day. She would go for a long, brisk walk, she would sit for an hour in the coffee shop two blocks up the street, just as she had seen other women do. In search of some new friends, she would smile at everyone, and hope someone would speak to her. She would register in a fitness program, and join something, maybe volunteer somewhere, so that she would have some place to be a couple of times a week. Maybe she should sign up for a university class. Maybe she would even get herself a grief counselor, the way widows tended to do, to keep what she was told would feel like approaching madness at bay.

No, scratch the grief counselor. There was no way she would ever tell anybody that Roman had been unfaithful to her, who knew for how long, and that she had been too stupid, too preoccupied, too smug to even notice. And now she was beginning to feel too uncomfortable about what she suspected were a lot of things about their marriage that so conflicted her that she didn't know how to properly grieve for him.

She had a whole week to fill before she left for Hart City and Vonnie's big dinner; instead of going back to obsessing over the murder, she would spend it trying to turn her condo into a more comfortable and welcoming home; she would go through all the tons of papers she had had to put in her basement storage locker – Roman's old tax records, and whatever other documents he had squirreled away over the years, farm records, his old grain permit books. A mere brown envelope under her door didn't have to mean the end of normal life, she told herself indignantly, if a bit uncertainly.

But once in bed, she forgot her stricture to herself and found herself mentally going over who had been the powerful people in provincial society back in the sixties: the Chasen family, in the brokerage business and insurance and including at least one MLA; the Fever family, still very much alive with business tentacles stretching – well, who knew where: grain marketing, agribusiness, a grocery store chain, but no politicians that she had ever heard of: the Shapiros, who made their money mostly in shipping in Europe, didn't they? But there had been a family of them in Ripley, she was pretty sure, living in a mansion on an acreage outside the city. Raising race horses, collecting nineteenth-century European art, among other hobbies only the wealthy could afford. Did any of these families besides the Fevers have sons?

After them – or before them, she wasn't sure which order made more sense – there were the politically power-ful from the Premier on down to the local fire chief, although those of course kept changing. To pinpoint the ones in office when Zara died would require a review of her old research. After that, who was there left who had power? Religious leaders? Not a chance. Nobelists? None in Ripley although Hart City had one. Maybe one of the young real estate moguls who were always getting their pic-tures in the paper? Not that she could think of any of their names, and they had a tendency to disappear, mostly because their businesses had gone bust. Still worth looking into, though.

Somewhere, in that narrowed-down mass of men then between the ages of about fifteen to maybe forty or even fifty-ish at the time of her death, Zara's killer lurked.

After an entirely frustrating morning of sorting exactly one box of Roman's papers and throwing them all out as no longer of any consequence to anybody, and trying to carry out her resolution, in the afternoon she went for a walk around the reservoir, one of the most popular walking areas in the city. Other walkers nodded and smiled at her as she threaded her way along the asphalt path, trees and an upward slope on one side, and a few trees and a drop down to the water's edge, now with a fragile coating of ice around its borders, on the other. She headed west, and from a low hill at a spot clear of trees, she saw the jagged line of the Rocky Mountains against the sky, rising in startling clarity above long miles of dark, coniferous forest, snow-covered and gleaming in the cold afternoon sun, and for a long moment she forgot everything in awe of their unanswerable beauty. In awe that there was still some vast part of life greater even than wealth and corruption, cover-ups and murder. Greater than her own pain and feelings of betrayal, of having been robbed of the ability, the right, to grieve.

A helicopter was making a wide circle overhead, but it was high enough and the circle wide enough that its noise didn't bother her. Before long it was joined by another helicopter circling at a lower altitude, and it was soon clear that they were focusing on the area where she and so many others were walking. Lost in thought, Fiona only half-noticed them, and, not having been a city-dweller for more than forty years, it didn't occur to her that their presence had any particular significance. In Calgary there seemed to always be at least one helicopter beating the air overhead. A woman who looked to be at least eighty walking on the same path Fiona was on, stopped, turned to her, and gesturing upward, asked, "What's up? Somebody spot another darn bear?"

Jolted, Fiona realized that indeed that must be the reason for the helicopters. A third helicopter had arrived, and another woman who was just approaching from the site direction, replied cheerfully to the questioner, "I was walking down at the water and I came across fresh bear scat. You probably shouldn't go down there until the wildlife officers find it and catch it," she aimed this last remark at Fiona, perhaps somehow spotting her as a newcomer in need of advice. She was thirtyish, wearing jogger's apparel, slender and strong-looking, and seemed nonchalant at having nearly stepped in fresh bear scat. One of the helicopters went whirly-gigging off toward the shining towers of downtown, while the other two moved off down the valley to the far end of the reservoir to hover there over the wild land belonging to a First Nation's Reserve.

Fiona decided she had walked enough for one day, but she wasn't ready to return to her condo, and all those papers of Roman's, just yet.

It was another half hour before she arrived at the coffee shop at the trail's starting point, out of breath and windblown. Thankfully the place wasn't too full. She tossed her jacket onto a chair and joined the line. Moments later she was back with a newspaper tucked under one arm, her small zippered bag under the other, carefully balancing a mug of coffee. She made herself comfortable, tasted her coffee, set it back on the table, and unfolded her newspaper, feeling urban and sophisticated, and pleased with herself.

A male voice said, "Mrs. Lychenko?" Startled, Fiona looked up. A man sat in the chair across from her. No one she knew, or had even seen before. No, wait a minute! There had been that retired police officer who had met her for coffee when she was working on her book, then told her he believed that a serial killer had killed Zara Stanley, that he was still out there and had killed other people since, that he would kill her if she didn't stop asking questions. He had thoroughly frightened her, not over the serial killer business, which she had thought at once was nonsense, but he himself, the way his eyes had grown small and hard, boring into hers. If there had been a serial killer in Ripley, she asked herself, where were the missing people, the dead bodies, the unsolved murders? She had tried to seem attentive to his theories, taking notes that she later threw out. A few months later she had run into him again, and he had seemed amiable and friendly, just another old duffer, so that she half-wondered if she had actually seen what she had seen in his eyes that day.

Wasn't this the same man sitting so close to her that their knees were practically touching? She stared at his square, slightly jowly jaw, his greying, whiskery cheeks under a ball cap, at the nondescript glasses set low on the bridge of his nose, the team jacket he wore. Was it or wasn't it?

"Yes?" she said, finally, trying not to give away her confusion.

With one hand he took off the cap, set it on his lap, and with the other brushed the top of his head as if checking to see if he still had hair. Not much, Fiona thought, but refrained from saying.

"I read your book," he said. Oh, a fan, Fiona thought, relaxing, smiling at him.

"What did you think?"

"Full of mistakes," he said.

"Really?" she asked, surprised. "How do you know that?"

"It doesn't matter," he answered. His voice had gone gruff. She was going to say, Well, it matters to me, but he leaned toward her, fixed her eyes with his, his face so close she drew back at little. "You meddled once," he told her, his eyes gone hard and small, just as the retired cop's had. "Don't meddle again." For a long second he kept his face close to hers, his eyes on hers. *"You will be sorry if you do."* He spoke each of these last words separately and distinctly, then turned his head away as if not he but someone else had just threatened her, rose in one quick movement, lifting his cap back onto his head, straightening it while he threaded his way among the few people, and was gone out the door while she sat, paralyzed, in her chair.

No one was paying any attention, they were chatting or reading their newspapers in silence or texting away, oblivious to the fact that Fiona had just been threatened by a stranger. Unless it *was* that old ex-cop again. She wished she had had the presence of mind to demand to know who he was and why he was harassing her. Loudly, so that everyone would see and hear. She couldn't remember the letters on the team jacket. Or had there been letters?

Some lousy kind of sleuth I am, she told herself angrily. Her breath had slowed again, and she drank a little of her coffee to calm herself. She found, after a moment, that she was indeed frightened, but only in a vague and distant way, not with the heartstopping immediacy of the incident of the glaring man on the highway. Of course, she had been alone then.

Now a female jogger plopped herself down in the same chair, not looking at Fiona, but studying a heavy black wristwatch as if for data from Cape Canaveral.

He had to have been following me! I didn't know I was coming here so he couldn't have known. Her body gave a small jerk at this thought, enough that the jogger, who was now unzipping her tight jacket, taking off her cap so as to shake out her long hair, glanced at Fiona in an assessing way.

"I just forgot something," Fiona said to her, smiling self-consciously so that the jogger went back to adjusting her clothing. Fiona rose, leaving her coffee and newspaper where they sat, and went out of the café. He knew where she lived, knew how to find her. If she didn't stop asking questions, what would he do to her? Car accident, mugging, poisoned umbrella – which made her laugh in an unhumorous way – or would it be by spreading vicious stories about her? Stories that had the ring of truth to them, stories that she couldn't disprove? They would have to invent; there was nothing shameful in her past at all. Even my parents led blameless lives. And Roman – that he had deceived her with other women wouldn't make her look criminal, nor him either.

She was taking the stairs up to her floor when it crossed her mind that it was very stupid to send someone to threaten her when his very threat would tell her that she was on the right track, that she was somehow close to something big, close to the answer. If he, or they, knew how utterly clueless I am…she told herself, unlocking her door, not finishing the thought.

Resolve was beginning to grow in her again: If I am on the right track, and apparently I am, I will never stop now. I will just be a lot more careful.

Chapter Ten

L ooking around, Fiona saw that it was, as Vonnie had promised, a gathering of everybody who counted: the Premier and his wife, the glamorous Lieutenant Governor and her stylish husband, several cabinet ministers, mere MLAs by the dozen, judge after judge, and, judging by the gold on his scarlet tunic, the provincial head of the Mounties, as well as Ripley's notable citizens. Wasn't that the self-important television and radio talk show host Giff Trumball over there at an inner-circle table? And the local police chief across from him? And wait, over there, wasn't that Rudy Kovalenko, that old flame of hers and Vonnie's, as well as of who knew how many other women?

She could feel herself suddenly flushing with pleasure that her boring widow's life was abruptly not so boring after all, and moved her eyes over the at least two hundred others she failed to recognize, some looking dazed and uncomfortable, or huddled into themselves at their tables, staring straight ahead, grim expressions on their faces as if this whole business was something to be endured, and still others rushing between tables to greet friends with hugs and air kisses.

Not always friends, Fiona noted: Some were clearly making their presence known to important people they didn't know: the careful smiles, the hands kept at the sides, the gracious, not-quite bowing retreats. She watched with interest, as if she were attending a play, reminding herself, I have zero currency: I'm old, neither beautiful nor rich, I don't have an important position, I'm not married to an important man, I hold the key to nothing any of these people care about. Only genuinely kind people or old friends would give a darn that I'm here.

She weighed this thought carefully: How can it be that I lived all those years in this province and know hardly anyone in this room, while Vonnie seems to know everybody? But this was too disheartening; it was her own fault, she knew it, and vowed not to let this undeniable moment of truth get her down. Your only value in this province, she told herself (and a dangerous one at that) is going to come through that brown envelope. So keep your mouth shut; sit still, watch, listen and learn.

She had lost Vonnie on their slow way from the smaller room where the reception had been held, down the wide hallway and into the crowded and glittering ballroom where dinner would be served, but she found their table and her place card, and sat. She could see Vonnie, wearing her shiny new medal, moving from table to table, finally ending up at one not too far away in an animated conversation with people Fiona didn't recognize. Hugs and kisses, my god, a man even kissing her hand, although in a half-humorous way. Vonnie looked splendid in her silk gown with its artfully creased shawl collar, the big medal hanging from it on the left side, and her diamond earrings flashing light. She had dieted herself into a pencil slim dress that Fiona would have called simply gold in colour, although a dull gold, the dress surely some designer number. She had never thought Vonnie and Jack had that kind of money. But, possibly, with the divorce about to happen, Vonnie had thrown caution to the winds – like I did, she reminded herself ruefully, recalling Vonnie's incautious stare at Fiona's dress and a faint frown – Fiona wasn't sure about what – that she quickly smoothed away.

"You look amazing, Fee," she said. "Amazing. And I love your dress! I love love love it!" Fiona still wasn't sure if she'd erred by looking too good, or by not looking good enough.

An overwhelming, deep-seated yearning swept through her; yearning for the low, grassy hills behind their farm, for the single ravine back there that had a stream trickling through it during the spring melt, and where crocuses grew up the south side, poking their heads through snow when the north side was already dry and hot, where blue herons sometimes nested, and the occasional bald eagle perched for a while, maybe on its way west through the mountains to the sea where it belonged. The deer, the damp soil, the scent of the air. For an instant she wanted to be there so badly she nearly cried.

But then, her table's couples started to arrive, the men in tuxedos, the women in their carefully subdued gowns, as if dignity was to be preferred over fashion or the too-resplendent; greetings and introductions were being exchanged, and people were seating themselves, smiling and looking around. Vonnie made her way over and Fiona dutifully spoke to everyone as Vonnie introduced her. A minister of the crown sat next to her – Arts and Culture, she thought she'd heard, but she'd missed the man's name entirely. He was unprepossessing: short, balding, a little overweight. She saw at once that his thin, elegant wife in the pale pink dinner suit was the controlling one in the family, the one who would restore order to the table if it were required, her manner thoroughly personable while clearly she was being as impersonal as possible. Quite a performance, that, Fiona thought, not precisely admiringly.

Evidently such women acted as gatekeepers, establishing codes of conduct, and by ignoring or brushing off anybody who deviated in the smallest way from them, ensured that for the most part, nobody did. And why? she wondered. Because if anybody was vulgar, or too friendly, or not appropriately worshipful of convention and the people who represented it, such behaviour would devalue all of them by breaking down the separation between them and the rest of society, those who couldn't be trusted to behave with such rigorous propriety. Zara flashed before her and quickly disappeared.

Or maybe such women never even thought of such things. Maybe they only cared to hang onto their power, most of it acquired through the achievements of their husbands. Maybe that is all it is, Fiona thought, just pride. That, and vanity. But, what do I know? I've never been in that position. It never occurred to me that I could be this during that time when Roman was doing so well out there in the world. I preferred staying home with a good book. Or was that merely another kind of pride? She suspected it was – pride, and not engaging for fear of failure.

Across from her was an excessively tall man – even seated his head was above all the others at the table – very spare in his figure, wings of white hair carefully brushed back, his long, bony nose gleaming, his jowls pink over skin rinsed by pallor. Already he looked bored to death. Beside him, his grey-haired, rigidly-coiffed wife dressed in navy crepe, sat motionless, looking vacant, although when someone came from another table to greet her, she rose with dignity. They were the Kipps; Malcolm Kipp was the only name Fiona had remembered of those she'd been introduced to, partly because it was familiar.

He had once been Ripley's Crown Prosecutor, his name appearing over and over again in the newspaper, so that everyone must have gotten so used to seeing it that they stopped noticing it, as she had long since done. She remembered then that Kipp hadn't had the job for longer than twenty-five or so years before his retirement, that the man who had been prosecutor when Zara was killed was William Porringer, who had been kind of a rake, (if anybody still used that word) athletic and movie-star handsome, and trailing gossip about his probable affairs – hadn't there been that red-headed secretary who claimed to have given birth to Porringer's child and wanted support? A big scandal squashed in practically seconds and nothing proved. Not too many years after Zara's death he had been killed in a "single-vehicle roll-over accident at only forty-eight years," according to the paper. At something like three o'clock in the morning on a country road. That was when Kipp had taken over as prosecutor.

Nobody had ever known what Porringer had been doing out there at such an hour. His long-suffering wife, left with three young children, had said a lot of incoherent things between sobs, accusing everybody and his dog of her husband's death. Everyone said she was clearly deranged by grief. And Fiona knew it could well have been true: Absolutely you could be deranged by grief, although, she was discovering, sometimes grief would also clear your head.

Kipp's evident boredom was either insulting to the rest of them, or it was simply the boredom of someone who has been through this sort of thing ten times too many already and could barely manage to get through yet one more dinner. His wife turned to say something to him and put her hand on – my gosh, Malcolm Kipp was in a wheelchair. Had she ever known that? The newspaper never showed the wheelchair, but wait – hadn't somebody told her he had had polio as a child? Never mind. None of this meant a thing.

She stared frankly at Kipp now, hardly aware she was studying his face, trying to see some wisdom in it, and seeing nothing but that milky-eyed absence. Surely he would know all about his predecessor's death – he would have access to all the records. She became aware of his wife gazing back at her and, trying to hold her expression steady as if she hadn't noticed, Fiona moved her eyes back to the table in front of her. On her left Vonnie leaned past Fiona to engage in polite conversation with the minister's wife, and across the table Mrs. Kipp had begun to chat with the husband of a couple sitting next to her husband whose names Fiona had forgotten. The Master of Ceremonies on the dais was clearing his throat into the microphone. *If any living person in this province knows what happened to the investigation of Zara's death, it is Malcolm Kipp. Bill Porringer was the one who really knew, but he is dead. But Kipp would have had access to all the files. Surely Kipp knows.*

She berated herself for not being smart enough to have seen it ten years ago. No, no, she thought, drawing in her breath so suddenly that Vonnie leaned toward her and mouthed, "Are you okay?" Embarrassed, Fiona could only nod and dig a tissue out of her evening bag as if she were about to sneeze. She was saved from having to pretend by the MC asking them to rise for the singing of "God Save the Queen."

But he refused to talk with me, and I thought that whatever I needed would be in the official documents. I didn't need him, I thought. How stupid, when almost certainly, as the link between the police investigators themselves, the Chief of Police, and the Attorney General's Department, he had held the key to the whole business. Or so she thought, but had to admit to herself her lack of knowledge of how the justice system worked. But then she thought, eyeing him, surreptitiously this time, what he knows is as sealed off from me as is the hidden government file.

Waiters were appearing carrying trays of individual salads while others poured wine, one arm tucked correctly behind their backs. She glanced up to find Malcolm Kipp's mild bluish gaze fixed on her. When she met his eyes, he did not lower his, but instead said, in a voice pitched too low for her to hear well but instead to some degree read his lips, "You wrote the book about the Stanley case." No one else at the table, attacking their food with attentive delicacy, appeared to have noticed. She nodded. He continued to stare at her and the clouded quality of his eyes dissipated at the same time as the blue deepened. She felt he was appraising her and then he seemed to decide she was nothing to worry about because he dropped his gaze to his plate and picked up his fork. She waited, her eyes still fixed on him, but he didn't look up again.

Before she left Calgary to join Vonnie for the celebration, she had printed the file number on the back of a painting that needed reframing and had delivered the painting to a framing shop. They were backed up, it would take a couple of weeks, she'd been told, and she'd said, no problem, just call when it's ready. The brown envelope itself and the original piece of paper with the name and file number on it, she had taken to the bank and put in her safe deposit box and had put the key into her purse. As for the number itself, wanting to have it with her at all times in case she needed it, she had written half of it in tiny letters in ink on the arch of one dress shoe, tucked up against the heel, and the other half in the same place on the other shoe. She had thought of simply memorizing the number, once would have done so in perfect confidence that it would be there when she needed it, but those days of perfectly-functioning memory were long gone. The shoe trick was hardly inviolable but, remembering the man who had threatened her in the coffee shop, she thought it would take anyone searching her things a while to find it.

Vonnie was bending toward her again.

"You really picked a dress that does wonders for you," she whispered. "You look great."

"Thanks, Vonnie," Fiona said. "But that dress of yours is the most gorgeous in the room. Perfect on you. Are you having fun?" An expression that Fiona couldn't quite read crossed her friend's face.

"To be honest – and I never thought I'd say it – I wish to hell Jack were here. It seems so damned unfair that he isn't." She dropped her head, but not before Fiona saw the rise of tears in her eyes. "It's no fun getting dumped when you're nearly seventy." But then she glanced up at Fiona, her eyes clear again, and said, "Sorry, Fee. It's no fun being a widow either, is it?"

"None whatsoever," Fiona said crisply. "But it gets easier. Have you seen Jack at all lately?"

"I don't want to see him," Vonnie hissed. "But a few days ago I had to, to sign the documents. We're still fighting over money and property. I'm determined that if he goes, he'll go with as little as possible. See if he loves his teenage blonde more than he loves land and cash. But the truth is I think he's been hiding money for some time. I've told my lawyer that."

"Surely Jack wouldn't have...would he?" Fiona said, thinking of the large sum of money in Roman's safe deposit box, and money in the trust account in Edmonton, the one with no beneficiary. How did he get away with that? Why did he do it? More to the point, where had the money come from? Had he just diverted some grain sales income from their joint account? Had he made a profitable business deal that he hadn't told her about? Could he have been up to something illicit?

She thought, I have to track down Livana Kirby. I have to face that tomorrow. I need to go back to the beginning and slowly walk the path I think he took. And I think it starts with the beautiful Livana, and with China, where I believe he met her.

The main course was being served, and soon there would be speeches, and then the after-dinner reception during which the crowd would dwindle and dwindle and those given to excessive drink would reveal themselves, and deals would be made, of which there would be no official record, and maybe, just maybe, faces surreptitiously pointed out for the purposes of...what?...following? Investigating on the sly? Intimidating?

She looked up from her ruminations to see that everyone at her table was quietly angling their chairs to face the dais where the Premier was rising to make the evening's first toast. Kipp's expression, she noted, had changed not one whit; still that look of a boredom so vast it was not much different from death, as if he were no longer present in anything but body, his chin tilted upward so that the light glinted on his long nose and on his prominent cheekbones with their flush of delicate pink.

As the Premier's voice rose and fell, Fiona thought about what Kipp's predecessor had written in his report on the death of Zara Stanley. The coroner's jury had rendered its official verdict that she had died from asphyxiation, because once Zara's battered face had been cleaned of blood, bits of bone, mucus, and whatever else was found there – pieces of flesh, she supposed – the tell-tale "pinpoint hemorrhages in the eyes" had been discovered, and bruising on her chest that might have been made by someone kneeling on it, or putting a heavy weight on it. But Porringer had written that the jury's verdict was that her death was caused by blows to the head. She had put it down to simple carelessness, or possibly to overwork so that he had written it in haste.

What if Bill Porringer had, for reasons best known to a crown prosecutor, done it on purpose? This would have been less alarming if there wasn't on record documents presented by the lawyer of a wrongfully accused man from an entirely different case that revealed what Fiona suspected were not mistakes, but downright lies, written by none other than the deceased Bill Porringer, about the man's past history, lies that had seen him indicted and taken to trial years before the documents came to light. How shocked everyone had been at this discovery, which had been all over the papers. But then it just passed away, and nothing at all in a legal way was done to the perpetrator, one William Porringer, at least partly because of the accident that killed him. End of case. Problem solved.

Now she wondered, glancing at Kipp again and then

back to her plate, was Porringer stupid or merely incompetent? Or maybe malicious? Kipp could know the answers to such questions. He was the one with access to the files, with the same police chief to have a drink with after work, or go golfing with, or whatever such people did so they could pass information to each other that they didn't want others to find out about.

They were rising now, lifting their glasses, muttering variously, *To the Queen*, then seating themselves with rustling, thumping and the occasional tinkle of crystal and cutlery.

Could Porringer have been advancing some legal cause? Is it easier to convict someone for murder who hit their victim over the head, than someone who smothered her with a pillow? Her research had indicated that suffocation was a hard crime to be sure had occurred. Had Porringer, she suddenly wondered, been writing his report in collusion with the chief of police? That chief, Norbert Giles, had been dead at least ten years – no, closer to twenty. But she was sure that both Kipp and Giles had been in office at the same time, for at least a few years.

But, she told herself, the crown attorney does not represent the police: He represents the people. Oh, gimme a break, and she snorted, and then pretended to blow her nose on the lace-trimmed hankie, once her mother's, that she had tucked up one long sleeve. *God! I am such an idiot.*

She was interrupted in the middle of her thoughts by a drafty rustle of taffeta and a life-threatening blast of *Thousand Nights* perfume. Marigold Martin, AKA Marjory Popowich, was bending close to her, her brittle blonde hair brushing Fiona's cheek.

"Fiona, darling!" she said. "I'm so surprised to run into

you here!" Fiona managed, just, not to let her expression reflect her desire to punch her. But Marigold wasn't paying attention anyway. "Malcolm, you old panther, you. I thought you were fed up with dinners."

Malcolm Kipp nodded slightly, something resembling, but faintly, a smile moved his lips while his wife, whose name Fiona abruptly remembered was Margaret, fixed her eyes on Marigold as though by staring hard enough she might induce the woman to autocombust. Marigold was impervious.

"What on earth are you doing here?" Fiona asked, in as carefully a dumbfounded tone as Marigold had just used on her, as if this would be the last place a Marigold Martin, or rather, a Marjory Popowich, would ever be invited. Beside her, Vonnie dropped her head and made a strangled sound into her curled fist.

"Ah," Marigold said, lifing her voice and putting a pretty tinkle into her laugh, "I'm here to catch some footage of ole Blair Fever getting his medal at last. He's over there." She pointed in front of them and to their left. Fever chose that moment to stand conspicuously, as if in the general low level buzz of conversation he had heard Marigold, and began walking to the platform as people clapped. He stood out, not only because he was so much bigger than average, but also because his hair had always been so blond (and he wore it in a high wave as if to catch everyone's attention) that he had earned the nickname (not used in front of him) of "The Albino," although for some weird reason his eyebrows were dark. Did he maybe bleach his hair?

Marigold, in her dazzling aqua gown (definitely over the top, and chosen to stand out in this room full of blacks, pale blues, off-whites, and greys – and of course Vonnie's muted gold), had already abandoned Fiona's table and was giving instructions to the cameraman who had materialized from nowhere and who was, even then, flicking on his camera. Heads went up as Fever mounted the dais, in the glare of the too-bright television lights his hair shining so lustrously he appeared to have a halo – *my goodness he is still a handsome man* – to even more applause, and stood at the podium, smiling modestly, as if embarrassed by the adulation. Fiona was sure he was not.

Fiona had paid no particular attention to the evening's medal recipients other than Vonnie and a Cree elder wearing a beaded and fringed white deerskin dress with matching beaded moccasins that rose under the dress's hem. She had spoken in so soft a voice, but clearly and without hesitation, and then had said a few words in Cree as well, dignity emanating from her as she received the medal and then went back to her seat again on the dais. Vonnie, for once, seemed just a touch cowed as she went forward for the Lieutenant Governor to pin her medal on her chest, pleased as punch, yet somehow humbled.

But in all this, Fiona had pretty much ignored the four men who were also presented medals, although she had to admit that she had noticed how elegant Blair Fever's tux was. Besides, Fever was the only person being doubly honoured, both for his past exploits on the football field, that had brought national attention to the province, and for more recent business decisions – some of them murky, although that might just be Fiona's failure to understand business – that had made him and a few other important people tons of money. Not that Fever needed money. For years his father had been the wealthiest man in the province, money made in a giant grocery chain, as well as in agribusiness and who knew what else. But, Fiona suddenly remembered hearing, the family's original money had been made in large-scale bootlegging during prohibition. Blair Fever nevertheless wore the air of someone who knew himself to be above the common herd.

Not that Fiona knew him personally, but wherever a pretty girl was, Fever would show up sooner or later, and she'd known several girls who'd dated him including, it was rumored, Zara Stanley, as well as…She found she couldn't remember: Had he dated Marjory Popowich? In those days so long ago Marjory had been not so much beautiful as what young people now would call "hot". A Marilyn Monroe figure that she emphasized by wearing tighter sweaters than anybody else dared, and the usual pencil slim skirts, also tighter than the other girls'. Her hair was bleached even in high school and she was always trying to attract male attention, something feverish even, about that insatiable desire for attention. Feverish? Hmmm, Fiona thought. But wait, wasn't she too young to date Fever? She wasn't much more than a child in grade nine when they – herself, Vonnie, Zara – were seniors. Maybe she dated him after high school.

All eyes were on the dais as Fever extracted a folded page from his breast pocket, smoothed it flat, and began his speech. Beside Fiona, Vonnie had arranged herself in an elegant, although noncommittal, pose, her chair pushed back from the table, her legs crossed at the knee so that the walking slit in the side of her skirt opened to reveal her slender calf and ankle, arms resting casually on her chair's arms, hands dropped downward from the wrist, back comfortable against the chair's velvet, and her chin tilted upward just enough that she appeared alert and interested although her expression revealed nothing else.

Ah, Fiona thought, Blair Fever was chosen to give the thanks from the recipients, not Vonnie. But Fever was oh-so-wealthy, while Vonnie was not, nor even married to a rich or powerful man, didn't even have the good sense to live in the capital city where she might insert herself among the rich and powerful. No, Vonnie was decidedly a minor player, awarded this honour to give the appearance of even-handed egalitarianism. Maybe there even was even-handed egalitarianism.

Fever was making a joke that made no sense to Fiona, nor did Vonnie smile, although across the table, Malcolm Kipp's pale cheek had wrinkled briefly. Fiona studied Fever as well as she could from a distance: that insanely white-blond hair, even his wife's paled beside it; impossible from this distance to say what colour his eyes were; heavily built with the broad shoulders, thick neck and big hands befitting the football player he had once been.

And what about the woman Fever had married? The engagement and wedding had been the social event of the season all those years ago, one that the city's finest had prayed to be invited to. The bride was quite a few years younger than Fever himself, and the province's upper class (to the extent that the province had an upper class) had seemed a trifle dubious about the marriage as if the beauteous Rickie Beauvais was marrying down, Fever's family being rich, but purely commercial and entrepreneurial with that bootlegging beginning, while Rickie's were actually connected to British aristocracy – not that anybody cared about that, of course. Fiona resisted the urge to snicker at her own – admit it – snide disclaimer. But the aristocratic connection was real: a younger son of a lord or a baron or something of an ancient British family, its name in the Domesday Book, had, for whatever reason, come to the NorthWest Territories of Canada in the late nineteenth century, took up land, and slowly built one of the biggest ranches in the province. From this impressive beginning, after the ranch was broken up and sold out of the family around the 1950s, the Beauvais family had branched out to be appointed senators and heads of various boards of major charities, arts organizations, and worthy institutions of historical explication and preservation. Rickie's grandfather had been a 'Sir'; not that anybody was certain what that meant besides wealth and, of course, connnections that Blair Fever would otherwise never have had, and surely wanted for himself. He already had everything else.

If she leaned to one side in her chair and looked past Kipp's right, she could just make out Rickie Fever's slender white shoulders, the sheer pale grey stole she was wearing having slipped down her back, and her smooth wave of shoulder-length platinum hair gleaming in the television lights turned on her as well as on her husband on the platform above her and a few feet away.

Fever had finished his very short address now, and after shaking the premier's hand, was making his way down to the steps, shaking hands with men who thrust theirs out to him without the gracious smile or the deferential shrug, an emperor barely acknowledging his vassals, threading the short distance to his table and seating himself beside the gorgeous Rickie, who had turned to smile at him. A smile, Fiona noted, that he didn't return.

Rickie Fever who, with the lavish application of money, still looked about seventeen although she had to be sixty at least, had distinguished herself by doing good works, and by the way in which she always carried the air of someone to the manner (or the manor) born – as indeed she was – an inborn sense of position that nothing untoward Fever ever did, despite being her husband, could touch.

While the clapping was still going on, Veronica leaned close to Fiona and whispered, "That scum," apparently referring to Fever. Fiona, surprised, turned to look at her, but Vonnie had turned away and was now speaking to the Minister. Across the table Margaret Kipp was whispering to her husband, who was nodding, although so faintly it might have been an early Parkinson's tremour, his expression not changing, his eyes hooded.

Fiona had heard that Fever had many friends who cared a lot for him, that he could be a good friend and a hearty compatriot. Yet there was a hint she sometimes thought she picked up on in newspaper items of a certain – she couldn't identify it – a certain ruthlessness. Lately he hadn't been in the news much but, she acknowledged, we are all getting too old for shenanigans. Although, come to think of it, Roman hadn't been and neither had Jack Sorrel. *They never get too old*, Vonnie had told her, and she had laughed at the way she'd said it, as if she were Dorothy Parker or maybe Zsa Zsa Gabour. Oh, lord, Fiona thought, half the people here wouldn't have a clue who those women are. But who of the famously beautiful or famously witty was there left in the world? Anybody at all?

Vonnie was bending close to her again.

"I'll tell you when we get back to the suite." Fiona nodded, reached for and squeezed Vonnie's hand for no reason, just to let her know she cared for her and was proud of her. That whoever else might defect, they had each other.

ll around the room now people were pushing back their chairs and standing, beginning to move out toward the final reception or standing in groups chatting. Vonnie was standing too, saying goodnight to the Minister, then talking to a couple Fiona didn't know. Slowly, she rose herself, wondering what to do while she waited for Vonnie to finish her rounds. Malcolm Kipp and his wife, too, were making their slow way around the table, Kipp's wheelchair being pushed by a young man in a plain black suit who had appeared out of nowhere.

As they reached Fiona, who hadn't expected them to stop or even to acknowledge her existence, Margaret Kipp put a hand on Fiona's arm. Startled, Fiona looked down at her, at the flesh crinkled at the top of her too-low-cut evening dress, and sympathy came over her because she too knew what it was to be old, and to have ugly crinkles where there had once been plump, enticing flesh.

"Malcolm would like to talk to you." Fiona glanced up, but Margaret's husband had moved on, seemingly oblivious to his wife's not being behind him – goodness he was tall, even seated in a wheelchair, his head nearly level with the young man's who was pushing him – but in a flash, Fiona understood that he knew very well, but did not want anyone else to know that he wanted a meeting with the notorious FLL, author of that (she could see now) not-nearly-scandalous-enough book about the unsolved murder of Zara Stanley.

"Why, of course," Fiona said.

"Perhaps during this coming week?"

"Where?"

"In Ripley, where we make our home and have," she laughed here, "ever since Malcolm became Ripley's Crown Prosecutor." She put out her hand, ostensibly to shake Fiona's, but instead tucked a folded piece of paper neatly into Fiona's palm. Then she nodded in a gracious manner, as if she were Queen Elizabeth herself, and moved on toward her husband's retreating back. Fiona, rattled, turned her head to see where Kipp was and found him in conversation with Blair Fever. That gleaming hair was easy to spot anywhere. Rickie Fever was nowhere to be seen.

Now Vonnie was touching her, saying, "Let's not hang out very long at this reception. I'm tired, and besides, I think I've spoken to everybody I need to. We can just show up for a few minutes and then we can go up to the suite, have a drink together, and catch up on history."

They followed slowly at the back of the crowd until they had made their way out of the ballroom, into the room of the final reception. At the far end a few people were already crowded around the bar, and Fiona was pleased to see that there was, this time, no receiving line.

"I'll get us wine," she whispered to Vonnie who was already talking to one of the other recipients, the faceless ones, as Fiona thought of them: grain barons, or tourism heroes, or fund-raisers par excellence. The aboriginal elder seemed to have left the gathering as soon as the dinner ended.

With the two glasses in hand, she turned from the bar to find Vonnie at her elbow and behind her stood a slender, white-haired man only a couple of inches taller than she was, whose face was familiar.

"Rudy! It's been years!"

"Years and years," he agreed, leaning forward to brush her cheek with his lips. In the high school they had all gone to, such sophistication as this evening was had been beyond anybody's dreams; it belonged in the realm of movie stars, to a mythical New York city and Paris, France. They were laughing now, as if they'd all had the same thought at the same time.

"What's the opposite of how the mighty have fallen?" Fiona asked, beginning to suspect she shouldn't drink this last glass of wine. But hadn't she dated him in high school? Hadn't he been such a lovely, lovely boy? Who had, in fact dated everybody. And yet managed to do it without causing rancour among the many girls who'd gone out with him.

"Ozy-man-dias?" Vonnie asked, more or less irrelevantly, but then, "No" they all said, and broke up laughing again for no good reason.

"Where have you been? What have you been doing? Where's your wife?" He was still so handsome, even silver-haired, even sort of...wrinkled. This was the first moment she'd felt anything close to having fun all evening.

He was divorced; no, not remarried; he had gone to law school, and had started his own practice, years ago, one of his sons practised with him now: Kovalenko and Kovalenko; yes, he still lived in Ripley.

"I liked your book," he said to her, his manner abruptly serious. "I admired the hard work you did; it must have been tough. Lots of door slams and hang-ups, I bet."

"Not to mention a super-abundance of lies," Fiona said, suddenly just as serious.

"It's too bad," he told her, not looking at her, "because Zara deserves better. She deserves a little justice." Vonnie was speaking over her shoulder to someone. Rudy and Fiona's eyes met, and Fiona saw honesty in his, and was moved, so that she looked away, blinking. But he went on, "Tiny little Ripley, just a smaller version of the great cities of the world. Its venality, its corruption, its deaths, as real as in Rome or New York, just on a smaller scale; just for less profit." Fiona was shocked at his cynicism, it seemed so out of character. Or had she always recognized the wrong man in him, and was chagrined that she had seen so little – only his good looks and his charm, never his wisdom.

That perfume again; a screech of delight or maybe it was just drunkenness, but here was Marigold again, cuddling up to Rudy, kissing his cheek and leaving a pink smear on it that already he was reaching for a tissue to rub away, but the smile he gave her – Fiona saw at once that something had gone on there. She felt a twist of jealousy and was hugely annoyed with herself, Margie being so much younger, still so pretty no matter how she had achieved it. Men were a bit dumb about that kind of thing.

"Everybody's here!" she cried, apparently meaning "all the important people in the province." Or did she mean, everybody from high school? To Fiona's relief both her microphone and the cameraman had disappeared. "Congratulations, Veronica. I know you really deserved it." Vonnie was about to reply, but Margie had turned her face back to Rudy. "I was telling Fiona here that rumour has it that Zara's killer took a souvenir."

Vonnie looked startled, and raised her eyebrows at

Fiona. It wasn't until she saw this little 'face' of Vonnie's that Fiona realized that not everybody was as preoccupied with Zara's unsolved murder as she, and apparently Marigold, was, and would find this sudden conversational swerve more than odd. She rolled her eyes at Vonnie; Marigold, intent on Rudy, missed it.

"Where did you hear that?" Rudy asked easily, as if the abrupt switch of topic didn't rattle him in the least.

"Troy Venables," Margie said. "Remember him?"

"Sure I do," Rudy answered her. "Big guy. I think his father was somebody important in the police department, wasn't he? In the bad old days, I mean." Ahh, yes, Fiona thought. They all talk about the 'bad old days' as if there wasn't a lot of 'bad' still going on. What an admission of all that wrong-doing on the part of officials! Some of them were just criminals too! Or at the very least, more interested in their own careers and what would 'play well' with the public than with getting justice for Zara. Not true of lots of them, she scolded herself. She had seen the unspoken sorrow on the faces of some of them, old men now, but about Zara's age when she was killed.

But wait, Rudy's remark to Margie finally registering: So maybe Troy Venables did know something! I never knew his father was a police officer. How did I miss that? In her state of mild inebriation she couldn't quite sort out if this was something important or not.

"So, are you coming to my movie when it opens?" Marigold/Margie/Marjory inquired of Rudy.

"Well, of course, if you send me an invite," he said.

"You know I will," she purred, at least, that was what Fiona thought she heard. The noise level was, if anything, getting higher.

Margie looked over her shoulder at Fiona, smiling in a sly way and Fiona noticed that Rudy had lifted his free hand and was resting it against Margie's lower back. As she watched, he dropped it. Margie gave a little kick to her skirt then, forcing the fullness to the back so she could walk – what an over-the-top dress that was – gave a cute little wave with her fingers, mouthing, "Toodle-ooh," and melted into the group standing next to theirs where she began airkissing cheeks again, and cooing to people who seemed to be accepting her presence unreservedly. At least, the men were.

I will forget Marjory Popowich, she told herself. She swallowed down something that might have been a cough or a sob, saw that Rudy and Vonnie were talking cheerfully to each other and would have run for the ladies room, but people were so packed into the room now that she knew it would be hopeless to try to slip away. It would involve screaming and punching, and she doubted she could do that, even though, it occurred to her, she really wanted to. Which made her laugh again, so that the other two broke off their conversation and turned to her.

"What?" Vonnie asked.

"I think I'm drunk. What's the opposite of mighty?"

"What?"

"The opposite of, 'How the mighty have fallen.'"

"Oh," Vonnie said, understanding that Fiona meant the three of them coming from such humble origins and yet standing here, equals, at least for this one night, to the mighty. She paused. "Weak. Powerless?"

"Impotent," Rudy said, and for a second Fiona was taken aback.

"You're right! Good choice! It should be: How the impotent have risen."

They both stared at her as if wondering about her sanity, then they all began to laugh again. Vonnie and Fiona were leaning into each other, giggling helplessly, close to falling over with laughter, when Rudy, gazing at them with an amused, non-censuring smile on his lips, gave them something like a small, ironic bow, turned and slipped away through the crowd. Only Rudy could slip away in this tightly-packed crowd, Fiona thought. He could do anything, people liked him so much. So why was he divorced?

By the time the two of them had stopped laughing and stood, side by side, as sober as if at a funeral, their wine glasses empty and held in both hands at their waists, the place had begun to seem merely unbearably noisy, the crowd drunken, all dignity having evaporated. Without speaking, they began the difficult passage out of the room, single file, then across the wide hall to the shiny, brass-trimmed elevators, where they got on alone and were taken up to the small suite that Vonnie had splurged on, saying to Fiona that she couldn't imagine lying alone in a hotel room after such an event, no Jack to talk over the evening with, or to say loving words of praise to her. You'll have to do, she'd told Fiona. But we'll have our own beds.

Once in the suite, neither spoke while Vonnie opened the complementary bottle of wine set on a tray on the coffee table and partially filled the accompanying two glasses. They sat facing each other on the long sofa that would open to be Fiona's bed, having swung their legs up like two teenagers, and each leaning against her corner, although Fiona, the taller, had to bend her legs to fit. All that was missing were fat plastic curlers and face cream.

"Congratulations, again," Fiona said, raising her glass and sipping. "You were going to tell me something about

Blair Fever, but I can't remember what it was. Oh, yeah. You called him scum."

"And scum he is."

"Why?"

"He cheats on her. He's even been seen in public with other women. Has no qualms about humiliating Rickie. But she is worth ten Blair Fevers. I'm surprised you don't know all this. Everybody does."

"I think you have to move in the right circles," Fiona answered. She had set her wine glass on the coffee table, untouched after the first sip. She felt sober now. "I mean, it's not the kind of thing that would be in the paper."

"Mixes with some really bad types, I've heard. Helped the Mafia move into the province people say."

"But – they gave him a medal tonight!"

Vonnie shrugged, making her medal swing, so that she touched it with her hand, not seeming to notice that she was, cradling it in her palm.

"I don't know about that. Maybe the people on the committee don't know the stories about him, or maybe they think it's all just malicious gossip. Or else he gave some big donations somewhere. I hear that the big thing is to get yourself a nomination. I was lucky. The Western Arts organization nominated me so I don't owe anybody a thing." She yawned, setting her glass on the table too. "I'm worn out. It was a great day, except for no Jack." She sighed, leaning her head back, and Fiona was afraid she would cry.

Fiona sat up straight then, swung her legs around and stood briskly, tottering a little.

"Are you ready for bed?"

Not speaking, long-time housewives falling into the familiar routine, they threw the cushions off the sofa and opened it to its full size. It was already made and Fiona found pillows in the entry closet. They began undressing, each in her own space, hanging their gowns regretfully, pulling off panty hose with relief, putting on night clothes, using the two bathrooms to remove make-up, brush hair and teeth. Vonnie got into bed in the large bedroom and Fiona into the sofabed in the living room. They put out the lights and lay in the semi-darkness, the door between them open so that they could see each other. The city had quieted at last, and there was no sound from the wide hotel hall, no footsteps, no drunken voices, no doors shutting.

After a while Vonnie called softly, "Fee, did you sleep with Rudy in high school?"

"No," Fiona answered. "I was a virgin in high school. Did you?"

"Yes," Vonnie said. "He was my first – no, I'm lying – he was my second man." Another long silence. "Do you think he was saying he's impotent now?"

"Who can tell," Fiona answered. "I hope not. He's such a nice guy."

"There's always Viagra," Vonnie pointed out.

"Hope springs eternal," Fiona said. Then it came to her, "The opposite of how the mighty have fallen: It's, ummm, From lowly things…mighty champions grow. No, I've got it: 'Mighty things from small beginnings grow.' Dryden." Another silence. "Who was your first?" she asked Vonnie.

"You wouldn't know him."

"What happened to him?"

"He got married. Nothing happened to him. Who was your first?"

"Guy I dated in second year university. He was –"

"I know. An engineer."

"Yeah."

"So did you go out with him a lot?"

"Never saw him again once I…succumbed. Stay away from engineering students. The first one I dated tried to rape me. Or was he an Arts student?"

"Tried?" Vonnie said. "If he had really wanted to, he would have succeeded." A chill entered the room, both of them thinking of Zara Stanley.

"You're right," Fiona said. "Anyway," yawning, "it was such a long time ago and I'm sure he got married and had babies and became a credit to his community."

Vonnie said, "Like we all did." Fiona didn't say, except me, I didn't have babies. Mustn't think about that. "Vonnie, did you ever know Livana Kirby?"

"I met her once, not that long ago, actually. She's pretty rich, I guess. Or she acts like she is. Still has a thick accent. I don't know when she came to Canada. Or from where, come to think of it."

"Is she still beautiful?"

"Oh, you know. I was at some society women's tea here in Hart City and I wound up at the same table with her. Volunteers in the arts, I think. What made you think of her? Do you know her?"

"It's just such a strange name. I think I must have heard somebody say it tonight, and I wondered about it."

"I can give you her address and phone number," Vonnie said, yawning. "She lives in Hart City and she'll be on the Arts Committee's lists as a donor." Too startled to reply, Fiona said nothing. She could hear Vonnie tossing in the other room, the bedclothes crinkling and rustling, then pillows being punched. "No way can I sleep. I'm too excited. I wonder where Jack is tonight."

"Don't think such thoughts," Fiona admonished.

"At least you know where Roman is," Vonnie pointed out.

"Most of the time I was married to him I had no clue where he was."

Vonnie was out of bed now, pulling on her dressing gown, and padding into the living room where Fiona was sitting up in her makeshift bed. Vonnie had brought pillows and plopped down beside her, lifting the blankets to cover her feet and legs.

"Is that really true?" she asked Fiona. It was well into the witching time, Fiona thought, when the world darkened and at the same time floated luminous over the void. Some unnamable feeling came low in her gut, hitting her so hard that for a second she couldn't breathe.

"*I don't think Roman was faithful to me.*" It was a whisper.

"What?" Vonnie said, turning her head to look into Fiona's face. Fiona met her gaze.

Vonnie started to say something but then stopped herself and after a second said softly, "I'm sorry, Fiona."

Fiona said, "You knew, didn't you." Vonnie kept silent. "How long have you known?"

"Jack told me ages ago," Vonnie said. "Fee, I'm so sorry. But he did love you, you know."

"I'm beginning to doubt that," Fiona said, lifting her voice to a high, feminine note, as if she were saying that she doubted a certain dress would fit, or that there would be time for lunch, to keep herself from crying.

"Join the club," Vonnie said, finally.

"What shall we do?" Fiona asked. Such a depth of silence there was in the world; so deep it was a presence itself. Cry?

Rage? Hit things? They lay side by side, gazing straight ahead into the shadows. Fiona spoke at last. "It was because we couldn't have children, I think."

"You could have adopted?" Vonnie asked, gently.

It was odd that they had never talked about any of this over the years of their friendship, but Vonnie was having her babies, and raising them, children from whom Fiona had kept a polite distance, helping out now and then. Vonnie, seeming to have sensed that it was hard for Fiona to be with Vonnie's kids, didn't ask her too often, relying most of the time on Jack's mother, and then, after she died, on teenagers from the village. Fiona would always be grateful to her for that, and yet, she had never sat down with Vonnie and told her the whole story.

"When we married we expected to have children. We decided three would be about right. Roman said we'd have two boys and a girl, and I said, no way: two girls and a boy." Vonnie seemed about to speak, but Fiona went on. "We actually chose names. Roman wanted WASP names because his own name was Slav, and that was a burden to him in the province. You know how things were then." Vonnie moved a finger in agreement. "Thomas, he said, and William, or James. I chose the girls' names. Melody, Melissa, Madeleine. He said, What's with all the 'm's? I told him that they all go well with Lychenko. Melody Lychenko. That was the one I chose finally. Doesn't it have a nice musical sound?"

"It does," Vonnie said, "Melody Lychenko," trying it out. "It really does." She had named her own daughters Anne, and Sandra, and Sarah.

"Should I go on?"

"Of course you should," Vonnie said, and touched Fiona's hand where it lay next to hers on the quilt.

"We waited five years before we finally went to the doctor. It turned out that although Roman's sperm count wasn't high, it was in the normal range, that the problem was most likely me. So, I went through examinations and tests, but none of the experts could find anything wrong with me. No endometriosis, no failure to ovulate, no malformations, or missing or malfunctioning parts.

"The doctor said," Fiona went on as if reading from a paper, "ten percent of the infertility cases we deal with have no identifiable cause, and around another thirty percent seem to be caused by some combination of factors of both the husband and wife's situation, also not always ones we can identify or help." Fiona sighed, went on. "There was no in vitro fertilization to consider then, or hormone treatments, or whatever. I hated the thought of it anyway, I was never sorry we couldn't do that. We could only wait and hope, at the same time as we were trying to get used to the thought of being…childless." She still had trouble saying 'childless.'

"But adoption?" Vonnie asked.

Roman had been against adoption, Fiona told her. "And I was never the kind of girl who couldn't wait to hold her first baby, who yearned for babies. I had no strong desire to go out and adopt one either."

"Did he hold it against you? That there were no children?" Vonnie asked. For the first time during her long recitation, Fiona felt tears starting in her eyes, and refused them permission. Because Roman didn't mention their childlessness as the years passed, she assumed that he was accepting of it, and didn't have any great regrets.

"We got on with our lives," she said. She saw now that that had meant that they had grown farther and farther apart. "Maybe it's harder to feel really married, to stick to the rules, if there aren't any kids. Do you think so?" she asked her friend.

"Maybe," Vonnie said, dubiously. "Although having them apparently doesn't matter either."

Fiona knew that Roman's disengagement from her had begun after those long sessions with the doctors which ended in that fog of uncertainty that she had never tried to beat her way through, instead telling herself not thinking about it was the best route. After all, there was nothing she could do about it, and, for all she knew, she still might wake up one morning pregnant, she still had time.

Yet, she thought, all that – the testing, the results – happened in the months before Roman decided to go to China on that delegation, and made it clear that he did not want me to come with him. And I hardly noticed at the time that that was what had happened.

A bone-searing sadness spread from her gut upward into her chest and throat, until even her fingertips ached with it, her ankles, the soles of her feet. With that pain was itself the knowledge of how wrong she had been in so important a facet of her own life, and of her life together with Roman. It was, at last, the acknowledgement that should have come then, thirty-five years ago, of what it meant to be childless, specifically to her, Fiona, as a woman, as a wife. She would not admit it as a loss, wouldn't admit to her grief and so, she saw now, by this failure of her own she had lost even more.

Chapter Twelve

She woke before Vonnie did into the stuffy darkness of the hotel suite. She made her uncertain way to the bathroom, pausing on the way to hold back one of the heavy curtains to see what was happening outside. It was still dark, but to the east at the horizon there was a faint line of paler grey with a hint of gold along its bottom. Her mouth was dry, her head aching. She supposed she should be grateful that three glasses of wine made her ridiculously drunk, where when she was young they would have made her only giggly and voluble. Now they also left her with such a hangover that she vowed never again to drink even one glass of wine, all the while knowing that in an hour she would feel close to her regular self, seventy being what it was and mornings more difficult generally than they used to be. At least she hadn't been too drunk to hang up her dress last night. Her marvelous dress. Where would she ever wear it again? Now that Vonnie's event was over she felt foolish at having spent so much money for one evening.

Now she remembered what she'd completely forgotten the night before: the little square of paper Margaret Kipp had pressed into her palm after the dinner. She searched and found her evening bag. As she had thought, it held an address in one of the city's posher districts, in the old part of town where great trees, elms, maples, poplars, lined the streets on each side, the lots were enormous, and the houses were actually small mansions, some built as early as the late nineteenth century. Houses that, when she was a girl, could only be viewed by most of the city with the kind of envy that said that you knew you would never ever be fortunate enough to live in one of them. There was a phone number, too. So she was to call and make an appointment, not just show up.

There came a groaning and a thumping of bedclothes from the other room.

"Are you up, Fee?" Vonnie called. She had to stop, clear her throat, and try a second time. "What time is it?"

"Eight-ish," Fiona said. "What's your hurry?"

"Meetings," Vonnie called back. Her lamp went on. "Oh God, I feel awful. I ache all over. Damn high heels. Would you order up some breakfast?"

Water began to run in Vonnie's bathroom.

By the time the breakfast cart arrived both Vonnie and Fiona were dressed, Vonnie in a smart blue suit and another pair of slightly lower high heels, Fiona in pantsuit and flats. They pulled up chairs to the small table and Vonnie poured the coffee.

"Don't forget to give me Livana Kirby's address," Fiona said.

"Why are you suddenly so interested in her?"

"Remember thirty-five years ago when Roman went to China?"

"And you stayed home like an idiot?"

"Yeah," Fiona said. "That time."

"So?"

"Livana Kirby was on that trip. I'd like to collect her impressions of it. It was after Nixon went to China, a few years after Trudeau had gone too, and it was a different China than today. I thought I might write an article about it. But…with Roman gone…"

"That's a great idea. You just need some meaningful work to get you rolling again. I wish you'd move back to Ripley."

"Sometimes I wish it too."

The light outside was growing stronger, sending a faint ray into the room through the vertical crack Fiona had made between the curtains. In its clarity Vonnie's makeup appeared garish, accenting her wrinkles, the tiny droops at the corners of her mouth. Fiona looked away, dismayed for both of them.

Oblivious, Vonnie was going on. "Come to think of it, it's a puzzle where Livana Kirby got all that money."

"Maybe her family had money," Fiona suggested. "When are you going to give up the farm and get a smart condo overlooking the river?"

"What year did Nixon go to China? Late sixties?"

"1972 and don't change the subject." Fiona said. Vonnie sighed.

"I suppose I will soon. Maybe in a year or so. I hate to leave the farm and the girls don't want me to sell it because they were raised there; it will always be home to them."

"Let them blame Jack. It isn't your fault you have to sell and move."

"They'll blame me anyway. I'm a mom," Vonnie said. She rose and opened the curtains wide so that the room lightened and Fiona clicked off the lamp on the breakfast table. They were both surprised to discover that it had snowed in the night.

After they had eaten Vonnie opened her laptop, and

found Livana Kirby's address and phone number for Fiona.

"I shouldn't be doing this, privacy and all that, so don't tell her it was me who gave it to you, okay?"

Fiona nodded. "She must be pretty old by now," she remarked.

"No older than us, I don't think. But then, we're the oldest people left on the planet, aren't we."

Fiona was wrestling with herself over whether to tell her friend what she was really after. When she examined her silence, she could see no good reason for it, other than that Vonnie might tell others. But she won't if I ask her not to. And she already knows all about Roman's unfaithfulness.

"Okay," she said. "Here is why I want to talk to Livana Kirby."

Even as she spoke to Vonnie about her true reasons for looking up Livana, she was thinking, I should have forced Roman into a conversation with me. By 'conversation' she meant a mutual truth-telling, a confrontation that couldn't be escaped. But she saw then too, that to have done that probably would have meant the end of their marriage. And I couldn't face that. So I kept silent, pretended not to know what I knew – what I must have known.

"So that's why I'm looking up Livana Kirby. Not just to see if she can tell me why I got that envelope with her ex-husband's name on it, but because I think Roman started with her."

"That was a thousand years ago," Vonnie said, surprised. "Why not start with the years just before he died?"

"Because I want to understand," Fiona told her. "Because I want to begin at the beginning and not stop until I get to the end. I hate not knowing about my own life. I hate being a dupe."

"But, you're going to see her? What will you say? What do you think she will say?"

"I want to see her in person. I'll just ask her about the China trip, and while she's talking, I'll…listen, and make up my own mind." Vonnie was staring at her, moving her eyes over Fiona's face as if she were looking for something she hoped would be there. Fiona was reminded of the man who had pulled up beside her in her car and stared at her like this, but in such a hostile way.

"That's brave," Vonnie said, at last, her expression softening. "Completely crazy. But brave."

"If I find her, I find myself," Fiona said, then frowned, as if she had just heard what she had said, and was surprised, not sure what she meant. She was still debating whether to tell Vonnie that she hoped Livana could tell her something useful about Livana's former husband, Evan, something that might help her to understand why his name had been inside the brown envelope slipped under her door. But that would be going too far, she decided. It was still way too speculative.

After a long moment she stood briskly, straightening her pant legs, tucking her blouse into place, buttoning her jacket, then unbuttoning it again. She went to the bathroom and gathered her toiletries, placed them onto the top of her folded clothing in her small suitcase, then closed it and zipped it firmly. At the sound of the zipper whisking around the case Vonnie stood too.

"I have an interview downstairs in about ten minutes," she said. "I'm not heading back to the farm until tomorrow. Then this afternoon I see bloody old Jack. I will ask him, 'What happened to you, Jack? Do you think you will never be *too* old, as I am? Do you think that the day will never

come when you will yearn for what you and I once had?'
And he will back up, turn red, snort, and refuse to answer
me. End of story."

Fiona went to the closet, removed her gown and folded
it carelessly into the case she had brought it in, dropping
the shoes she'd worn with it on top of the dress. She
reached for her coat, put it on, and said, "Vonnie, you are
still beautiful. You will always be beautiful no matter if your
skin sags and your body loses its shape. You're smart, you're
capable, and you've done wonders with your life. You've
done it from out in the boonies, not from some mansion
here in Hart City, or in Ripley. I think you deserve that
medal and another one besides. And don't you ever forget
it. Jack is a moron."

Sitting in the car she had rented on her arrival at the Hart
City airport, across from the high rise where Livana Kirby
made her home, Fiona took out her cell phone and was
about to dial the number Vonnie had found for her when
she changed her mind. She put the phone back in her
purse, got out of the car, locked it, crossed the street, and
went into the lobby. At the directory, where there were only
apartment numbers without names beside them, she
pushed the buzzer for Livana's condo, and waited impatiently. She was surprised to find that all her qualms had
vanished somewhere on the drive from the hotel. Behind
her cold November light bullied its way between blackened
tree branches to spread over the thin layer of snow covering
the streets and sidewalks. Her back and neck had tensed
and the air seemed to have acquired a crackle, yet she wel-
comed this; it matched the determination growing in her

heart and gut. *This* was the place she wanted to be. Then Malcolm Kipp.

A deep-throated voice, accented, said, "Yes?"

"Mrs. Kirby?" No reply. She went on. "I'm Fiona Lychenko, Roman Lychenko's widow. May I come up and speak with you?" Silence followed, then the loud buzz of the door being unlocked. Fiona opened it, walked into the lobby to the elevators. It was only when she was rising to the fourth floor that she began to wonder what she would say, and whether her daring to come here to talk to this stranger wasn't just posturing on her part. Or foolishness. I should be chasing down that file number, she told herself, but she still had no idea how to go about that. Unless I request it through the Freedom of Information Act. But if all she had was a number, how could they give the file to her? They couldn't. She knocked briskly on the Kirby door as if she had every right to be here.

At first she could hear nothing behind it, as if there were no one there at all, then there was a soft thumping sound, and the door opened to reveal a short woman in a blue and green flowered muu-muu, her aggressively dark hair cut in an elegant cap-shape, a not-very-welcoming expression on her face, a face Fiona found very recognizable still from the photo she had seen. When she said, "Come in," and turned away Fiona saw she was using a cane.

A flood of light poured from a curved bank of windows that ran across the end of the living room she now found herself in, a white room: white curtains, white carpet, white sofas, the swathe of white broken only by colourful cushions on the sofas – pinks, scarlets, deep reds.

"What a beautiful room," she found herself saying before she had actually considered whether she liked it or not. 'Striking' might be a better word, she thought, as she sat on the sofa Livana indicated before seating herself across from Fiona in a small, white velvet armchair.

"I grow tired of it," Livana said. She set her cane carefully against the chair, tucking the handle in beside her so it wouldn't fall to the floor. "You know what I mean?"

Fiona nodded. "I can't seem to move myself out of sloth to actually do any decorating even though this place I bought really needs it," she said. Livana snorted, stretched her neck as if it hurt her, pointing her delicate chin upward, then slowly lowering and rotating her head back to face Fiona.

"I am stiff in mornings," she said. "Now, you come to see me." Fiona was taking in the small tables beside the armchairs and in front of the sofas: sort of Turkish, she thought, round, with pie crust edges all in a dull gold, and their surfaces covered with minute designs in colours she couldn't quite pick out – blues, dark reds, tarnished black. Was Livana maybe Turkish? On the table to the right a few silver-framed photos stood, all black and white, of a girl child in a white dress, and then a posed studio photo of a pretty young woman, and another of her beside a younger Livana.

"I want to know more about the trip you and your first husband –"

"Only husband!" Livana intervened, lifting a finger as a lecturer might to insist on a point.

"Excuse me. I'm referring to the government trip you and your then-husband took to China in 1980. My husband was on that trip too, and I want to compile a record of his life as an activist for the *Western Canadian Farmer*. That's why I'm here." Livana stared directly into Fiona's eyes, her own eyes seeming to grow larger and blacker.

Fiona gazed back as if she were accustomed to this and would not be shaken. Even with the darkened skin, loose along the jaw-line, the too-thin penciled black eyebrows Livana's former beauty was evident. Out the windows, she became aware, was the expanse of a large, treed park. How lovely it must be in the summer, she thought. At the moment, far across the park the expanse of dead grass with its fresh covering of snow gleamed with light, the tree trunks and branches damp and black as the sun warmed them.

"Good story," Livana said. "I commend you." Then she smiled, slowly. "I make tea."

"Oh, no," Fiona said, perhaps ungraciously, but she wanted only to pursue what she wanted to find out, and ignoring the "good story" remark. "I just had a large hotel breakfast," – untrue – "And…uh…" Livana was giving her that look again.

"Has been very long time," Livana answered, looking somewhere over Fiona's head to the space behind her. "I remember it all," dropping her eyes to her knees. "All of it. Such a cold country it was, so very cold, I remember. All these…" she lifted both hands and spread them wide, "Extensive, big, long…halls and all these silk banners." She paused, shaking her head. "Your husband, Roman, I liked him." Fiona was tempted to ask, how much did you like him? but bit her tongue. "Why you not come too?"

"I'm not sure anymore," Fiona said. "We didn't have any cattle, and our neighbours would have looked after our couple of horses. The dog could have gone into a kennel or the neighbours could have fed him. I didn't really want to go, I think, and when I could see that Roman was pushing me to stay home – he had all these good reasons: To make sure the place wasn't vandalized, to look after the ton of mail he always got, to attend some conference in his place that he seemed to think was important, not to interrupt my own work at the newspaper – I can't remember it all. But..." here she raised her head, focused her eyes on Livana's face which she found so compelling, such strength in it, she was like a little rock sitting there across from her, "I think now, these last few days, I mean, that he wanted to go alone. He didn't dare say so out loud, but he wanted me to stay home. He was up to no good, I guess."

"Why you say that?" Livana asked, her eyes flickered to the table with the photos of the child and the young woman on it.

"Because...after his death I found certain...things... were not as I expected. Didn't make sense."

"So, now we know!" Livana said, suddenly and loudly enough to startle Fiona. "You want to find out what he was up to. You found money, I think." Fiona could feel her face abruptly flushing, she might have made an "uh" sound, as if all the air had abruptly departed from her lungs.

"Yes, money. Too much money."

"You know about this?" Livana tossed out one hand in what seemed to be contempt, and nodded once, firmly. "Bribe," she said. Then she laughed, turning her head to indicate the large, glamorous room in which they sat. "Bribe," she repeated, lifting her hand and tossing it lightly from the wrist, to indicate the entire condo. Fiona's heart was pounding so hard she thought the noise was keeping her from hearing right.

"Bribe? Bribes? Roman? You?" Livana was smiling calming, nodding her head, 'yes,' again. "Who paid you bribes? Why? What for? When?"

"Long story," Livana said, shrugging, lifting her hands,

palms up. "I tell you. But first, I make tea. No, coffee. You need whiskey?" Fiona thought, yes, I need whiskey, at least partly to assuage a bit the effect of her thankfully diminishing hangover, but she said, "Coffee would be good."

"Brandy," Livana announced, already out of her chair and leaving her cane behind – she seemed to walk perfectly well without it – went to a gleaming, distressed gold sideboard beside the door through which Fiona had entered. There she poured two brandies and brought them back, setting one on the table beside Fiona, and one on the table beside her armchair.

Fiona, of all things, found herself giggling, the sound growing and deepening into a strange, guttural laughter, her face reddening, her eyes beginning to stream. She couldn't stop laughing, until she realized she was crying. For a woman who was widowed, who had nothing left of her life, entirely too much was going on; she couldn't get a grip on all of it. She extracted a tissue from her bag, wiped her eyes, and blew her nose.

"I'm sorry," she gasped. Livana made a dismissive gesture. "I cried plenty too," she said. "Women cry, I think, eh?"

"Total waste of time," Fiona, the cynic, returned.

"All right," Livana began. "You came here to find out what Roman was up to." Was her English growing better, too? "Or so you say. But this is mixed in with that murder case you were so interested in, that book you wrote about Zara Stanley." Fiona nodded slowly. Evan Kirby's name, on that page in the brown envelope. And all three of them were on that China trip. She took a deep breath, fixed her eyes on Livana.

"Did you and my husband have an affair on that trip?"

"What does it matter now?" Livana asked. Her tone was

sober, quieter, almost melancholy.

"I'm going to find out the truth about my marriage if it kills me," she said. "I mean that. So did you?" Livana nodded again, but slowly, not looking at Fiona.

"Yes, we did. Evan was in meetings a lot when the rest of us weren't, or only some of us went with him, the important ones. I wasn't important, just a wife, and Roman wasn't important then either. Evan, he was more than he seemed then, and so sometimes late at night he had to go out. And...Here, I'll tell you what no one else knew, only Roman." Fiona waited, holding her breath without realizing she was, moisture breaking out on her palms and between her breasts. "Evan has a very mean side. He beat me, and when he left for his meeting, I went to Roman. That's what happened." That innocuous looking little guy! Fiona thought. He beat his wife?

"Once when he was so drunk he couldn't stand up he said that he had killed a girl and that he wasn't afraid to kill me too. Drunken ravings." She shrugged. "Then he only wanted to scare me. But another time he said rape. Who? I asked. He wouldn't tell me. Held up two fingers. Can you believe this? This time I did believe him. I was afraid what in time he might do. So, I left him."

Yet Livana looked anything but cowed. She looked, instead, steadfast; she looked determined, a determination that had transformed itself into a soul-deep unyieldingness that, Fiona thought, would not soften even in death. This little woman frightened her just a bit. Even as she was in awe of her.

"When were you divorced?"

"Divorced in 1981."

Suddenly Fiona thought, a bribe paid for this apartment?

"How long have you lived here?"

"Yes, bribery paid for this place. So I would keep my mouth shut about what I knew. I held out for quite a lot of money. He threatened to kill me to frighten me, but I am not stupid and I am not afraid. I had ways of protecting myself."

"But…What are we talking about? What did you know he didn't want you to tell? And Roman?" Before Livana could answer Fiona understood: "You put that envelope under my door, didn't you? Why didn't you just tell me what you knew? Why the cloak-and-dagger stuff?" She found she was indignant, but she couldn't sort out what she should be saying; there no longer seemed to be a straight line through this conversation. "Have you seen the file? How do you know about it?"

"I found it in Evan's desk – when he was in government here – long before China trip, long time ago. He came home before I could do more than glance at it, and copy down that number. I never saw it again."

Fiona put both hands up and, for a second, held her head in them as if to control the turmoil inside, then put them down again, taking in a slow breath through her nose. What should she be asking?

"But then…why do you think I should see it? How do you know it's important?"

"Because he was so angry when I found it. I was looking for stamps, I said. He slapped me. Stay out of my desk. Something from police chief, I saw." Fiona thought, *he was making documents about the murder disappear so nobody could ever properly revisit the crime.*

"How big was the file?" she thought to ask.

"Oh, thin, thin," Livana said. "A few papers, that is all. I only saw one page, but he thought I saw it all. But I said, no, no, no, I didn't, I didn't." She clasped her hands as if in prayer and raised her eyes upward. Fiona saw, this was Livana persuading Evan.

"Then, what was the bribe for?"

"When I decided to divorce him, he said I would get nothing, he would take our child, I'd had an affair, he would see to it that I starved if I left him, I said, okay, I saw everything in the desk, I have the file number, I will tell everyone. I told him, too, a letter would go to the newspaper if anything happened to me, that it was all arranged. He believed me. But I was lying. He got money for me to keep me quiet. I took it and I have kept quiet, until now. I thought it better to have the money. But now, I think I was wrong."

"Why didn't you just tell me this?" Livana shrugged. She lifted her arm and pointed to her wrist: Fiona saw that what she had thought was a bracelet was instead a medical identifier. Heart? She wondered. Livana said, as if reading her mind, "Heart." A sober silence followed, before Livana spoke again.

"I go to you anyway to get you started again. I can't do it myself. It is very dangerous still, you know. He made me swear to tell no one or he and his friends would ruin me."

"How?"

"The way they always do: pin something on me, spread vicious rumours that would make me kill myself, whatever. There are people to do that to people who betray the powerful ones. Don't you know that?"

Fiona put her elbow on the sofa's arm, cupping her forehead with her palm. "But – *what is it you know?*"

"I know who killed Zara Stanley."

A loud buzzing filled the room. What air was there to breathe? What should she do? Where could she hide?

Abruptly, she had to void her bladder. "Please, a toilet," she gasped, standing clumsily. Livana pointed, and Fiona followed her pointing finger out of the room.

In the small powder room by the entrance she shut the door and leaned for a second against it, breathing hard as if she'd been running and couldn't catch her breath. She snuffled, as if she had a cold, and had to breathe through her mouth. Fumbling, she pulled down her slacks and underwear, and sat on the toilet. It was as if a siren was going off in her head.

Dear God, I have got to calm myself. She began to breathe deeply through her nose, forcing herself to hang on through long breaths that her body screamed to end. Finished, she cleaned herself, pulled up her clothes, scrubbed her hands vigorously, and refusing to gaze in the mirror even once, went back to the living room where Livana sat, her head leaning against the upholstered chairback, as if she were very tired. The act of moving briskly was calming in itself and the feeling of strength she had had when she rang the doorbell a half hour earlier had returned, although her body felt sticky with old sweat, and her mouth was dry.

"Tell me who killed Zara." Fiona said this as she sat again on the sofa. Livana shook her head, carefully, no.

"Why not?"

"Because it is no good without proof. I have no proof and neither do you. If I tell you, and you go to the killers, they will know you know – it will be on your face, in your voice, too. No, better you keep on digging. I help you."

"But how do you know who killed her?"

"I saw things; I heard things; Evan and his friends, they talk. I am not stupid. And he knew all kinds of things the public doesn't know. Secrets. Cover-ups."

"I don't know who we're talking about!"

"Doesn't matter," Livana said. "I gave you what you need; you must find the trail, find the evidence, make a case that nobody can ignore."

"Are we talking about your ex-husband?" Livana shrugged slowly, not looking at Fiona. "He half-way claimed he did," Fiona pointed out. "He said 'rape,' too.

"He was drunk, very, very drunk. He might have dreamt it; I think, too, he was talking about somebody else."

"Did he – did he – rape you?" Livana didn't move or speak. Then she nodded her head slowly, still not looking at Fiona.

"When drunk," she said.

Fiona said, a whisper, "I am so sorry."

They sat together in silence for several minutes, Livana resting her chin on her palm, her elbow on the chair's arm, head turned to gaze out one of the tall windows. Fiona stared at her hands lying loose on her lap. Finally, she spoke.

"I think that I've already figured out one important thing from your brown envelope: that we've all been look-ing in the wrong place all these years. Zara Stanley was killed not by some drifter, but by someone she knew, someone everybody knew. And further," she paused to straighten and draw in a breath, "that it seems that the highest officials then grouped together secretly to protect the man they knew had murdered her. I doubt very much that even the police officers who were doing the investigation knew why they were pulled off the case, or why their inves-tigation failed."

Livana seemed smaller, sitting across from her in the big armchair, smaller, older, less vivid. How very odd, as if the secret she had carried all these years had filled her with a kind of dark, even unwelcome, power, and now that she had passed some of it on, she had shrunk.

Fiona didn't care about Livana, she wanted to finish her thought. "There is only one reason they would do that: if the killer was in some way prominent enough and/or powerful enough that he could insist on this protection and receive it. Because who was Zara Stanley? A poor country girl with no lineage, no land, no money, no connections, with nothing. Nothing but her great beauty. And I am so angry," she said. "I am so angry I could kill someone myself."

Across the few feet between them Livana watched her. Fiona had an abrupt, eerie sense that she had in some way become Livana, that she had picked up Livana's passion, her cold rage, her necessary deviousness, that she was not mild, passionless Fiona anymore. She was both terror-stricken at this and vastly proud.

"Don't kill," Livana said. Such a strong voice from this small woman; it echoed. "Get the killers. Get the men who covered up for the killers. Get them all." She paused. Fiona was thinking, *So the rumour was always right: there was more than one killer.* Rage was rising in her again and for a second she couldn't hear Livana, who had gone on speaking. "But be careful. Try to keep your searching a secret whenever possible. They *will* go after you. They have to. If you solve this mess, if you find the string and pull it, what you find at the end could bring down – " She broke off, shaking her head. "This is a dangerous business. Or maybe, they will offer you money to shut up, as they offered me. I took it." She lifted her palms again, shrugging. "It was a different world then. I don't think you will take it. What would happen if you refuse money, I don't like to think. Oh, the mud that will be slung at you."

Fiona considered, imagining that moment when the knock came on her door and some innocuous man she would never notice on the street stood there offering her money, threatening her in subtle ways. Or maybe he would try to kill her. Maybe he *would* kill her. She was quiet for a long moment while across from her Livana waited, studying her.

"I'm an old woman," Fiona said. "I have no husband, no children, nothing to lose. To get justice at last for Zara, that is all I want."

She stood, took a last sip from her brandy, replaced the glass onto the little table, crossed the room to shake Livana's hand. "I am thinking the file number is an old Justice Department file. Or maybe it is a special secret file that belongs to the premier's office. I suspect I'll never see it." And if I never see it, how do I find the killers? There has to be a way. You knew I saw Evan? I'll go again and I'll be less polite this time." They were at the door into the foyer when she remembered. "What about Roman? What did he know? He still had about a hundred thousand dollars stashed away in a couple of places, and the bills in the safe deposit box weren't really old bills."

Livana said, "He knew the story when I did, because I told him, but he didn't use it for years. Then it was safer not to let on what he knew. He came to see me every now and then. Some years ago he told me he wanted to buy more land. So then he went to Evan. Maybe he had some evidence. This I don't know. Have you been through his papers?" Fiona shook her head, no, although she had, but when she had done that she hadn't been looking for evidence of wrong-doing. It seemed to her that there was something else she wanted to ask, but what it was, she couldn't remember.

"That child in those photos in the living room: Is she your daughter?" Livana nodded.

"Yes. She is grown now and gone away. I see her once a year. We write, we phone." A smile hovered on her lips, tender, thoughtful.

Fiona told her, "I am going to see Malcolm Kipp. He asked me to. More lies, I suppose. How will I get to that file?" A rhetorical question as much as anything, but still…

Livana said, "I don't know," softly. She was leaning against the wall now. Fiona had opened the door into the outer hall, glancing back once, then turning away toward the elevator as Livana took a step forward to close her door.

The last thing she saw was Livana's eyes, curiously luminous after the impenetrable black they had been at first, nearer to clear brown now, with flecks of gold, as if light had finally entered them. She thought of Emily Cheng, how she hadn't really seen anything in her eyes, could only guess at their colour, dark she thought, but it was the lack of light in them that had confounded her. Now why was that? Because, she thought, surprised at herself, dark secrets do things to a human soul, they kill it, bit by bit. The light slowly goes out. Abruptly, she wanted to weep, thinking of Roman, thinking of her own complicity, letting him make a fool of her, determinedly refusing to see. And now, such shame she felt.

Out of nowhere she thought, Evan Kirby raped Emily Cheng. She would still have been Emily Zhang then. Fiona knew what it had been like in the sixties if you were raped, before the hippies arrived in their remote province. Probably even after. You told no one. The shame was yours;

there was almost no recourse: police officers were men, the courts were male, and they leaned toward believing the man and to blaming the woman. You could only pray not to get pregnant.

But if he did rape Emily, it could have stopped his advancement in the civil service if Emily told the right people. She was lovely-looking and wildly intelligent; she would not scream and sob and threaten; she would be cold and clear-headed so that they would listen. And act. But Emily used her good mind and decided to blackmail him instead.

Fiona tried to put her finger on why this puzzled her: Because Zara was killed in 1968 and Kirby didn't marry Livana until a year or so after that. Emily worked for him in 1969 or so. Hardly noticing where she was going, Fiona walked out of the elevator, through the lobby, opened the glass door and stepped into the fresh, chill air.

Emily had to have found the file first, probably not long after Kirby had taken it from Livana and moved it to his office. She had access to all his files, she was never stupid, and she hated him. I bet she bided her time until she thought what she knew would work *for* her, and not just get her killed.

Over the years that Fiona had been thinking about the murder and asking question after question of person after person she had been learning about the world. What had so slowly been unveiled to her had hit her bit by bit, but what she hadn't realized was how the bits and their power to erode her view of life – she saw now how childish and benign it had been – had been accumulating, until now, at this moment, her whole body felt invaded by horror and disgust.

Chapter Thirteen

She was on the sidewalk in front of Livana's building now, and in the crisp air the horror was evaporating; she could breathe again, and things – the world – seemed less appalling. The late fall sun was near its zenith, casting a thin yellow light across the city. The night's light snowfall had begun to melt on the roads where cars had made tracks revealing the black asphalt beneath. Tiny crystals of ice glittered on tree branches wherever the sun hadn't reached, and exhaust from cars was white and pink as if it were cotton candy instead of lethal gas. She stood on the sidewalk looking about in a daze, not sure why she wasn't moving, or where she should be going. She felt that she forgave Roman for this infidelity, if not for the others she was sure had followed it, but then wondered at herself, and filed it away to think about when this was all over.

She noticed that a small black SUV parked far down the block behind her car had someone in the driver's seat, a man, she thought, but she couldn't make out his face with the glare of light across the windshield. She kept her eyes moving past this, as if she hadn't seen him. She could see no exhaust, so he was sitting in the cold, an odd thing to be doing. *You're paranoid*, she told herself. But she hadn't convinced herself sufficiently about this not to notice that when she drove away the car started up and pulled out too. But the thing was, she feared not for herself, but for Livana. And yet, wasn't Livana clever enough to play the feeble old lady card?

Her heavy accent, and the fractured English she spoke, had disappeared for a while. What could that be for? Was she simply crazy? And how did she manage things among the socially elite women she spent time with? Or maybe she went to fund-raising events only now and then so didn't have to put on an act for long at a time, or did so in a less dramatic way. If you couldn't speak English properly, then people you barely knew wouldn't be getting into long, in-depth conversations with you. And nobody would be afraid of a little old lady so weak she had to use a cane. Livana, Fiona realized, was working to present a smaller target.

And now, however carefully, she had broken her silence. If anyone found out, what danger she would be in.

She needed to phone the Kipps and see if she could make an appointment. But in the meantime, she decided, she'd go to the airport to exchange her rented car for a different one. She felt sure if whoever was following her saw her turn into the car rental lot at the airport, he would assume she was doing this in preparation for flying home immediately, but probably wouldn't wait around to see her get on the plane.

All the way to the airport she kept checking the rearview mirror to see if the car was still behind her. Sometimes it was, but a few cars back, and sometimes she couldn't tell if it was there or not. At one left turn though, she had gotten a glimpse of the driver two cars behind her, and saw only that his hair seemed to be silver, and his nose small and straight.

By the time she had been through the inspection and paperwork to return the car and rent another, he would be long gone. Her mind kept turning to, and then skittering away from the things Livana Kirby had told her: Murder covered up; the truth too dangerous to tell; ill-gotten gains, piles of money; Roman in possession of those ill-gotten gains.

She thought now of Ibsen's play *The Enemy of the People*. The doctor in the play wanted to shut down a town's water system as unsafe because of corruption, but people argued with him that shutting it down would do more harm than good in the end, and who was he, a single individual, to alter the town's future in such a way? Who did he think he was? God? Sometimes being right is not the best thing to be, and thinking this, Fiona faltered in her stride toward the line of car rental booths. How does one decide what the right and best thing to do is, they not being the same thing after all? Sometimes, she thought, being an English major is a definite handicap.

Then she thought, hesitating, I suspect that I will not succeed anyway. Most of the people who did this are dead; I bet, if I get the proof and take it to the right people, the officials will probably pin it all on some dead guy. Or they will succumb to what has become inevitable, they will decide to throw somebody to the wolves, and then, if they have to, will find ways to put a cap on the resulting formal investigation's scope so that the full truth is buried forever. She thought grimly that if being seventy wasn't good for much in the general run of life, it certainly helped her understanding of the world to have been a fifty-year reader of newspapers, listener to the news on television and radio, and reader of magazines that often ran stories exposing "what really happened." After twenty years or so of it, even the most naive and optimistic would begin to see patterns forming, repetitions of behaviour, the same responses by governments and their agencies to revelations of corruption or official lying.

Sometimes before the face on television even opened his mouth Fiona knew what he would say. If she had long ago lost her naivety in that particular regard, available to any citizen, she had never gotten used to it, never failed to be disgusted and angered. She sighed at her own intractability, wished she could shrug her shoulders and walk away, but not this time. No, she said to herself, I will do everything I can to publicly identify Zara Stanley's killers, and let the chips fall where they may. And from now on I will be very, very careful.

As she drove from the airport in her new rental car – this one a silver sedan chosen because it looked exactly like hundreds of others on the road – planning to get some lunch, then make the two-hour drive to Ripley, and call the Kipp household to make an appointment, she suddenly remembered she had also planned to see Evan Kirby one more time. This required thinking about, and she made a turn onto a side street, and sat while she tried to remember why she'd wanted to go see him again.

I thought I could get something out of him. I thought I wouldn't stop at the desk, but walk right into his room and catch him off-guard. But that was before I saw Livana, and found out what I found out. If I ask him directly about the file, he'll lie, and then have me thrown out. Besides that, he knows who killed Zara, and he does not want me to know, so if I go again, he will alert...who-ever...that I'm still on the trail. No, it's too dangerous to go near him again, especially when I think I've lost the man who was following me.

She was about to put the car in gear and drive out into traffic again, when she thought of Marian. I should call Arnie, see if there is any news about her. She dialled Arnie and Marian's house in Vancouver. A woman whose voice she didn't immediately recognize answered.

"Angela!" her much-travelled, peculiar niece. "It's your Aunt Fiona. How are you? It's been ages. It's so nice to hear your voice."

"Uh, hi, Auntie Fiona. It's good to talk to you. If you don't mind, I'm expecting a long distance call..."

"Never mind," Fiona said, remembering now what Angela was like. Eternally focused on something else. Fiona hadn't seen her in maybe five years, or talked to her since then. It was surprising she'd even come home merely because her mother was dangerously ill. "How is Marian, and where is she?"

"Still in Vancouver General, but she'll move out to rehab next week. It's all set, according to Arnold." When Angela was fifteen, much to her parents' annoyance, she had started calling them by their first names.

"Does this mean she's better, or worse, or no different?" There was a long pause and a rustling sound.

"You should come and see for yourself," Angela said. "I really have to go now. Bye, Auntie." With Angela, it was ever thus. Off saving the natives in the rainforest, or the slums of African cities, while her mother nearly died, her own brother disowned her, and her father gazed helplessly at her, wondering how on earth they had ever created such a daughter. She'd been a difficult little girl too. Fiona remembered when they all thought Angela would grow out of it.

She was about to put the car in gear, when she remembered that she was to call Malcolm Kipp. She found the paper Margaret Kipp had slipped into her palm – was it only last night? – and taking a deep breath, dialled the number.

Margaret Kipp answered.

"Kipp residence."

"This is Fiona Lychenko. We were at the same table…"

"Of course, of course. Can you drop in about four?"

"Certainly," Fiona said, hiding her surprise behind a matching brusqueness. If she started driving immediately she would be in Ripley in lots of time.

Once out of the city, though, she felt confused and uneasy and concluded that she needed to mentally go through the interviews she had done and the material she had collected from them. Taking stock was necessary before she saw Malcolm Kipp.

"Brown envelope," she said out loud, then "Evan Kirby" and "file number." This was information that she had in hand and knew was accurate if it revealed nothing much. Then she said, 'Interviews' and then, 'Evan Kirby' tapping her fingers on the steering wheel and then accelerating around a beat-up half-ton, clearly a farmer's work truck. "Hostile," she declared, referring to Kirby, and "nothing, nada. Emily Cheng: Hostile, nothing." Well, this was getting nowhere. Okay, how about, "Livana Kirby." She slammed the heel of her hand against the wheel in exasperation. How could it be her head was so full of *stuff* when she'd interviewed a mere three people and only one had had anything to say?

Try a new tack: What did she want to know? Answer: Who killed Zara Stanley. Who were the possible candidates? She knew she should be thinking about the sons of the rich and the powerful fifty years ago. The first name to pop into her mind was Blair Fever. Her chest clutched for a second at the name, as if her body knew something her brain didn't, but she hurried on mentally.

The then premier had two daughters, no sons. The next one was childless. Who else was powerful? The leader of the opposition, she supposed. Who the heck was that? Oh, yes, and he did have a son, although she couldn't remember his name. But both the former leader of the opposition and his son were dead, killed in huge pile up in a thick winter fog on the TransCanada highway years ago. Who else? Mayors? Somebody had pointed with zero evidence to young unmarried police officers, one retired cop had even said to her with a puzzled frown on his face, "If this were a TV show, it would turn out to be a cop who did it." But who would take such profound and long-lasting steps to protect a mere young cop? Nobody, she concluded. Unless he was a friend of the guy who *would* be protected. Unless he was there too. She remembered again that Livana had said without a second's hesitation, as if she took it for granted Fiona knew this, 'killers,' not 'killer'. But no, she told herself, there is no way I can start with the companions of the real killer. I know absolutely nothing about any of them; I have to start with the leader.

Well, let's just suppose it was Blair Fever. Here she had to remind herself that she was alone in her car and if she said any of this out loud, there was no one to hear it. *"Be bold, Fiona, let your mind leap over the same old stuff. Go somewhere new.*" Because of his powerful father, Fever would definitely have gotten protection. And if he had friends with him who knew the truth, protection for them could be bought too. Not to mention that they would come from his social milieu; they wouldn't be petty criminals or street kids. They'd be children of the powerful too.

Where was she going with this? Find out who Blair Fever's friends had been? And how would she do that, she asked herself morosely? Check old newspapers for clippings of Fever with his football team? Or check the old high school yearbooks to see if they would give her any information? Or university yearbooks? They'd stopped printing them a long time ago, but she knew they'd been produced every year over the period she was interested in. At least she'd know who'd been in classes with him.

She wished Roman were alive so that she could ask him to ask around among his many acquaintances if anybody knew the answer. But Roman was not alive, and before she could sink under the tide of newly confused sorrow, a new realization struck.

All that time I was working on my book about Zara's death, interviewing all those people, talking to everybody, telling Roman all about it, he knew. The whole time *he knew* who killed Zara.

Chapter Fourteen

It was not until she was driving into Ripley that she noticed how the sky had lowered and turned a steely, smooth grey. Snow on the way, she told herself, and then, can't be, it's too early for real snow. She had not once had the feeling that anybody was following her out of Hart City or on the highway; probably she had nothing to worry about here in Ripley. Nonetheless, she parked underground at the downtown shopping mall, planning to pick up a cab on the street to take her to the Kipp's house. But, lost in thought, she had forgotten to find a cab and found she had passed right through the commercial area and was walking on the narrow sidewalk on one side of a major road while vehicles whizzed past only a couple of feet away. It had begun to snow, although lightly.

When she realized what she had done, she hesitated and almost turned back, but decided to keep going to the next intersection where the road she was on narrowed, and the adjacent roads led into residential areas. But, still no cabs in sight, she gave up looking for one and turned left toward the subdivision where the Kipps's house was. As she walked, the snowfall grew thicker and thicker until, to her surprise, it had happened so fast, she couldn't see beyond a half a block ahead and snow began to pile up on her shoulders and hair, even on her eyelashes so that she had to brush them with her glove to knock off the build-up.

She plodded on in her neat low-heeled shoes, drifts of airy snow piling up on the sidewalks and streets burying them so rapidly that the demarcations between them were vanishing. She was lost in rumination, her nose beginning to run so that she felt in pockets for a tissue, and when she found one, discovered she was crying. She mopped at her eyes and cheeks, but her eyes continued to run, and every minute or so she would have to wipe away the moisture, fearing it would freeze to her face.

After a few more moments walking, she stopped, looked around, and realized that she didn't know where she was. She stood there for a long time in the falling snow, growing colder and colder, bewildered and at the same time numb, trying to solve this new puzzle. *I'll go to the nearest corner and find a street sign.* Not able to see the edge of the sidewalk, she slipped off and fell, hard, jarring herself right through her chest and abdomen. She got carefully to her feet, brushing her slacks and the arm and shoulder of her coat off as best she could and using her shoe, carved out a line in the snow where the curb was so that she could get back on the sidewalk. She kept her head down, concentrating on her passage, Roman's deception a dark weight hovering behind all her thoughts.

Why did he come home at all? Why did he stay married to me? Was I that repulsive to him? She thought then that she probably was, and lifted her head to look up to see if any ray of light could be seen to say that the blinding snowfall was ending. But there was none. Only this thick, endless white. Why didn't I see that his silences and his absences weren't necessary? That his return to me each day was only that he didn't know what else to do with himself yet? That he was biding his time? That when he sat across from me at breakfast and ate the eggs I'd cooked for him and drank the coffee I'd made – my perfect coffee – I had become the absence. He saw no one across the breakfast table from him. He had already moved on.

She slipped on the wet snow that was turning icy underneath, fell again, got to her feet, her hands and knees were smarting with the force of the fall, and again brushed the snow from her pant legs. But she was at an intersection. Where was the street sign? She reached out, moving her arm to the left, waving it carefully back and forward trying to connect with a post. Eventually, stepping this way and that, she found it. The two attached street names were coated with a thick layer of the light, air-filled snow, and were too high for her to reach them, so using both hands she shook the pole hard while snow fell off onto her head, and she had to shake it out of her hair and brush it off her shoulders and collar.

Ah, only two more blocks to the Kipp's house. She leaned a shoulder against the still quivering post: I can't do this. I am in no shape to talk to anybody. How can I even keep my mind on anything after what I have just realized? Because I have to, and she pushed herself off the post and put one foot in front of the other, wiping her eyes now and then, knowing she was nearing the Kipp house and thought to check her watch. How long have I been walking? She thought, maybe an hour, although she didn't feel so much tired as frozen and as if battered all the way by a great wind.

But the snow was diminishing now, the flakes no less large, but fewer and fewer, and a glow of sunlight was beginning to tint the white air yellow. Only a half block to go. Again she stopped, brushing snow off her hair, her shoulders, her coat all the way down to its hem and then her pant legs below that, and her neat black shoes now rigid with the cold. She scuffed them hard on the sidewalk to remove the layer of frozen snow that had built up on the soles, and opened her purse in an effort to look into her compact to fix her hair and makeup, but it was no use, the compact clouded over and she couldn't see herself. She hoped that if her eyes were red from crying the Kipps would think this was from the cold.

She turned up their sidewalk and pushed the buzzer not even noticing the house itself other than that it seemed to extend a long way on each side of the front door. What would she ask? Nothing, she told herself. He asked me to come and see him; I don't have to have anything in mind. In a moment the door opened and Margaret Kipp was ushering her in, taking her coat, offering her a pair of slippers to replace her frozen, scraped shoes.

"You walked? In this weather?"

"It was fine when I began," Fiona said. "After it started there wasn't much I could do but keep walking." She was being led down the wide hall with polished hardwood floors and matching wainscot, then into a room on the left where Malcolm Kipp was seated in a vast upholstered leather chair. A light afghan thrown over what she saw now were twisted, unnaturally short legs – the illusion of height was produced by his long back. His wheelchair sat beside him and an old-fashioned fireplace in which a fire burned was to his left. He greeted her cordially, asking his wife to bring them all a brandy. Brandy? Again? She was afraid she might laugh. Of course he would sit in a Masterpiece Theatre leather armchair beside a wide wine-brick fireplace, the flames burning brightly, and a pipe – yes, a pipe –

sitting on the table by his chair. Of course he would offer brandy.

"You wanted to see me?" she asked, as she sat across from him in a smaller, wingback armchair. He said nothing as Margaret Kipp came in with three brandies on a round silver tray. Do these people really live like this? As if this were Victorian England and they the stuffily well-off with the good connections? But how good the scent of the brandy was, how warm the fire. She let her head rest on the chair back and felt she might go to sleep, might sleep forever. But, she thought, I *was* asleep, for years I've been asleep, deliberately, willfully so, and now it is time to wake up. She sat up straight and looked as directly as she could at Malcolm Kipp.

"I refused to see you once, a long time ago, when you were working on your book about the Zara Stanley murder." She had forgotten he still spoke with an English accent despite many decades in Canada. Surely this was deliberate.

"You said you were too busy. Or rather," remembering now, "Mrs. Kipp did."

"I seem not to be too busy now," he replied. "I'm not sure how I can help you as it was not my case. You understand that I was still in England when Zara Stanley was killed. It was my predecessor, William Porringer, who handled the inquest."

"Yes, I'm aware of that." She waited. Waiting is an art – somebody had said that.

"What do you want to know?"

"I finished my book three years ago," she pointed out.

"I am sure you still have questions. I'm told your book didn't find solutions to the puzzle." "Puzzle?" she thought. Surely the word is "crime." "What do you want to tell me?"

"What do you need to know?" Fiona realized that Margaret Kipp was sitting on the sofa to her left. She had a sense that Margaret Kipp was the one she would have to answer to if she let slip any accusations or asked questions that were too rude or direct. What to ask? Not to give away too much, not to miss an opportunity.

She cleared her throat, sat up straighter.

"You were a powerful man in Ripley once you became City Prosecutor. You knew everyone, all the men who counted: the mayor, the fire chief, the police chief, the MLAs and the MP. The wealthiest. You were privy to more than official documents and official secrets, although you had access to those too, by virtue of your office. You had to know the backroom stuff too: the gambling dens, the brothels, the petty criminals who carried out the designs of the serious criminals – the ones wearing suits and sitting in offices. After your twenty-five years in the job you knew it all. In fact, probably a good deal sooner." Between them the fire crackled and hissed and Kipp lowered his eyelids slowly and lifted them again to examine her.

"This is true, I suppose, in a way," he said, "although you seem to think that there was a great deal in the way of secrets for me to know. There wasn't. This is a backwater. It is a small town."

"So why did you want to see me?"

"I'm an old man. I am tying up loose ends."

"I'm a loose end?"

"I put that badly," he said. "I meant to say that I am trying to fulfill all and any obligations that I failed to fulfill along the way."

"So my asking to speak with you becomes an obligation to have a conversation, however belatedly."

"Indeed."

"And yet," Fiona said, fiercely, "You have nothing to say." A log fell in the fire with a splintering thud throwing a shower of sparks. Margaret Kipp shifted positions, as though she meant to attend to the fire, then thought better of it.

"My dear, I still have some of the obligations of an Officer of the Court. I cannot speak about this matter at all. I will never be able to speak about it. And in any case, I haven't anything to tell you. The police failed to find the killer, and Bill Porringer filled out the proper reports to that effect."

"He filled out the proper reports to his own satisfaction, inventing as he went," Fiona told him. Kipp blinked twice, rapidly. "It is public knowledge." Her tone verged on exasperation.

"Only one example," he said, his tone still mild. "A momentary lapse. I never knew him, but – people talk. He wasn't reliable, I've heard."

"I know of another example," she said. "Two of his momentary lapses." Again, Margaret Kipp shifted her position, and cleared her throat very softly. Fiona was trying frantically to think what she wanted from him. I want to know who killed Zara Stanley; I want to know why the investigation was shut down; I want to know what he knows about that.

She wondered if, once he had taken office, he had made documents disappear too as Kirby seemed to have done, or maybe knew others who had. But not much use asking that, he would surely deny any such activity or knowledge of it. Probably he had done no such thing. If she got too aggressive undoubtedly he would report it to the police chief.

Would there then be more phone-tapping and being followed by the police in marked cars so that she knew this was meant to be a warning to her to stop asking questions? Would it be worse this time around? Hey, two dozen pizzas might arrive at my door, and she almost laughed out loud. Would have, except that she was thinking about a car accident, like Bill Porringer's; how easy it would be for someone to kill her that way. But Porringer was long dead before Kipp had even come from England; Kipp had nothing to do with that, and nothing to do with those documents that had been less than truthful.

But Roman took a bribe. They can say that I knew about it, that I shared in the money. They must have a record some place of somebody handing money over to him. There must be a slush fund for dirty tricks, for bribery. Who has a slush fund? Didn't governments have their ways of handing over loot to the corrupt in order to keep a story out of the papers, to…she gave up. This was pure speculation, mostly gleaned from murder mysteries and television shows and movies. Ripley was indeed nowhere. Such things didn't happen in 'nowhere.' But bribes had been paid by somebody to, among others, her own husband.

She set down her brandy glass with a distinct 'crack' and Kipp – she could hardly believe it – flinched. Ahhhh, she thought; I *am* a threat, and for the first time she believed he did know something about that long-ago murder, although what it was she could only guess.

She was about to ask Malcolm Kipp about what he knew about Blair Fever when she realized she'd probably be giving away her hand to the enemy. She snapped her mouth shut again, then, flummoxed, said, "You can tell everything that you know when you are called to a hearing in a courtroom about this matter. When it all comes out, as it will, I am sure." He smiled in a distant way.

"If I live so long," his tone mildly amused. She decided to ignore this.

"I take it you read the book. Tell me if you found inaccuracies. Or show me the places where I should have paid more attention."

"I must point out again that if I had any knowledge of who committed the crime, I would be unable to tell you anyway. Nor could I tell you about evidence you don't already know about, or police actions that took place when I was still in England, that remain private police business. Your book, given what you were able to find out, is accurate enough. That's what you wanted to know?"

"Accurate enough," Fiona said. She laughed a little, "Given that it is not the real story at all." Kipp gazed back at her, not blinking, but there was, she noted, a kind of haze over the blue of his eyes, as if he had deliberately thrown up a screen himself so that he couldn't see her clearly. Why would that be? Because he knows there are those who think I may have to be done away with? Or at least ruined? And being at heart a decent man – she was surprised to realize that she had come to believe this – he does not want to be a part of it.

As if he could read her thoughts, he said, "I am sorry about this. How terrible that murder was and what a shame it hasn't been solved. I wish I could help you, but my hands are tied, and anyway, I wasn't here when it happened. And those who were are dead anyway."

She sighed then, gazed deliberately around the room,

peered around the wing of the chair to look at Margaret Kipp who, disconcertingly, fixed her eyes on Fiona's and was staring at her, Fiona thought, as a hawk stares at its prey. For the first time she felt hostility coming off her. It isn't just her husband she wants to protect; it is this cushy life, this position. Well, who could blame her.

She rose clumsily, stiff from her falls and from being seventy instead of thirty, said, "Thanks for the brandy," and began to walk from the room. Margaret was getting up from her sofa to go ahead of her. Near them, Kipp reached for his wheelchair, taking off the brake so as to move it closer. Seeing this, Mrs. Kipp went to him and, in a smooth, clearly much-practised maneouver, helped him into it. Nobody spoke while this went on. Fiona was about to continue through the doorway when she paused. "Tell me," she said, as if there hadn't just been hostility bordering on a quarrel. "What happens to old government documents? I mean the tons of them that must be generated every single year."

"Some are destroyed," Kipp said. "Nowadays a lot is digitized."

"But somewhere in Hart City there is a warehouse, I'll bet," Fiona said, "where government documents are piled to the ceilings. I hope they have a decent filing system."

"I'm sure they do," Kipp replied, as if from a great distance. The three of them began to move through the doorway, Mrs. Kipp pushing Malcolm first, then Fiona. In the foyer, their parade came to a stop.

"And there must be top secret files somewhere too," Fiona said, pushing off the slippers she'd been given by Mrs. Kipp. Mrs Kipp dropped Fiona's shoes, dry now and warmed, noisily onto the floor in front of her. One fell over sideways.

"I'm so sorry," she said, but Fiona didn't bother to look up.

"I wonder where they would be. I doubt in a warehouse. I doubt in MLAs' homes or the homes of the Deputy Ministers or other officials. Locked up somewhere in a fire-proof room, maybe."

"It takes an imagination to write books," Mrs. Kipp said, for the first time seeming amused. "Top-secret files!" She shook her head contemptuously.

"Are you suggesting there are no secret files?" Fiona asked.

"I suppose there are," she said. "But you're talking about old, old paper files, which I doubt even exist anymore. You'll have to try that warehouse, I guess." She laughed humourlessly.

Fiona considered, putting on her coat, buttoning it, turning up the collar, resting her scarf loosely over her hair to protect her ears against the cold, pulling on one glove and then the other.

"I believe I'll have to try the Justice Department," she said, looking directly at Kipp. "And the Attorney General's office." If this alarmed either of the Kipps, neither gave a sign of it.

Margaret Kipp had opened the outside door, regardless of the cold sweeping into the foyer. She held it back a long way, and Fiona turned and went through it without saying good-bye, not surprised when it immediately thudded shut heavily behind her, the Kipps having succeeded in so padding their lives that even their front door refused to make an unseemly noise.

Chapter Fifteen

The snow had stopped, the swaths that had so confused her were reduced to a thin coating covering sidewalks and streets, and a narrow stream of water trickling down the gutters. Getting her bearings now, she knew that if she walked maybe three blocks, she would arrive at a commercial street where she could get a taxi back downtown to the mall where her car was parked. The brandy – she had been so cold that she had drunk all of it as if it were lemonade on a hot day – had flooded her veins with warmth and she walked briskly, or as briskly as the fear of icy patches under the snow cover would allow her, so that in only a few minutes she arrived at a busy street lined by boutiques and cosy cafes. Gratefully, she went into one, ordered soup and a sandwich, and demolished them so quickly that she could hardly believe it herself.

She was in the parking garage, looking for her car, when her cell phone rang.

"Hi, Fee." It was Arnie and she felt a glow of warmth at his voice. Her heart was rushing back from a world of ice and snow and bitter cold to one where warmth might again be found.

"I'm so glad it's you. Is everything going as planned? Is Angela any help to you?"

"Help?" he said, laughing, and she laughed too. "No,

Angie had to attend to some crisis in Chile or somewhere so about a half-hour ago she took her bundles and bags and headed out again. That girl!" he said, although not angrily.

Cars moved slowly past, some of them thinking she was about to back out and waiting impatiently for her parking place. Tough, she thought.

"Marian is doing well. A physiotherapist comes every day; they get her up dragging herself around. There's a speech therapist who works with her for a few minutes a day. Progress is happening, but I have to admit, it's not coming very fast."

"It's early days," Fiona said. He made a sound of agreement.

"We're finally ready to get her into the rehabilitation facility so that's why I called you. It'll happen tomorrow. Got a pen? Here's the name and address of the place." Fiona fished out her notebook and pen and wrote down the information. He said, when they were done, "Are you coming out again?"

"I suppose I should. But I didn't want to be there if Greg and Angela were there too. I've been waiting to hear that she was ready for more visitors too. Sort of string us out so that she has constant family coming to encourage her, but not all at once."

"Greg leaves in a week," Arnie told her. "Maybe you could plan to come after that?" She realized then that he wanted to see her, that despite his children's visits and Marian's increasing alertness, he was lonely. She found she was touched.

The smell of exhaust was suddenly overpowering, the people trudging by with their shopping bags, silent and shadowy figures, a tableau in some dull Hades.

"Come and see us," he said. "Marian needs you, Fee."

"I will," she said, and was cheered that there were still people in the world who needed her.

Her plan had been to head back to Calgary, but once out on the highway she knew she was too tired to try to drive so far, and anyway, didn't she have more people she wanted to see? For a second, she thought of turning back and finding a decent downtown hotel, but caution returned and she decided instead to stay at a certain motel she knew of in a roadside community perhaps a dozen miles out of the city. Or she could go to Vonnie's. But Vonnie was still in Hart City and likely wouldn't be back before, at the earliest, tomorrow. No, it would have to be the motel.

As she drove she made a mental list: Roman cheated on me with – probably – a series of women; he let me write that book knowing the whole time who killed Zara and why and never said a word about it; he took a bribe and by doing that he contaminated me too. But her mind skittered away from all of this. She couldn't seem to focus on his… his… But she couldn't find a word for it all. Why did he marry me? she wondered. He got involved with another woman really soon as far as I can tell, and there was never that…passion…between us that I so craved. It was as though we were never more than two separate people and no matter how I tried I couldn't open him, I couldn't get him to share whatever went on inside, and as the years passed, it got worse and worse. That their lack of children was the root cause of it didn't quite satisfy her; surely there was more to it than that.

But she had believed in his fidelity, his sense of responsibility toward her. That, she had trusted. But it was all *pro forma*, she said out loud. *Pro forma*, repeating it, liking the sound of it. It seemed to her that she was behaving strangely, that feeling so satisfied at having a cold Latin term for Roman's attitude toward her was probably not quite right. That she ought to be screaming, out of the car kicking the tires, throwing herself in the snow, beating her fists against the earth. To find at my age that my marriage, my whole life, has been a lie from beginning to end.

But she couldn't manage rage, and once again she saw that impermeable although clear wall between herself and Roman, and between herself and her feelings about Roman, and felt now only weariness and sorrow. For a moment, her resolve to carry on trying to find out who had killed Zara Stanley dwindled and nearly died. But something powerful rose up in her gut, so that her muscles clenched, and she took a deep, long breath in through her nose. She would keep on for Zara; she would keep on for all the many girls and women who were brutally raped and murdered and no killers ever brought to justice; she would do it for the daughter she had never had.

The long blare of an air horn coming from the highway shook her out of her reverie. She was trying to remember why she married Roman. I liked his ambition, she thought, and I was uncomfortably close to thirty; I thought I'd end up an old maid. And we'd put in five years together already. It seemed crazy to walk away from that. I thought I loved him. Maybe I actually did, then. But once we were married, and he seemed not to want to grow closer to me in the way that I thought was natural in a marriage, that I thought *was* marriage, and when children wouldn't come, I began to give up, began to get interested in my own work, began to accept his silences and his absences as if we'd made some kind of an unspoken pact.

But we hadn't, she thought. We simply never spoke of it. He would put his arm around my shoulders in public, sometimes even taking my hand, she'd thought because he loved her, but now she wondered instead, was it to tell the world he was a faithful loving husband in case anybody out there thought otherwise? She wondered now why she hadn't insisted he stop his constant travelling, leaving her alone for days and weeks at a time. She remembered the way he sometimes wouldn't even answer her questions, as if he had unaccountably gone deaf. Why had she allowed it? But one mental step in that direction, she saw, would lead her to things about herself and her own lack of ambition and feeble desire that she couldn't endure to know.

She thought of the view out her sitting room window, the one window that faced the pasture that they mostly didn't use, and that had never been plowed. The slough there, the bluff of poplars. Mornings and evenings deer came to drink, more than once a moose, and it was commonplace to see coyotes trotting across the field, or the occasional fox. Birds in the spring and fall: wild swans, even pelicans once or twice. Was that what she had stayed for? That and the ravine behind the house with the crocuses and the wild roses?

Abruptly, she signaled, put her foot on the brake and pulled onto the shoulder. This was crazy; she had more work to do; she needed to be in Hart City where she could look up old newspaper reports about, at the very least, Blair Fever. Who were his friends?

She realized then that, out of sight of her conscious mind, she was thinking that Fever was the main killer (if there had been more than one), and she couldn't recall when she'd started thinking that way. Hadn't she heard more than once when she had been researching her book that Zara and Blair had dated? But was there any record that he knew Zara? Zara liked having her picture taken and men liked to be photographed with her. Maybe somewhere there was a photo of them together.

He had been on that China trip too, although that could have been a coincidence. The Fevers had a hand in so many ventures that ordinary people had taken to referring to Fever Senior as "Yellow Fever," implying his inexorable, ever-expanding, silent and, quite possibly, although unprovably, virulent reach. But he had been dead for years.

She had been watching in her rear view mirror to try to figure out if she was being followed, and had seen no one who sparked her suspicions. Then she realized that the reason nobody was following her was that she had hidden the car from him, that until Malcolm Kipp phoned whoever about her visit – she was sure he had – they all thought she had flown back to Calgary. "They" whoever "they" were. Government lackeys, maybe police or private detectives, or the killers themselves, or their minions. Once they figured out she wasn't in Calgary they would take up the search again. And if someone was now watching her condo – she reflected, thought that quite possible – that person would report that she wasn't there. What to do?

She had arrived at the motel a dozen miles out of Ripley, parked, went in, and was about to offer her credit card when caution took hold and she gave the clerk cash. With that same feeling of having stepped over some line into a surreal other-world, she registered under the name of Mr. and Mrs. Alfred Baron of Winnipeg, telling the clerk her husband would be along in an hour or so and accepting a second key for him. She asked for a room at the back away from the highway. "Because of the noise," she told the young clerk, but really so that her car wouldn't be visible to anybody driving by, not that anybody knew what car she was driving. But it did have a sticker on it saying it was a rented car.

It was nightfall by then; she went straight to her room, took off her coat and shoes, turned on the television to the news, and lay down on the bed feeling so exhausted that she got up only once to make sure her door was securely locked, and another time, much later, to undress and put on her nightgown.

All night long cars and trucks roared down the highway on the other side of the motel. Every time she fell asleep a long, swooning roar from an eighteen-wheeler would wake her, she'd fall back asleep again, only to be lifted to wakefulness once more. Toward morning, though, she fell into a deep sleep, and dreamt Roman had come to see her, smiling at her as he had done when they first met. He was about thirty years old in her dream, dressed in khakis, a wool sweater and leather team jacket over it. Then he walked away from her across a plowed field, glancing back over his shoulder more than once, not to ask her to come with him, not in love or regret, or even friendliness, but in a cold, disengaged way that chilled her without actually frightening her, and that woke her. It was seven in the morning, and she was starving.

By ten she was back in Hart City having had bacon and eggs in one of the endless number of bad but fast and cheap restaurants along the highway into the city. By eleven she was downtown, seated in a cubicle at the public library pouring over microfilm of the society and the sports pages of old *Hart City Herald* newspapers. Eventually, she gave up on the sports pages. Blair Fever was in them a lot for a few years, but either alone or with a team, and in team pictures there was no way to tell who his friends were. From the early sixties though, there were a number of pictures of him with a variety of attractive women on his arm at various formal dinners, either of the type she had just been to with Vonnie, or fundraisers for one cause or another. None of the women on his arm was Zara Stanley. Twice the couple standing with him were the same people: Andrew Hallett and his fiancée, Bridget Summerfield.

Hallett was shorter than Fever, and probably weighed seventy-five pounds less. He was black-haired, judging by the photo, also darker-skinned than Fever, and had a short, straight nose over a small, well-shaped mouth. Even in a photo Fiona could tell that he was fastidious in his clothing and grooming. Bridget was a bit blurred, a brunette, tiny and slim. Beside her, if you ignored Fever who loomed over her, (and looked as if he were drunk besides in one of the photos) Hallett looked tall and masculine, a shorter Gregory Peck type but without the lines in his face.

Gregory Peck! she thought. Who even remembers that handsome man? She saw no trace of humility in Andrew Hallett's face, rather, now that she thought of it, it projected only vanity. No wonder the small woman beside him blurred. It wasn't just a smudge on the original newspaper, it was that such a man, having the vanity usually attributed to women, would have to have a permanent girlfriend who would subordinate herself to him.

So who the heck is Andrew Hallett, she wondered. He probably went to high school in Hart City so I would never have known him. She sat for a moment, her elbows on the desk that held the microfiche reader and tried to think: I'm here because I've decided without a single piece of evidence that Blair Fever best fits the profile of someone for whom others would bond together to make sure any serious crime he committed never came to light. Why? Because people don't seem to like him despite his status as a former football hero; because rumors abound about his unsavoury private life. I am here trying to find who his friends were around 1965, earlier or later, so that I can try to assemble a probable – no, a possible – cast of villains.

Suddenly she thought, did Andrew Hallett go on that trip to China? But she hadn't brought her "China file", as she now thought of it, with her. It was back in her apartment in Calgary, lying (deliberately) in full view on the dining room table with the title, "Memoir, Roman," printed in big letters on it. She had thought about it and to make the file bigger, had thrown in the pages printed out by the woman in the Prairie Farmers' Commission archives about other exploits of Roman's, and had located in her own box of papers a few programs from events she had attended with him, ones that had his name on them as a speaker. She hoped that rendered the photo of the China delegation harmless. Now she thought about it, there had been someone in the photo who might have been Hallett.

. Abruptly she got up and, leaving her coat behind on her chair but not her purse, and the microfiche reader running, she went into the reading area to a free computer, called up "Canada 411, Find a Person," and typed in 'Andrew Hallett, Hart City.' His address came up at once, or at least, an "A.R. Hallett." She copied it down and his phone number, not that she had any plans to call him. On impulse, she backed out of the site she was looking at and went to the digitized file for the *Hart City Herald*, which didn't kick in until 1980, and typed "Andrew R. Hallett." Click, click, click. Several references came up. Next she tried, 'Andrew Hallett' and then, 'A.R. Hallett.'

She realized her palms were sweating, and she rubbed them on her slacks, tossed the lock of hair that had come loose from her beauty parlour hair-do from her eyes, and waited. Another half-dozen. Carefully she wrote them all down. Her search took her an hour, but when she was done, she'd seen a couple more photos of Hallett, and she knew now that he was off and on an alderman who once ran for Hart City mayor, but was defeated; he made his living as a lawyer, his father having been a lawyer to Blair Fever's father. He was now a partner in a moderately successful law firm that specialized in trade law: contracts, international trade treaties and so on. Boring stuff, purely background, not in itself of any importance.

She went back to the microfiche and microfilm readers to do a last quick run through the *Hart City Heralds* from the mid-to-late sixties. Before long she ran past a society page about a big wedding, then halted, and rolled back to it. Sure enough, it was more than half a page on the wedding of Blair Fever to the lovely Erica (Rickie) Beauvais, noting at once that the bride's dress was spectacular. Fiona supposed she didn't remember the wedding because it had taken place in Hart City, Blair Fever's stomping ground, rather than in Ripley, the city closest to the bride's country home.

But there they were, in their bridal splendour, each with five attendants. She peered closely at the line of grooms-men. Yes, Andrew Hallett stood closest to the groom. The others were familiar names: football players, or if not, she knew their names as those of prominent families – the sons of rich people or high-ranking officials in the government. She was about to make a note of the names of all the attendants, Rickie's too, when it occurred to her to check the date of the wedding: December 1, 1968. Zara had been killed October 13, 1968.

Cold sweat prickled on her chest. Six weeks before Fever's big, society wedding, Zara's delicate face had been smashed, her skull too, she had been raped and, still breathing, she had almost certainly then been smothered with a pillow, a few feet from the closet that held several brand new, unworn, expensive formal dresses, the tags still on them.

Ideas tumbled over each other: What if Zara had dated Blair, who was already engaged to Rickie, although Zara didn't know that. What if he had promised Zara some sort of future with him in order to get her to sleep with him – fancy balls and dinners with the province's *créme de la créme* (hence the dresses), trips to exotic locations, with the hint of an engagement, maybe even in the end, marriage. And such was Zara's ambition, her confidence where men were concerned, her romanticism (that of course this would happen to her given her great good luck in being so desirable), that she had fallen for his lies? When she heard of his engagement – that would have been in the papers Fiona felt sure, and the date of the wedding would have been in the paper when the engagement was announced – she had confronted Fever, threatened to go public with their affair, to tell his bride of it, and then, maybe, to tell his father. That last would have done the trick; it would have sealed Zara's fate. Surely Fever's father would have wanted nothing more than for his son and heir to marry into the British aristocracy. That would be the cap on the long career that had made him one of the richest men in the province if not *the* richest. Surely if Rickie and her family found out that Blair had been sleeping with the daughter of poverty and the backwoods when he should have been faithful to Rickie – should have been trying to be worthy of her and her lineage – they would call off the wedding. And Fever's father would be so furious he would – it was impossible to imagine what he would have done. Disown his son? Throw him out of his family? Disinherit him?

Or a pregnancy! What if Zara had been pregnant? It was before birth control pills were in common use, before safe, legal abortions were available. But no, she had read the coroner's report and there was no mention that Zara was pregnant. It had seemed to her that the coroner had looked especially for that, because he had reported on that, just as he had reported that her hymen was torn, but that the remains of that tissue usually stays until the first childbirth. She had assumed that these were questions the police had wanted answered – reasonably, she had supposed, as they would help with the investigation – although her flesh crawled at the degree of violation that even after her appalling death poor Zara had suffered.

No, at the time of her death she had not been pregnant, and so her murder was not because Fever had been trying to keep his bride-to-be and his father from knowing about an illegitimate child.

No, Zara had threatened him with exposure and the end of his and his father's plan to marry above himself, and although Fiona believed that all murders were a kind of insanity on the part of the murderer, this murder would respond to rational dissection.

Satisfied by her morning's work, if also shaken and sickened, she knew her concentration was shot; she wanted only to escape from the cubicle and the library, from what she had found there. She put away the materials she had been using and shut down the reader. Now she wanted the anonymity of Calgary, she wanted to go into her condo, to shut and lock the door and know no one would breach it. There, she would feel safe again.

Outside on the library steps she was pleased to see that the day had warmed, that she didn't have to worry about icy roads. She got into her rented car and headed out for the highway and Calgary, planning to turn her car in at a rental agency there instead of taking it back to Hart City and flying home. But first, she pulled into a service station where she began to fill the gas tank. Next to her, a heavy young man, unshaven, with earrings, a nose ring, tattoos on his fingers, and a spider-web design on the side of his neck, had gotten out of his half-ton from which a radio blared, and leaving the door open, began to clean his windshield. Fiona was going about her business, when suddenly she heard, "Kirby," coming from the radio, and "foul play."

If the gas hadn't stopped running, she would have poured it all over her shoes. The man got back in his truck, slammed the door shut, and roared away, spraying wet snow, thankfully, mostly on the gas pumps that separated them. Her hands shaking, she managed to screw the gas cap back on, nearly got in and drove away, then hurried inside to pay. Which Kirby? Evan probably. Or Livana? But I just saw her, I was just there yesterday, no, the day before yesterday. She was fine when I left.

A radio was playing inside the gas station too, and she listened, but all that emerged over the buzz of the freezers, the hissing of the glass doors as they opened and shut and the click and dings of the cash registers was soft music. She said to the attendant, a tall, skinny male barely out of his teens, who needed a shave (or was that the fashion?), "Did I just hear something on the radio about a murder in Ripley?"

He shrugged, intent on ringing in her gas. "Uh, yeah, I think so."

"What was it?"

"Some old woman, I think," he said. "I dunno." He smiled and handed her her change and receipt, and was already looking beyond her to the next customer. She rushed back to her car and drove away hardly noticing that she had, but in a moment she was passing a strip mall and she pulled in and parked, trying to still the inner quaking, trying to get her mind to work.

Her cell phone was ringing, and after some fumbling, thank heavens the caller didn't hang up, she found it and answered it with a shaky-sounding, "Hello."

"Did you hear that?" It was Vonnie.

"I think so, I mean, sort of, I mean – what did you hear?"

"The police found Livana Kirby's body in her condo. They said she'd been dead only a couple of hours or so, that her housekeeper-cousin found her and that they suspect foul play, but they wouldn't say how she died. Said she was the former wife of the distinguished bureaucrat, Evan Kirby, now retired. They didn't say 'bureaucrat,' I forget what they called him. 'Senior official in the last government.'" Fiona had begun to shake, her teeth chattering, she couldn't speak.

"Are you there? Are you all right? Where are you?"

"I'm just leaving Hart City." She had to clear her throat.

"Did you go to see her after you left the hotel?"

"I did," Fiona said. "She was perfectly fine when I left. There was nobody else around that I saw." She had decided not to mention the man in the parked SUV.

"Why on earth would anybody kill her?" Vonnie asked. She made a swallowing sound followed by the rustle of paper.

"Where are you?" she asked Vonnie.

"Still in Hart City. One more meeting and by three I'll be on my way home. Where are you going now?"

"Home to Calgary," Fiona said, her mind still on Livana's murder. But, she thought, nobody saw me go into her condo. Only that man who was watching. But who was he? She began to think, Andy Hallett, but maybe not, she hadn't had a good look at his face, this was after-the-fact witnessing: It wasn't witnessing at all.

Vonnie asked, "What do you think this is all about? Just a random-robbery-with-violence? I mean, she was rich, after all."

Fiona was calming down, but she couldn't remember what Vonnie knew and what she didn't, and so she said, "Probably. Don't you think? I mean, why would anybody want to kill her? She was a harmless old lady, used a cane, never learned to speak English very well…"

"Guess what, Fee," Vonnie said in a harder voice. "Livana Kirby wasn't even a European. That is, she was born here. It turns out she was a Ukrainian farm girl from Vegreville. How about that? Her cousin, was a sort of housekeeper for her, Olga Welland told them. That's how they found out she was dead. I bet that friend couldn't wait to finally out Livana's deceptions. And she wasn't that old either. She was only sixty-one."

There was a cousin in the building? Had the cousin seen her, Fiona? Had she maybe seen the killer? But Vonnie was saying, "She and Evan Kirby had a daughter apparently. She'd be about thirty-five or forty by now, wouldn't she?"

"I never thought of her," Fiona answered. "That poor girl, to lose her mother that way. How terrible. And her father dying now too. I suppose the cousin will tell her." Vonnie murmured in commiseration. Fiona, trying to change the subject, asked, "Have you recovered from your big dinner?" Why had they killed Livana? Because she knew too much; she knew everything, and then Fiona had appeared at her apartment door. *Livana had to be gotten rid of.* Would they next go after her? Why wasn't she telling Vonnie all this? What was she covering up? She was confused enough to put her palm flat on her forehead and hold it there. Oddly, the coolness had a sobering effect.

"It's terrible about Livana and I have my fingers crossed that the police catch the killer." Vonnie said, "Must hang up, friend. The meeting will start in a minute."

After they said their good-byes Fiona sat in her car trying to figure out what to do. Should she phone the police and admit to being there? Or should she wait until they called her – if somehow they found out she'd been there.

So they *would* kill, she thought, whoever they were. It sure wasn't Evan Kirby himself, she thought. He can't even walk, he would have had to hire somebody. She thought of the man watching Livana's condo. But he followed me to the airport, she reminded herself, so, unless he went back, he couldn't have done it. But I don't know exactly when it happened, and she thought she should get out of the car and buy a copy of the Hart City newspaper, as soon as she could trust her legs to carry her.

She thought of Livana again, sitting in that light-filled, glamorous room with her cane and her fake accent and trumped-up history and her fear. What she had missed, or hadn't properly cottoned onto when she'd been there, was Livana's fear. She had easily seen her rage and her exhaustion. Now she knew that the condo had been permeated by fear, that the very air had been saturated with it. She'd been so curious, and then so frightened herself that she'd missed or failed to identify it.

But why did Livana choose now to tell me how to find the killers? After all these years? Because she must have known Evan is dying and she hated him so much she couldn't let him die without retribution. Or, she couldn't tell anybody earlier because she had taken a large bribe. Or maybe she was dying herself – that medical bracelet she had shown Fiona. Unless that was fake too.

She got out of the car, went back into the filling station and bought the Hart City morning paper.

According to it, Livana Kirby had been found dead on the kitchen floor of her "luxurious" Hart City condo, a bullet from a small-calibre gun in her head. The investigation was being pursued "vigorously," and the police were requesting that anyone who had seen Mrs. Kirby in the last few days, or who knew anything about her friends, her family, or her visitors please call a certain number.

Fiona had been about to write the phone number down, but her hands were shaking too hard, so she tore it out of the newspaper. The report went on to say that Mrs. Kirby was a prominent member of the city's social elite, that she had been married to the former Deputy Minister of Justice, Dr. Evan Kirby, that they had one child, a daughter who was a television producer currently living in New York City.

It struck Fiona then with full force that if Olga told the police she had been there, she would, even now, be a suspect.

Chapter Sixteen

He could watch either the front door or the back door, she thought, as she drove into Calgary; one person can't watch them both. Come to think of it though, maybe he would just park at the narrow lane that was the only way into or out of the complex. Would she be up to parking the car on the street a block back and climbing over the back fence so that anybody watching the lane wouldn't know she had entered the complex? She supposed she could do it if she had to, although it was a high chain-link fence. But if they had stationed people to watch the front or back door or both, it wouldn't matter if she climbed the fence or not, they would recognize her. The next step was one she had already thought of a dozen times: A break-in, a murder disguised as a home invasion and robbery? A carefully staged suicide? But I haven't any proof of anything, she whined to her attackers. Honest! She would have laughed if it weren't all so frightening.

The only way I can get into that condo without being seen is if I get into somebody else's car and duck down so it looks like the driver is alone. But who? Carla, her next door neighbour, always drove to work and back. Fiona once commented on how heavy the traffic was; Carla had said you had to be very careful during rush hour, how a moment's inattention could spell disaster.

It was 5:00 p.m. right now and if Fiona was right, Carla would be negotiating Crowchild Trail even now on her way back from work. She had no clue what make Carla's small car was, but it was a new shade, an intense cobalt blue. She decided to take a chance. She would park the rented car around the corner on the street that ran perpendicular to hers, but a block east from her condo complex's only entrance road. Then, leaving her bag in the car, she would walk back another block away from the complex to the corner off the main street, the fastest route home for Carla, flag down her neighbour when she slowed at the corner, and beg a ride the rest of the way. If she doesn't come, then what? I'll go to a hotel and figure it out in the morning.

But she hadn't stood five minutes on the corner two blocks away from the road in front of their condo enclave when Carla came driving around the corner, saw Fiona, and when Fiona waved urgently, pulled over to the curb. She was frowning at the same time as she was smiling politely, a feat Fiona didn't think she'd ever seen before, so that Fiona knew that Carla was mystified and concerned, but also slightly irritated at the interruption in her routine.

"I just twisted my ankle. I can't go another step. I need a ride the rest of the way. I'm really sorry to do this to you."

Obviously relieved, Carla said, "Of course, of course. I'm happy to drive you. Do you need to go to Emergency?"

"Oh, no," Fiona responded, doing her best to sound assured, although in pain. "It's a twist, not a real sprain. It'll be fine in the morning."

Already the entrance to the condo was only a half-block away and Fiona, who had begun scrabbling in her purse as if searching for something, made an abrupt movement, the purse tumbled off her knee to land upside down at her feet, the contents spilling over the floor. Carla braked.

"No, no," Fiona said, "Keep going. I'll find the rest in the parking garage where the light is better." But she kept down, pretending to be feeling around on the floor of the car, so that anyone watching would think the car held only the driver.

The days were getting shorter and shorter as the year wound on to its end, and thankfully the outside light was poor for spotting somebody behind a window in a moving car. Once parked inside the garage, Fiona opened her door, swept the rest of her belongings up into her bag, thanked Carla profusely, walked with her to the elevator, remembering to limp and accepting Carla's offer of her arm to lean on. Together, they rode up to their floor.

She had one bad moment when she thought maybe he would be waiting in the hall, but the hall had no nooks or crannies to hide in; people coming and going would notice him as not a resident, and would surely have called the police immediately. She thanked Carla profusely, refused her offer to come inside with her and get her set for the evening, unlocked her door and went inside, stopping herself in time from putting on the light.

She would have to manage without light, and was grateful that she hadn't pulled any of the blinds when she'd left which, even though it was only a couple of days past, now seemed aeons ago. This way light from the streetlights and the moon would stream in so that she could see to do whatever she had to do. First, make sure the door is locked, get some food, then try getting some sleep. Feeling only marginally secure, she wondered how wise it had been to come home at all.

It was a while before she thought of checking for phone messages. She'd talked to Arnie today already, and also to Vonnie, and there wasn't anybody else she could think of who might call. Nonetheless, she lifted the receiver and there was the telltale beep-beep-beep, so she keyed in her personal identity number and waited, her palms dampening.

"You don't know me," a woman's voice began. "My name is Connie. I knew Zara Stanley really well and I have something to give you that you need to have to know who killed her. Phone me at this number for instructions. Then erase this message." The voice went on to leave an odd-sounding phone number that Fiona figured must be a cell number, even as she was frantically, in the semi-dark, scribbling it down. She hadn't even taken off her coat and, with trembling fingers, she was clicking in the number the caller had given her.

The same woman's voice said, "Yes?"

"This is Fiona Lychenko…" She would have gone on, but the woman interrupted her.

"Meet me tomorrow at noon in the Medicine Hat mall," she said, a husky whisper as if she were cupping the receiver in a hand so her voice wouldn't travel beyond it. "I have something to give you."

"Something? What?" Fiona asked. "Who are you?"

But the woman said, "This is about Zara. It's important. Noon tomorrow, china department at The Bay. Look at the china dinner plate displays; don't look around. I'll find you," and hung up. But I just came through there, Fiona objected mentally to the dial tone, then, *now I'll never sleep*, which made her give a short bark of laughter at her ridiculous demurrals when somebody apparently had something for her that could be vital. But hadn't she heard all this before when she was writing her book? And none of it had amounted to a hill of beans. Still, this one sounded – she sounds as if she is as paranoid as I am. Maybe worse.

It was three hours on the TransCanada to Medicine Hat, and Fiona thought she should try to find a city map so as to take back roads out of Calgary in case anybody was watching. But nobody knows what car I'm driving, she reminded herself. But maybe they're smarter than I give them credit for and they've figured out I rented another car, maybe they know what it is. But how would they do that? She imagined a country road, graveled maybe, nobody around, from out of nowhere comes a...what? A big truck, a three-quarter ton diesel, black... *Stop it!* She told herself, but the picture completed itself before she could erase it: the truck inching its way up beside her on the narrow road as she pushed harder and harder on the gas pedal, forcing her onto the soft shoulder, so that she lost control of her car and was suddenly rolling over and over again and then upside down in the ditch. Then what? He stops his truck, comes over, and either shoots me or bashes in my head with a tire iron. For an instant sheer terror rushed through her, Karen Silkwood and all that. I watch too many movies, she told herself. Stop it right now. *None of that is going to happen.* She said it aloud, slowly, through clenched teeth.

The woman who'd left the voice message couldn't know that Fiona was familiar with Medicine Hat, this because more than once when Roman had business there she had driven with him, just for the change, and when he was in his meetings, she would take the car and drive, not so much in the city, as take the roads around it, leading in and out, studying the terrain, so very different from their farm in what was called "the parklands," where clumps of trees, low hills, ponds and sloughs were everywhere, making an inviting, bucolic landscape that belied, often, its true nature. This terrain was wide and open, mostly sky and low rolling land covered with short yellow grass, with occasional areas of badlands with their crumbling, yellow-clay banks protruding against the horizon here and there. She would drive and look, enjoying the driving, and the stark, forbidding landscape that she didn't have to live in (or make a living in), and with the prospect of a nice lunch with Roman ahead of her. Often, if they went on to Calgary, they would take back roads.

On such occasions it at first surprised her that Roman would be perfectly happy to meander over the back ways, looking at the countryside, the cattle, the oil rigs, the terrain itself, until she realized it was part of his work. How did the cattle look? How were the crops? What were the farmers seeding this year? How much native land was being plowed right now, or the reverse: How much plowed land was being seeded back to grass? He had committees to report to, but she had ridden beside him in quiet pleasure.

Never mind, she would eat, get some sleep, and would go first thing in the morning. It didn't even occur to her that she might ignore the call, stay home, or even seriously consider it as a hoax. Well, of course these ideas occurred to her, but they didn't stand a chance.

"You don't solve murders sitting around on your bum, Fiona," she told herself. "Or by passing up opportunities. You have to take a chance." But what if this woman was one of the bad guys and she was setting Fiona up? That sobered her but, in the end she had no way at all of knowing if she was or she wasn't, and the china department was a public place. If whoever contacted her looked scary, a man maybe, or more than one, she would scream and scare them off. Oh yeah, sure she would. More likely she'd lock herself in a toilet cubicle and still be there when the cleaners arrived at midnight. She almost gave up the idea of going at all, then told herself: *It is at such moments as this that you have to remember Zara.*

Even though she didn't feel sleepy, and expected to spend the night tossing and turning, she undressed, put on her nightgown, and climbed into bed. Either she was more tired than she knew, or it was the special comfort of being in her own bed, but the next thing she knew, it was morning and time to start the three-hour drive to Medicine Hat.

Go to the china section of The Bay and I'll find you there the woman had said. Be there at noon; look at the dinner sets; don't look for me; I'll find you. She couldn't help but feel that such instructions were over the top. She imagined that the woman was like herself: somebody who had seen too many television programs to be able to assess the situation very well in a real-world way; somebody who was doing her best, as she, Fiona was. For now, though, early morning having arrived and darkness not to be dispelled for another hour and a half, she had to concentrate on how to get out of the condo grounds without being seen.

Her building had a central section with a wing extending to the west and another to the east. Normally, because her condo was at the east end of the building, she used the stairs or the east elevator, but now, tiptoeing, trying not to make a sound, struggling to hang on to the collapsed kitchen stepstool she was carrying, she made her way down the long hall to the west end, took the stairs down (the elevator bell would ding), and anxiously, slowly pushed open the outer door. There was an embankment all along the back of the property, maybe twenty feet from the building, and immediately behind at its foot, a six or seven foot high chain link fence – a fence without a gate or any other opening in it its entire length. This was what she would have to climb to get away from the building without being seen. There had been another light snowfall during the night; she would leave a trail. Never mind; nobody would know whose trail it was.

She hurried up the embankment in the dark, glancing back to see that a few lights glowed behind blinds along the wall behind her, but no window coverings stirred as if someone were peering out. She went quickly down the far side of the embankment to where she was partly hidden from view at the foot of the fence. She opened the stepstool, set it against the fence, climbed over it not without *oofing* and a groan or two as she lifted first one leg and then the other to get over the top, carefully unhooking her coat from where it had caught on the top of the fence, prepared to jump to the ground below. If I break my leg she thought, but remembering long-ago gym classes, she tried to relax, and rolled as soon as she hit the ground.

She checked: nothing broken, nothing twisted, and couldn't quite suppress a glow of satisfaction. So much for seventy being the end of all life, she told herself. If a bad guy comes near me, maybe I'll just punch him out. She was a bit hysterical, she thought, because when it hit her that she was probably the first amateur sleuth in history to use a kitchen stepstool for her escape she snorted and had to use both hands over her mouth to keep from laughing out loud. One glance back to say farewell forever to her step-stool, and she moved on quickly, hoping to get to the car before first light.

The fence separated her complex from another one, more family-oriented, with treed grounds that faced onto a major thoroughfare. She hurried through the trees, out to the main street and started walking rapidly around the block, taking a circuitous route that avoided her own street and condo entrance, to the street where she'd parked the rented car. It was still there, and her two cases were undisturbed. It was hard to see with only the one streetlight, but there didn't appear to be anybody sitting in any of the cars up or down the block. She got into her rented car and drove away into the growing stream of early morning commuters. Before another twenty minutes had passed, even staying off the main thoroughfares, she was on the highway and heading southeast for Medicine Hat.

At noon she was browsing in the china department, feeling more foolish than worried, when she felt someone stop beside her. The woman was small and grey-haired, although appearing to be younger than Fiona by a few years. The buttons over her chest and abdomen of her worn grey coat were strained, and she had a hearty, straightforward and, Fiona thought, completely un-fake-able country look about her that soothed Fiona at once.

"Follow me," the woman said. Obediently, thinking it best to stay a few feet back, she followed the faded grey back toward the doors into the parking lot, then to a four-door sedan that had passed its best-before date some years earlier, and settled herself in the passenger seat. She turned to Connie and asked, hesitantly for a fearless sleuth, Fiona couldn't help but tell herself, "Can I see some ID?"

Connie looked surprised, then undid her seat belt, reached into the back, finally giving up because she couldn't reach the giant purse she had placed on the floor behind her seat, undid her seatbelt, got out, took her purse out, reached into it, turning her back on Fiona as if to keep Fiona from seeing what was inside it, and produced her wallet. She climbed back into the driver's seat, still holding her bag, opened her wallet and showed Fiona her driver's license. She was indeed named Connie Nordstrom, residing in a small town Fiona had never heard of, in the neighbouring province. Fiona decided that would have to do; she'd have to trust this woman.

"Sorry to have to do it this way," Connie told her, shoving the purse into the back through the space between the seats, "But this has to be secret, although you do have to know who I am. I'm going to drive us across the river to this nice coffee shop I know." As they drove, keeping her eyes on the road, she began to talk.

"Like my driver's license says, I am Connie Nordstrom. I'm Zara Stanley's first cousin on our mothers' side. I'm a couple of years younger than her – than she was. We lived on different farms and in different school districts, so after she was in grade four we went to different schools. She went to Springvale, and when I got to grade four they sent us the other way, to Premium. We used to see each other when we got bussed around to basketball or volleyball tournaments, or for music festivals and Christmas concerts, and one thing and another. But we were part of the same giant family and so we were together at every big family celebration all through our childhoods: Christmases, Easter, weddings, christenings, and every single summer as long as I can remember, at a big family weekend at Sullivan Lake. We'd all camp, and play ball and games and eat these enormous meals." She sighed. "It was really fun."

They were crossing the bridge over the river now, climbing the big hill, and turning left into a small commercial area Fiona hadn't known existed. Connie parked in front of a café, but didn't get out, instead turning in her seat to look at Fiona. "We were once pretty close, you know. The way cousins can be? But her dad was an alcoholic and mine was religious, so…that sort of separated us too. And then she grew up beautiful and went off to the city for high school and I stayed on the farm and pretty soon I was married." She turned back to the view through the windshield. "Should we go in?"

She was already opening her door, getting out, and reaching into the back seat for her overly-large faded black handbag. They went inside the café and Connie, spotting a corner where nobody was sitting went straight toward it. Fiona followed and sat down across from her in the low-backed booth. The waitress came at once while they were still getting comfortable, plunking two glasses of water and two menus down in front of them. The instant she left, Connie continued speaking as if there had been no break at all. As if, Fiona thought, she has been rehearsing this story for years while she waited for somebody to tell it to.

"But about six weeks before she died she came home for the weekend." She paused to sip from the glass of water. "I was still in high school, but I drove over to see her, and we went out for a walk. It was such a beautiful fall day." The waitress returned. "Two coffees," she said, not consulting Fiona. She was becoming more and more intense, staring at the tabletop, her grey eyes grown large behind glasses that, Fiona noted, had been out of style for at least ten years. "She was so happy! I can't tell you how happy she was. She said I shouldn't tell anybody, but she would be getting married soon, maybe in the coming winter. To some rich guy, she said. 'He's got so much money he doesn't know what to do with it all,' she told me."

"She said she'd borrowed some money from one of our cousins in Vancouver – he was an insurance salesman or something and he always liked Zara, too much, really – and she'd gone out and bought three – she even held up her fingers for me to count." At this Connie gave a small, inward smile, which vanished as quickly as it had come, and went on. "Three really beautiful formal gowns."

"I asked her why he didn't buy her the dresses and she said that she wanted to show him she wasn't just some country hick, she knew how to live too. Then she said, 'Look,' and she pulled back her hair and she was wearing these really pretty earrings. 'Gold,' she said, 'see?' Diamonds, just one little one in each. 'He gave them to me,' she said. She was looking at wedding dresses, too. I asked her, 'Zara, are you pregnant?' But she said no, she wasn't pregnant. They were careful. Neither one of them wanted a baby too soon. 'I just had to tell somebody, Connie,' she told me. 'I'm bursting with the news, but –' she almost said his name, you know – 'he won't let me tell anybody. Said he had to tell his parents first.' Of course, I tried to find out who he was, but she would only laugh and do this funny kind of show-offy, movie star walk to make me laugh, and wouldn't answer me. But I *know* who it was." At this, she leaned back in her chair, and glared so hard at Fiona, that Fiona, spellbound up to this moment, was taken aback. The waitress had arrived with their coffee and took her time setting it down along with cream and sugar, two spoons and some paper napkins.

"Two soups of the day," Connie said, not taking her eyes from Fiona's face. The waitress went away.

"Who?" Fiona was whispering now, leaning toward Connie. Connie moistened her lips, appeared suddenly to be shocked at her own audacity. She swallowed hard, and said, very softly, "Blair Fever."

"What?" Fiona was incredulous, not so much because of the name, but because of Connie's certainty, coupled with her own evidence-less guess. "How do you know?"

"They dated. There's a picture of them. It had to be him."

Fiona thought for a moment. "He's not the only rich man in the province."

"He's the only rich man she dated," Connie said. "And he's got this lousy reputation."

"Did you tell the police that?"

"Didn't have to. Her mom and dad did. It wasn't a secret then. His friends knew too."

"But it was never in the papers."

Connie lifted her gaze from the table, took her fingers from the handle of the coffee cup that she'd been toying with, fixed her eyes on Fiona's again, a crooked, non-smile on her face. "Yeah," she said, her voice dripping sarcasm. "Right. They're gonna put it in the paper that she was last seen with the son of one of the richest men in the country. Back in 1968? Are you kidding?" It occurred to Fiona that it was curious why Connie, having kept silent for fifty years, was suddenly coming into the open now.

"Why now? What made you get in touch with me now?"

"I just heard on the radio yesterday that Evan Kirby's ex-wife got murdered. Did you hear that?" When Fiona nodded, Connie went on. "Years ago I worked in his office.

I hardly even saw him and I don't know a thing about her, but I just thought, what's going on here? Is this what the dreams are about?"

Fiona drew back. "Dreams?" she asked, uncertainly.

"Dreams," Connie said, then opened and shut her mouth as if she had much more to say but had decided against it. Baffled, Fiona kept silent. How could this peculiar woman possibly know anything about Zara's murder? But then, she did say she worked in Evan Kirby's office. Best to wait it out, keep quiet and listen.

The waitress had returned, this time setting a tray down while she removed two bowls of soup, set them in front of them, then a plate with crackers on it, and soup spoons. Fiona waited for her retreat. "The police never questioned you?"

"Why should they? They didn't even know I existed, much less that I might know something. And I wasn't going near them. It wasn't safe; I knew it wasn't."

Behind them the café was filling, but no one was alone and nobody was paying any attention to her and Connie. "I'm sorry for ordering for you, but we have to get this done fast; I can't take this anymore; I haven't slept in weeks; it gets worse and worse. Nightmares…I saw you on TV back when your book came out and I read it and I knew you didn't have a clue. I meant to find you, I even got your phone number at the farm where you lived, but then you moved. I just found you again about six months ago. I meant to get to you, but I was afraid. I kept putting it off, and then the dreams started." She twisted her head away, screwing up her face, then after a second, her face cleared and she turned back to Fiona. "Look, I know stuff."

"What stuff?" Fiona asked, trying not to sound exasperated. All this drama, really, she was thinking, but her palms were damp, her heart was tripping lightly in her throat again, she couldn't quite catch her breath.

"When I graduated from high school, I hung around home for a year, packed groceries at the Co-Op. But I had this boyfriend and he got a construction job in Hart City, so even though I didn't want to go that far from home, I followed him. I got hired on clerking at the Legislative Building. About two months in he dumped me. Wouldn't you know it? Me stuck alone in Hart City. I was just twenty, going on twenty-one. Never been away from home before, but I thought I was grown up. Who doesn't at that age?" Fiona made a commiserating sound that Connie waved away.

"I worked in the central filing system. No computers in those days. You can't imagine how boring it was. All this stuff coming in day after day, and me having to find the right cabinet for it and the right place. File after file after file until I could have screamed. Then I got shoved up to Agriculture, to Evan Kirby's office, because somebody was sick and work was piling up and even if I was only twenty and not a college girl, I knew the alphabet."

Fiona interrupted. "You filed by words, not numbers?"

"Sometimes one, sometimes the other. It depended." Fiona decided not to ask on what.

The noise level in the café was rising, the coffee machines hissing, so that people had to raise their voices to be heard. Fiona leaned closer across the table. Their two bowls of soup sat cooling where they'd pushed them to each side. Connie began to talk again, whispering urgently, her face as close to Fiona's as she could manage across the table.

"I had to work overtime. They left me in this big office all by myself. My supervisor came and went, but mostly I was alone. And there were these two huge boxes of files and I wasn't supposed to go home until I'd put them all away in their proper places and I got another armload from the secretary's office. I'll tell you I was tempted to just jam them in any old place and walk out. But I didn't. I still believed that you did your work and you told the truth…" She snorted. "I picked up an armful of them. They were slippery and not all the same size or thickness, and I dropped the whole bunch on the floor and when I bent down to start sorting them – they'd sort of fanned out, so I could get them back together in mostly the proper order, thank god – there was my cousin's face staring up at me."

Connie fell silent, her jaw clenched, her eyes boring into Fiona's. "My cousin," she repeated. "Zara Stanley. So I didn't dare look at more in the file in case I got caught. I kind of slipped all the stuff that seemed to belong to that file back into it, and I stuffed it into my lunch bag, you know?" She leaned back and demonstrated. "Then I cleaned up the other files, pushed them into the drawers – I wasn't being too careful by then, I can tell you. And I went home. With Zara's file tucked into my lunch bag."

She leaned back, triumphant, light catching her glasses so that Fiona could no longer see her eyes. Sweat had popped out on Fiona's forehead, she had to swallow hard before she could speak. Fiona thought, that crafty so-and-so: Hide in plain sight! He had the file number, he knew the system, any time he needed the file he could go back and find it. And nobody else would ever look for it because nobody knew it existed. He didn't reckon on Emily seeing it, or a Connie Nordstrom – in fact, on any incompetent file-girl just shoving it any old place. Or maybe he was scared by something and this was all he could think of on the spur of the moment...

"Do you still have that file?" Connie, her lips tight, nodded yes, grimly, and patted her bulging purse. Fiona gasped once, then expelled air slowly through her nose to keep from shouting.

"All these years you've kept it? Did you ever show it to anybody? Tell anybody?"

"Only Kurt, my husband. He wanted me to blackmail a couple of the high mucky-mucks, but I wouldn't have none of that. I was too scared, and anyway, I didn't think there was any proof of anything. But I knew what happened to my cousin, and that was good enough for me. I kept the file because Kurt made me. For insurance he said. I should have given it to you back then when your book came out. But I just did not dare. I was sure disappointed you didn't figure it out. And nobody could even begin to guess that I know anything. I've never talked to a cop, never been asked a single question by anybody about what I know. I'd like to keep it that way." She closed her eyes abruptly and dropped her head, murmuring so Fiona could barely hear her.

"But these dreams – they get worse and worse until I'm afraid to go to sleep." After a second she opened her eyes, and raising her voice said, "It's that I see Zara, the way she must have been when she got murdered. All bloody, you know? And the look in her eyes – like she's just staring at me with those big blue eyes of hers. Just staring. She wants me to do something. I'll never get any peace until I get rid of that file." Again, Fiona thought, *Zara*.

"Why didn't you go to the police?" Connie's mouth opened and then closed again, and for the first time something like real anger appeared in the set of her mouth.

"Because I think the police are *involved*," she said, "At least, the police chief was. Maybe nobody else, but I couldn't take that chance. And who was left I could trust? Nobody I could think of. The Queen? The Prime Minister?" Disgust crossed her face. "I just waited and waited and had faith that someday I'd be able to do the right thing to get the man or men who killed Zara. And now is the time."

Chapter Seventeen

Fiona was listening so intently that all other sound in the café had dropped to a steady, muted drone. She opened her mouth to ask the obvious question, but Connie raised a hand palm out, toward her, silencing her.

"Read the file," she said, and pulling her coat around her to hide her fumbling with the purse that she had now placed on her lap. From it, she pulled out a worn brown, letter size cardboard file holder that clunked when she set it on the table by Fiona's elbow. "Take it," she said fiercely. "Hurry up."

Quickly Fiona slid the envelope onto her lap, opened her own purse, about half the size of Connie's, and stuffed the file in. There was something hard stuck in the bottom, so she could only bend the top part over in order to zip her purse again. But she had seen the number printed on the tab at the bottom, not all of it, and some of it was blurred, but enough of it to see that it was probably the number Livana had given her, that she had memorized, and recited to herself every day so that she wouldn't forget it, and didn't need to have it written on slips of paper anymore, or on the underside of her best high heels.

"I was beginning to think this didn't exist," she said. "I heard about it, but there wasn't any way I could get to it: I didn't know where it was, I didn't know if there really was one somewhere…" She was babbling with relief and excitement. So many years she had waited for this. They had all waited for it. She was blinking back tears of gratitude and relief.

Then it struck her that she was at last genuinely in possession of something that could get her killed.

A devastating wave of fear was sweeping through her, so fast and deep that her bowels for an instant loosened and, she was afraid she would faint. She forced herself to lean back casually, lifted her coffee cup to her mouth, her palms coldly damp against the cup's warmth.

Connie too had calmed; her skin had smoothed, where Fiona had been able to see behind the unfashionable glasses only blurred pinpoints, her eyes seemed larger and paler now. Connie might once have been a pretty girl.

"You'd get nowhere forever without it," Connie said, as if it were nothing, really, after all. She stood up, said, "I hope you can eat two bowls of soup," grinning in a haphazard, lopsided way, distracted, looked toward the door at the other end of the room. "I have to pick up Kurt so we can get home by dark."

"Wait!" Fiona said, so sharply that Connie stopped, and perched again on the edge of the seat.

"Did you know Emily Cheng? She worked there, I think. For Kirby. She was Emily Zhang then."

"She was Kirby's secretary, kind of lorded it over the rest of us. Well, she never even noticed me. Just came out of her office to ask for stuff or to give orders. I told her I was just temporary."

"So you collected files from her office that day too? Was that the pile you dropped? Did Zara's file come from

Kirby's office, or Emily's?"

Connie shrugged. "Could have been either one. The stack had sort of tipped over and I just gathered up all of it. I worried that I might have got stuff I wasn't supposed to take, but by then I was just plain mad. So I grabbed it all." She shrugged. "And, I phoned in sick the next day and I packed my stuff and I went home. That was that."

Without speaking again, she struggled to her feet and walked away, skirting tables and people. Once she'd gone, Fiona realized, among other things, that she had no way to get back to her car parked at the mall on the other side of town. Nor any way to find Connie again, either – wrong, she had her phone number. But clearly, Connie would not welcome being found again.

She wanted to pull out the file and start reading it right then and there, but glancing over her shoulder she saw two uniformed police officers coming in the door, froze, then realized that they were probably only stopping for lunch. She pulled the one soup bowl toward her and spooned in the now cool soup as if she were merely hurrying to complete a boring but necessary task, not tasting it at all, until the bowl was empty. Then, a half-made plan in her mind, she rose, paid the bill, and went out onto the sidewalk where eventually she picked up a cab that took her back to her rented car.

By this time she was sweating with her eagerness to get to the file, anxious to find a private, anonymous place where she could read it in peace and quiet and at last, find out who had killed Zara, and why. But she couldn't just go back home again. If she did, it would be the same old thing, trying to think of a way to sneak back into her condo without being seen; once in it, not being able to turn on the lights. Only this time, it would be worse, because this time she would be carrying the very pieces of information the bad guys didn't want her to have.

No, she would get a hotel room for the night and spend the day studying the file and figuring out what to do next, although she was already pretty sure what to do would involve hiding this file somewhere that no one would ever guess until she had figured out who she should give it to.

How long could she stay hidden? If people went into her condo, a private detective or someone like that, and listened to her phone messages – Had she erased Connie's message? She couldn't remember – or searched her place, what would they find? My old notes for my book, but they're no good to anybody. The file number? But so what? They'd know then that I know where to look, they'd even think I have the file. They'd re-double their efforts to find me.

Besides that, what if somebody reported that I'd been to see Livana? My fingerprints must be all over the place: the brandy glass, the sofa arm. Perhaps Livana was washing the glasses when her killer came for her? Maybe that's why she was in the kitchen. She wondered how he had gotten into Livana's apartment, unless he had told her some lie when she came to open the door, and not recognizing him maybe, from all those years ago, she had let him in. Maybe he had been wearing a uniform for some company and said he had come to check the something-or-other. Maybe she ran for the kitchen then, maybe – but none of this was relevant to what matters, Fiona thought. Livana couldn't have been murdered by her former husband Evan, but he could have sent someone. He could have sent – but who could he trust? He was blackmailing Blair Fever, she supposed, and maybe Andy Hallett too, if they were the killers. She couldn't guess who the third man might be, unless it was Evan himself.

She wondered suddenly where Kirby had gotten the money to pay off Emily Cheng. He was doing well, it's true, he was a lawyer, but even at that, unless there was family money, he wouldn't have been able to pay any sizeable bribe. Judging by the house Emily and Larry lived in, she'd gotten a substantial amount. Which in 1968 would be how much? Fiona thought back: In those days in Hart City or Ripley you could buy a house for maybe $10,000. But money bought more then than it does now, by a heck of a lot. I remember buying a new summer coat in about 1969 for $30. That same coat would cost around $150 today.

Could Kirby have put together a file that would put Blair Fever in jail? But if he was really involved in Zara's death and not just blathering when he was drunk – about who? Fever? – it might have put him in jail too – still, a bird in the hand. $10,000 wouldn't be much to Fever, or Fever's father. Once again, her brain faltered at all this speculation, all the directions her mind needed to go, but seemed to want to all at the same time. Like Stephen Leacock's horse, her mind was riding madly off in all directions. Or was that Stephen Leacock? Enough.

At last she had the file in her bag.

"This it?" the cabbie, a large, middle-aged woman asked her. They had arrived at the mall parking lot.

"This is fine," Fiona said. "Thanks." But her mind wouldn't stop its churning out of ideas even while she paid the woman, found her way to her car, got in, and drove to an inconspicuous motel she'd seen more than once from the highway. Small, cheap, out of the way. Even as she checked in, her mind was tacking back and forth, speeding up, slowing down.

Imagine he comes back to his office and this file he's put together has vanished. He asks his secretary where it went and she says it went with the boxes of files into the general file room. He'd say, 'oh,' and leave it at that. Then maybe after work when everybody has gone home, he goes to the filing room to look for the file himself. But of course, he can't find it, because it's gone. But maybe he finds other files and sees that they aren't where they're supposed to be and when he looks around at the tons of filing cabinets and the size of the room, he realizes that there is no way on earth he will ever find that file. It's lost, it's gone. That was never his plan; imagine his consternation.

And then maybe, after a while, he begins to think that might be a good thing. He's already collected. Why would he care if it's gone except that he wouldn't have anything on Blair Fever anymore, but Fever couldn't know that. But wait…Kirby must have made a copy. Maybe that's why the file was in his office to start with: so he could make himself a copy of it using the office machines. Maybe, a few years later, that copy was what Livana had seen.

By 2:30 Fiona was sitting quietly at the small desk in her new motel room nervously opening the file Connie had given her. The first thing she saw was that in addition to papers, it contained a flat box tucked into a fold stapled together at the bottom of the file. The box was slightly larger than one of the old compact disc boxes she'd thrown out when she moved from the farm. She lifted the box out of the fold it had been resting in, opened it and saw that inside was an old reel-to-reel tape. Nothing she could do about that right now. She pushed the file to one side of the desk, extracted the thin sheaf of papers, and spread them out on the desk in front of her.

An hour later, as she stood there thinking about the enormity of what had happened, all to cover up who the killers of one single pretty girl had been, and how the whole thing had grown and swelled until it was so large that there wasn't anybody left untainted by it, a savage anger rose from her gut all the way to the top of her head where it reddened her face and scalp, made her breath come fast and heavy; she felt she might be breathing out steam. She began to pace.

She had the answer now, she knew who the killers were, and the weight of this knowledge required that she go at once to the right people in order to start the wheels of justice moving. She paused, but who? Not the police, the Mounties, the government – then who? The media! Marjory Popowich AKA Marigold Martin. No, never. Marjory would be more likely to take the truth and sell it to the highest bidder. And as a local person, she didn't have the clout this business would require.

What about one of the investigative television programs? They did excellent work, and a lot of people watched their programs. But she didn't like the idea of having to appear on television herself, or of appearing even in shadow with an altered voice. She didn't like the idea of television at all.

A national newspaper: would one even be interested? There was only one, after all. If a story is big enough, she told herself, everybody will buy the paper to find out about it. Or, maybe the way to do it would be to blitz all the media at once: radio, television, newspapers. Would she dare take it out of the province? But, of course, she had to take it out of the province; she wasn't sure who she could trust within it. Toronto, then, and the *National Times*.

But more immediate problems intervened: she still couldn't go home; she had a rented car she had to take back or else call to extend its keep; she had to sort things out in her mind, because this was all too much and she could no longer make sense of any of it. Who might be after me right now? But she found she had no idea anymore. She was sure that the report that Bill Porringer had written that had false or incorrect information in it, if pursued, would at the very least embarrass the justice department and maybe – would it be possible? – reveal that officials had colluded in a legal process to weigh a case in the prosecution's favour. If so, she began to realize, *then* watch the examination of files that would probably follow by all sorts of lawyers acting for people charged in the past and found guilty under Porringer's watch! And the court cases that would follow!

As if that weren't bad enough, it would come out that Livana Kirby, Emily Cheng, and her own husband had taken bribes, paid for – another unfortunate fact that would surely also come out – by some of the richest people in the province. Yet it might be, probably would turn out to be, a fact that the payers' trails had been well-covered. Surely forensic accountants could look back and discover that in each case a large sum of money had appeared out of nowhere and gone into their bank accounts, or in Roman's case, into their safe deposit boxes. Would they be able to identify where the money had come from? How could she prove she hadn't known about Roman taking the money? Her reputation would be destroyed along with his.

Still, even with this file in her hand, she told herself that only one item constituted any kind of proof. *But it does indicate a conspiracy.* A conspiracy to subvert justice, right?

Or was the proper word 'suborn?' Whatever that meant. In the end, she supposed, this was all the whole mess was about as far as the big guys were concerned; it was about a conspiracy to prevent justice from being done. A long-ago conspiracy starting at the bottom and moving to the highest levels, because since that first agreement, others had to keep on covering up that original cover-up. That was why everyone was after her. That she might identify the real killers was part of it, but in the eyes of those who had control, the identity of the real killers was a side issue: the main one was the conspiracy.

Holy Cow! No wonder they were trying to scare her off. She couldn't get her breath, chills were running through her, all her courage, all her desire, deserted her, her knees weakened and she nearly collapsed to the floor, had to lean with both hands on the desk to hold herself up. *I can't believe it,* she kept saying to herself. *I can't believe it.* But the worst of it was that she did believe it.

She saw that if she dwelt on this, she would quit, go home to her Calgary condo, shut the door, and never go out again. She would not think of it again: she would do what she had to do, and – the journalist in her rebelling at the cliché – let the chips fall where they may. *Justice for Zara.*

She checked her watch. It was after 6:00 p.m. If she tried to find a way back to Calgary now she would arrive there too late to do anything meaningful, and she didn't dare go back to her apartment. Now she found, as she contemplated the three-hour drive back, a wave of exhaustion swept through her, so powerful that she lay down on the bed, letting her shoes drop to the floor, unbuttoning her jacket and throwing one hand over her eyes, began to breathe slowly through her nostrils, trying to relax.

"I'll just have a five-minute nap," she told herself out loud. "I can risk five minutes." Oddly, her mind had gone blank. All she thought about was how tired she was, how much she needed sleep, that she would be fine if she just had a nap before she headed out on the next, most important, most dangerous phase of her adventure.

It was two in the morning when she woke. For a long moment, she wasn't sure where she was and had to go through all the hotels and motels she'd been in over the last couple of weeks until she remembered: Medicine Hat, motel on highway. Then, I have to get to Calgary at once. I have to find the *National Times* bureau chief; I have to get rid of this file. And the car! I can't even phone the rental agent; there won't be anybody there. I have to get to the airport and turn in that damn car. Only weeks later would she begin to realize, under the circumstances, how bizarre her focusing on the rental car was.

Frantic because she had slept so long, she ran into the bathroom, used the toilet, splashed water onto her face, and without even pausing to brush her hair or her teeth, rushed to the desk, pushed the papers into the folder, made sure the tape was securely stuffed into it, then put the folder into her purse. Then she picked up the two bags she hadn't even opened, put on her coat, then stood, thinking, in the centre of the motel room.

Possibilities and contingencies raced through her mind, and she was trying to sort them, establish priorities, pick the most urgent thing to do. I have to get the file into the hands of somebody who would break open this major scandal, who would force the law to begin the struggle for justice for Zara. Whatever it cost. Whoever it cost. During this spate of frantic thinking she had moved to the window that overlooked the parking lot.

It was two in the morning and a man was standing by her car. Her heart leaped into her throat, sweat broke out onto her forehead. When she had parked the motel lot had only a few cars in it, even now it was barely half-full, but it was entirely possible that this man was an ordinary traveller who had just driven in off the highway having decided not to go any further tonight. She couldn't decide if the car beside hers, that hadn't been there when she parked, was his or had been there for hours. But as she watched, he turned away, and began to stride toward the hotel entrance. Then she noticed he wasn't carrying a suitcase or even a small bag.

Galvanized, she grabbed up her bags again and, throwing the plastic key card onto the desk, hurried out the door, turned left toward the stairs leading down to the back exit into the parking lot. By what magic had she wakened at just that moment? It was too strange; even in her haste and fear her mind fixed itself on her good fortune at waking at just the right moment, at looking out the window at that second. But she knew it, didn't even truly question its plausibility (although much later she would): Zara had wakened her; Zara wanted to save her; Zara wanted her terrible death to be avenged. Yes, she told herself, it had to be Zara. Or else there really are guardian angels.

Her bags banged against her thighs she ran across the lot to her car, unlocked it, threw the bags into the back, and drove off. Her destination was the Medicine Hat airport where she could turn in the car to their branch of the rental agency, pay whatever fine would be involved, and see about catching a flight somewhere as fast as possible. What if I can't get a flight right away? she asked herself, running a red light. But at this hour of the morning there was no traffic at all and she could drive as dangerously as she felt like. Then I'll grab a taxi and go somewhere. I'll figure out where when that happens.

It took her a second to realize that at two-thirty in the morning there wouldn't be anybody at the Medicine Hat airport either. And what if the man at her car was only a car thief? Or maybe he thought the car was a friend's or a relative's. She hadn't seen him touch it. Maybe he'd just gotten out of the vehicle next to it and was getting his bearings before he went into the hotel, and that was all. Maybe I ran for nothing. Maybe at least I could have had a shower.

Then she began to wonder how she could possibly have slept for eight hours. Could it have been eight hours? Surely not. Yet no matter how she counted, it came to eight hours. She felt her forehead crease into a frown, her hands grasping the steering wheel too hard. Have I lost my mind? Am I being driven crazy? Calm down, she told herself. After all these years you have the answer at last; years and years of wondering, and thinking, and worrying. You were worn out with it all. And overwhelmed with satisfaction at knowing the answer at last.

I know who killed Zara Stanley. She wanted to roll down the car window and scream it to the world.

No, she told herself: You were just so afraid of what lies ahead that you took a time out. That's all. A time out is not crazy. It's just…she pursed her lips, took one hand from the steering wheel to shake it out of its numbness from grasping so hard…It's just very unnerving – and inconvenient. I think it's called a *fugue state*. But that scared her too.

But she had to do something; surely the police were looking for her over Livana's murder. At this thought she took the next exit and drove into the local College parking lot, found a dark, quiet corner under some trees where two other cars were parked with no one in them, pulled in between them, shutting off the motor and with it, the lights, and sat in the darkness trying to calm herself, trying to think what to do.

er body felt clammy, even her face, and her clothes were limp and damp with sweat. *How many days have I been wearing this outfit?* She pulled opened the visor mirror to look at herself: hair not having seen a comb for some time, no makeup, all her wrinkles and age spots exposed for anyone to see. Her own eyes frightened her, so intense were they, so black, when as far as she could remember, the last time she had noticed them before Roman died, they had been their normal dark blue. *I look crazed,* she told herself; *no one will listen to me. I have to get to Calgary; I have to turn in this car. I have to comb my hair.* Each seemed as important and as difficult as the other.

She sat for a moment longer in the dark, trying to slow her breathing and to calm herself, then turned on the motor, put the car in gear, and backed out of her parking place. She would take back roads to Calgary to at least try to evade whoever was following her. *If,* she reminded herself. *If somebody is following me. The killers or their hired guns.*

Rather than going directly out onto the highway, she went out of the parking lot in the opposite direction, on the road that led through downtown that joined the highway outside of the city. When she reached the intersection only moments later, instead of entering the highway, she turned north onto a gravel road, and when after twenty or more miles, it ended because of the block of land used by the armed forces, she drove into the village on the land's borders. There she made a screeching turn and headed north on a narrow secondary highway. *Evasive action,* she was calling it to herself, and out loud, did a villainous *"har, har,"* and was grateful there wasn't anybody to hear how crazy she was getting. But the trick would be not to get lost, especially in the dark on strange roads, but she was sure that if she kept heading north and turning west at each opportunity while staying off the highway, it would be impossible to miss Calgary.

This was going to take a lot longer, but she couldn't worry about that. First, the airport to turn in the car – that would be just as easy as trying to phone while she rocked down a gravel road – then to the office of the western branch of the *National Times*. She put her foot on the accelerator and began to speed, prayed she had enough gas to get her to the city, or that she could buy more some-where on this godforsaken road once daylight came and gas stations opened.

She had headed north for half an hour checking in the rearview mirror every once in a while for headlights, but saw nobody who seemed to be pursuing her, in fact, nobody at all. She relaxed a bit then, but didn't let up on the gas. What did she care if she got a ticket, anyway? But damn it, she had to get to Calgary and, although at the thought of a ticket she had eased up on the gas, now she stepped harder again, and went racing down the road like any speed-crazy teenager.

Driving fast down deserted country roads in the hours before dawn, the sky growing more luminous as the searing silver of the stars slowly faded to softer whites, and shadows she knew to be grass-covered hills loomed charcoal and indigo at the bottom of the sky, she began to get a feeling of distilled excitement, even joy, then a sudden realization that she was a free woman – utterly free, and in control of her own life. It was, she thought, as if she, the woman she had faded into over the years and the one she really had been all that time had at last met each other, become one, and now she was full of power. Her! Fiona! Full of power!

She noticed she felt calmer, and pulled over to brush the knots out of her hair and apply a little lipstick. She buttoned her jacket and then her coat over her coffee-stained blouse and wondered how long she'd been going around with a brown stain on her shirt front. The sky had lightened enough that she could see a low smudge on the far horizon that was the city, and once again, she took the first secondary road north, and eventually west again, then, at last, a little north of the city, took the highway south into it and was back at the airport.

She picked up the *National Times* on her way in and while paying her bill and her fine at the car rental booth Fiona hung tightly onto her purse that had the file in it. In moments, she was in a taxi and heading downtown. From the newspaper she had found the location of the *Times* office to which she directed the driver, and in only a few minutes she had arrived. From the moment she had walked away from the car rental booth she had been growing more certain and feeling more in control, and now she paid the driver, got out with her bags, went inside, took the elevator up to the fourth floor and went down the hall until she found the office number she was looking for.

Inside, she found a pretty young woman typing rapidly

at her computer.

"Can I help you?" she asked.

"I'm looking for Steven," Fiona said, having forgotten his last name.

"He's off having a snack just now," the girl said.

"I'm his aunt," Fiona said. "Tell me where he is and I'll go to him."

"Of course," the girl said, her name tag said 'Mary Ann.' "He's downstairs in the café having breakfast." Leaving her bags behind with the politely reluctant Mary Anne, Fiona went downstairs.

The café was small and definitely on the grubby side, but there was only one customer, a heavy-set, fortyish, bearded man with horn-rimmed glasses, disheveled too-long dark hair, chowing down on fried eggs, bacon and hash browns.

"Steven?" He looked up, startled.

"My name is Fiona Lychenko. I have something important to…uh… You'll want to hear this." He wiped his mouth with a handful of paper napkins and mopped his palms, indicated she should sit.

"What?" he said, but he was not unfriendly. As she sat, he waved to the waitress lounging behind the counter, and held up two fingers, mouthing 'coffee.' Fiona took a deep breath, then a second one. Where to begin?

"I have come into possession of a file that contains material that is…inflammatory. It contains evidence that can clear up a fifty-year-old murder case. A case of some… notoriety. Worse," she said, leaning toward him, "It also contains evidence of a conspiracy at the highest levels to protect the killers. This is, I think, two issues: Catching the killers, even now, after fifty years, and dealing with the conspiracy. There is also perhaps – I'm not a lawyer – the possibility of charges of obstruction of justice. I don't think these issues can be fully separated." She was immensely pleased at her so cogent summary.

He was staring at her intently, assessing her; she could see his intelligence too, in his eyes behind the wonky glasses. She was glad she'd taken the time to fix her hair.

"The highest levels?"

"Starting with a long-dead police chief and going through the crown prosecutor at the time, also dead, to, I think, the office of the Attorney General, and carrying on to this day." He blinked, then blinked again.

"Here? In this province?" She shook her head, no. "Next door."

"What is the case?" He was looking at his plate now, moving his knife, then putting it back again. But he hadn't left yet; he hadn't walked away. Maybe he was relieved it wasn't in his own province.

"A beautiful young woman named Zara Stanley was murdered in 1968 in Ripley. She was beaten, quite savagely, raped repeatedly, then probably smothered with a pillow. The worst of it, if there can be a worst, is that it is thought that if she hadn't been smothered, she would have lived despite her injuries."

"Before DNA test were invented." She nodded. He thought for a moment. This was ringing a bell for him, she could see it. "That name – I think I remember it. She was a beauty queen, wasn't she? And in those days nobody ever got murdered in Ripley. That's part of the reason it was such a scandal. I do remember that, I mean hearing about it. I wasn't born then. But people still talk about it, and sometimes there'll be a story about it still." He lifted his eyes to her again. Silence. Then he asked, "You said you have a file?"

"I do." She had meant to say more, but the door into the diner had opened behind them, Fiona stiffened, she saw Steven observing this, and turned to see who it was. A couple of female office workers.

"Why did you come to me? Why didn't you go to one of those investigative television shows? Most people would have done that." Fiona shrugged slowly. She thought, he is giving himself time to think; he wants to know if I'm just another crazy or not.

"I think – I was a reporter once…" she laughed in embarrassment, "I even had my own column, until I got fired." She grimaced when she said 'fired,' "I guess I'm prejudiced toward print, toward writing. That's all. And maybe I didn't want to go on television. You know?"

"Hmmm," he said, as if he found this interesting and unusual. "What is it you want from me?" As if checking one more time to be sure she was serious.

"I can't go to the police with this stuff. I can't think of anybody else I can trust, although there are, I have no doubt at all, people who could be trusted with this. But it takes a national organ, somebody with clout who isn't involved with any of the people who are part of it, or who might have reason to want to stop this information from ever becoming public. And it has to be national; otherwise it could be shut down so fast – and there could be reprisals, too. There has already been one murder, since Zara's I mean. Two murders in total that I know of, unless Porringer's roll-over death wasn't an accident – he was the crown prosecutor at the time. No, I need a national outlet. I can still trust a journalist, can't I?" He drummed his fingers on the table top. The door behind them opened again, this time an old man the waitress seemed to know, greeting him cheerily by name.

"Why are you so jumpy?" he asked, as if he knew the answer, not looking at her.

"I interviewed people who are in the file," she told him. "I alerted them. I think I'm being followed, and I am afraid. Seriously afraid." He studied her again as if by looking hard enough into her face he might see whatever it was he needed to know. That I'm not crazy; that I really do know something.

"Do you have the file with you?" She hesitated, then nodded. Under the table she was clutching her handbag so tightly her hands hurt.

"I have to talk to my editor. Let's go up to my office." He threw a ten on the table and made his clumsy way out of the booth, with Fiona following.

In his outer office, he said, "Mary Ann, this is…"

"I know," Mary Ann said. "Your aunt."

"Right," Steven said, after a beat. "Will you make a pot of coffee and break out some of those cookies? Set it up in the back room." He turned to Fiona. "Let's go in."

Fiona followed him into his small office with its waist-high, greyed windows behind his desk looking out over a massive, full parking lot that surely couldn't contain cars that had anything to do with him. His desk was huge, its surface littered with paper, and a computer humming off to one side of it. Two chairs sat across from the desk and in the corner on her right was a small sofa with a coffee table in front of it. The coffee table had nothing on it and the sofa looked harder than the chairs did. He went round his desk, pushed a few keys on his computer before he sat, motioning for her to sit in one of the chairs across from him.

"This is just a sub-office," he said to her as if she had asked. "The main one is in Edmonton. Maybe you should have gone there."

"I didn't know," she told him, "and I live in Calgary so I wanted to be here."

When she looked up she saw that he had taken a tape recorder from a drawer and with thick fingers, was poking it into running. Seated, his fingers on his keyboard, he said, "Okay. Tell me the story from the beginning." When she looked surprised, he said, "The tape gets the facts, this" – indicating the keyboard – "gets the thoughts."

Fiona began talking, he interrupting now and then to clarify when something happened, or how to spell a name, or how she knew what she claimed to know. She began with a brief biography of Zara Stanley, as well as she could remember, and while his fingers tapped away relentlessly, went on to the rumors as to who had killed her. She told him about her own questioning at the time she decided to write her book, and about all the many details concerning the newspaper reports of the killing and the investigation that had left her with a dozen questions because they didn't look right to her, didn't jibe with what she knew otherwise, and that no one could – or would – explain to her satisfaction. But that she had finally managed to construct a narrative that satisfied her, had written the book, and that it was published to no fanfare, and the only place it sold well was in Ripley itself, because it was a Ripley story.

"And then I tried to forget it," she said. "Because I'd done what I could, and I could see no other way to go, hadn't a clue what more I might do."

"And then, one day," he said, taking his hands off his keys and looking at her.

"One evening, actually," she said. "I was getting ready to go to bed when I saw someone had slid a brown envelope under my door. That was the beginning." Without taking his eyes off her face, although she could see that he wasn't seeing her, he rolled his chair to her left again, put his hands on the keyboard, taking one off to comb his beard absently, then went back to typing. Click, click, click-click-click. Time passed; Fiona went on with her story, and he with his questions.

At last, he said, "All right. Now – the file."

He pushed his chair back from his desk, sweeping papers into a pile at the same time and tossing them onto the counter behind him. Then he crossed his hands across his abdomen and waited, gazing at her. The moment had come. She bent her head, unzipped her bag carefully, slowly, pulled out the file and set it on the newly-cleaned desk top between them, pulling her own chair around so that they sat nearly side by side, the file in front of them. Carefully she opened it. There was something in the air; it was more than silence – it was as if the very air was listening, fully attentive, and when she reached out to touch the papers she found her fear had vanished.

The first piece of paper was an official document from the Ripley prosecutor's office and addressed to the Chief of Police. It summarized the results of the coroner's inquest and ended with a four-line section, in italics and separated from the rest of the report, purporting to be a quotation from the coroner's jury's official verdict.

"I'd seen this document before," Fiona told him. Beside her he was perfectly still, listening and reading. "See? It says that the jury concluded that the deceased, Zara Stanley, had been killed by blows to the head. But that's not true: I managed, after insisting and phoning here and there, to get a copy of the official transcript of the coroner's inquest. The jury concluded that she had died of suffocation. Why would the crown prosecutor not say that?" she asked Steve. "Why would he pretend to quote from the jury and then write something the jury hadn't concluded at all? What was to be gained by that?"

"It's easier to prove murder by blows than it is by suffocation," Steve murmured, his fingers touching the signature at the bottom of the page. "More to the point, why would Kirby put this document into this file? So that he would have something on the crown prosecutor? That is, on William – what is it? – Porringer?"

Fiona said, "So that Porringer would never tell anybody what he knew, because if he had made a practice of writing whatever suited him in his official reports, then he would be afraid that all these many documents would be uncovered, his reputation ruined, and he might even wind up in court himself being sued by a lot of irate people who had maybe gone to jail because of his lies. Maybe it would be even worse."

Steve said, "But why would he do it?"

"I think because he was in collusion with the police chief to report in this way about the murder."

She glanced at Steve, and was surprised to see that in his intense concentration his appearance of lethargic scruffiness had disappeared. In its place was a powerfully-built man with the keenest eyes she'd seen in anyone for a very long time, and a delicacy to his movements, as if he understood as well as she did how vital were the documents they were perusing, as if they might literally explode.

"But Porringer is dead," he said. "Although the next

crown prosecutor would most likely know by now that Porringer's documents were often not accurate. Malcolm... Kipp, is it?" Fiona nodded.

"And he denies knowing anything about the case. Says as an officer of the court even if he knew anything he couldn't tell me."

"This alone..." Steve said, tapping the paper, shaking his head.

She put the document aside. Beneath it were two photos, one of a couple standing side by side holding hands, the man in a suit, the young woman in a simple formal gown, a corsage attached to one wrist. Zara Stanley and Blair Fever. The picture was in black and white, the edges uneven and curling. She turned it over for Steve to read: August, 1968.

"Zara was killed in mid-October," Fiona said, softly.

The second photo was harder to make out. It was taken at night, using a flash so that the back of the head of the man closest to the camera was unnaturally lightened, his scalp gleaming through his light-coloured brush cut. On the right, a few blackened rocks on the ground could be made out and the glow of what was apparently a nearby bonfire. Two boys, clearly drunk, sat side by side in sand, their arms around their knees, holding beer bottles, and laughing, looking about to topple over. Blair Fever, his uncoordinated grin betraying the degree of his drunkenness, and on the extreme left –

"This is Andrew Hallett," she told him. "This one was taken Labour Day weekend, 1968. The conspirators are all together here. This head with the brush cut is almost certainly Evan Kirby. I think this proves it was the three of them together." Steve was considering.

"Well, it is proof that Zara and Blair had been dating not long before Zara's death."

"And also," Fiona said, tapping the photo with her index finger until she noticed how grubby her fingernail was and drew it back. "This would be not long before Connie Nordstrom claimed Zara had come to her all excited about getting married to a rich man. This is as clear as if Zara is speaking to us from the grave: He *was* Blair Fever. And the other picture is proof – if anybody tries to deny it – that even then Blair and Andy Hallett were good friends. And this has got to be Evan Kirby." She paused. She could feel Steve thinking hard beside her.

"Evan Kirby *was* one of the murderers," she told him. "I was dubious from the start because he isn't a big man at the best of times and, I guess because it's hard to imagine him active and vigorous when he is so helpless right now. There was always that rumour about it being three men, not just one, but absolutely nobody had any evidence to prove it that I ever heard of, until Livana came along."

Steve stared first at one photo and then at the second one.

"She really was a beauty," he murmured, as if until he'd seen her photo he had doubted it. Not replying, faintly irritated with him, Fiona put the photos aside on the first document, and brought the next one forward, centering it carefully on the desk top. It was a photocopy of a letter, handwritten and signed by the Chief of Police.

With regard to the subject of our discussion of the 20th of October, I agree that such a line of inquiry would not serve the community well. We are instead pursuing a more specific cluster of possibilities and feel that that will satisfy our mandate if not quite achieve the outcome the public is after. But I fully agree that the other will achieve no particular good and will do harm to those involved.

To Fiona, no longer the naïve, benefit-of-the-doubt person she had been when all this began, *even when I wrote my book*, she told herself angrily, this seemed to be an agreement not to pursue the real killers. The letter then went on to other, more specific, local policing issues of the time, of which Fiona had only a vague memory. It was addressed to Mr. George McKenzie, who, Fiona knew, was then the Assistant Deputy Minister of Justice.

"Where could this letter have come from? For this file, I mean?"

"Evan Kirby or Emily Zhang Cheng," Fiona said. "Both of them eventually worked in Justice, but Emily not until a year or so after Zara's murder. But McKenzie could have kept the letter, passed it on to be filed, maybe by Emily, or another staffer, and Emily found it."

"Is any of this any good as evidence?" she asked him. "It's only proof of connections, but no proof of murder."

"A smart lawyer would find a use for it," Steve said. "What about that tape?"

"I don't know," she said. "You have to find a way to transcribe what's on it."

"Okey-dokey," he said, scooping it up and setting it on the computer keyboard.

"One last thing," she said, and felt him glance at her, so that she knew her voice had changed, grown more careful, yet throbbing with subdued excitement.

Last night in the hotel room after she had looked at all the pieces she and Steve had just examined, she had noticed a small lump in one corner of the fold at the bottom of the file folder. She had poked it out from the outside of the cardboard until it came loose, then turned the folder upside down. Out had fallen a gold earring: small, exquisitely fili-greed, a tiny diamond glinting in it, one of the old-style earrings for women who didn't have pierced ears, some sort of discoloration which might only have been dirt or tarnish on the part that clipped against the ear. She had realized that it had to be Zara's earring. It had to be that missing piece from the investigation that the police wouldn't iden-tify, saying only the killer would know what it was. The piece that the awful Margie Martin/Popowich had hinted to her about.

Fiona had felt as if Zara Stanley were standing beside her, a hand on her shoulder, and had to put both hands flat on the cold wood of the desktop to calm herself. Finally she extracted a tissue from her pocket and used it to pick it up the earring, then slid it back to where it had been.

It was evidence that the somebody who had compiled the file had been there that night and surely was a killer – Zara Stanley's killer. She had almost called Roman to come and see. She knew she didn't dare tell Vonnie; telling Vonnie would only put Vonnie in danger. She had known then only that someone had to know about this; she had to tell some-one. But she hadn't been able to focus, her mind had kept slipping back to the horror of the items that sat before her on the desk, what they represented, what she had just touched, and she wondered how Connie Nordstrom had been able to keep this material in her house all these years with this earring in it. Chills had prickled through her body, her fingertips puckering with sudden cold.

Steve was carefully not touching the earring, but gazing at it intently, then reaching past her, slid open a drawer and picked out a magnifying glass. She waited, hands loose on her lap, hardly daring to breathe while he examined the earring through the glass.

"That could be blood," he said, then breathed out softly through his nose. For a long moment they sat side by side, neither moving, the earring lying before them, dull and giving off the aura of weight despite its delicacy. At last, using the tissue she had used, he put it back into the bottom of the file, in the corner of the cardboard fold, just as she had done the night before. Then he stood and stretched, and she moved her chair back around the desk to sit facing him.

She said, "We know Zara dated Fever; we know Fever was friends with Kirby and Hallett and that they are most likely to have made up the gang of three. When Zara's roommate gets enough protection not to be afraid to tell what she knows…"

"And the earring…"

"They'll squeal on each other. That part will be over."

"The conspiracy will be harder, I think," Steve said. "To prove, I mean. Especially with all the powers lined up to prevent it from happening…"

"There were the bribes," Fiona pointed out.

"But were there bribes paid to officials?"

"Do you think the police chief or anybody like that got money?" she asked him, having never thought this herself before.

He shrugged. "More likely at that level it was a you-scratch-my-back-and-I'll-scratch-yours kind of situation." He rubbed his forehead, thinking. "They'll have to appoint a commission; there should be an inquiry," he said. "An inquiry will be easily forced, although you can bet the government will drag its heels as long as it can. That's where the truth will come out."

"If they don't figure out ways to limit the scope of the

inquiry, so that the real meat never gets examined."

He said nothing to that, tapping a paper he held in his hands, his expression gone internal. Finally, he said, "Come with me." He led her back into the reception room and asked Mary Ann, "How's that coffee?"

"Getting old," she said, "But it's still hot." Without another word, preoccupied, he turned, went back into his office and shut the door, then opened it again, and said, "I have to make a phone call. Take care of her," and shut the door again.

"Of course," Mary Ann said, pleasantly, to the closed door, then grinned and shrugged at Fiona. She beckoned her to follow her into a small room that opened off the reception area that she hadn't noticed when they'd come in, and that contained a printer, fax machine, a television set and other items of equipment she hadn't time to identify. But there was also another small sofa and an armchair, as well as a sink and cupboards, and an open door that led into a bathroom. Mary Ann had already placed the coffee and a plate of overly-large oatmeal cookies on the table. "There's sugar on the table and milk in the fridge." In the other room the phone was ringing. She departed quickly, closing the door behind her.

Fiona made use of the cramped bathroom, then threw water on her face, applied makeup, and brushed her hair, then poured herself coffee and ate two cookies. She was feeling somewhat better when the door opened again, and Mary Ann stuck her head around it to say, "Mr. Green is ready for you now."

Fiona followed Mary Ann into Steven's office where he sat behind his desk, a headset clamped over his ear with an attached mouthpiece into which he was speaking.

"Here she is," he said, indicating the phone on his desk. He pushed a button, shoved a land line phone toward her. She picked up the receiver and said, "Fiona Lychenko."

"Ross Williamson. I'm on the national news desk. Here's what I have in mind. I'm putting Steve on this, but I'm going to be putting somebody on the story at this end too, checking things out, doing background. If everything falls into place, we'll need to consult with you on the next step. I understand you have some, uh, material?"

"I do," she said.

"How do you know it's the real thing?"

"The person who gave it to me has had it since 1968."

"We'll have to see the...material. And also, we'll have to get our lawyers involved. Can't have the paper getting sued."

"All right," she said. "I don't like carrying this stuff around. It scares me to death."

"Steve will take care of it," he told her. "All right, put him back on." Fiona indicated to Steve he was to get on line. She put the receiver back on the cradle and waited, while Steve nodded yes, and said okay, okay, before he hung up. He gathered the documents, put them back in the file, but kept out the tape. "They'll go in the safe." He nodded behind her, but when she looked, she saw nothing.

"Where do you live?" he asked her, and when she told him in the south, but she didn't dare go home, he asked her if she had a car.

"Yes, but I can't get it either. I had to turn in my rented car so I'm travelling by cab."

"Is there any place you can go for the afternoon? A friend's maybe?"

"I'm new here. I have no friends and no relatives either.

I could go to a movie, I suppose." She thought for a minute. "No, if you could drive me to a motel nearby then I could spend the day there. I haven't had a shower in a couple of days, and I've been up since two. I need to calm down, maybe rest a little. What happens now?"

"I get to work on background. The guy in Toronto does his job. We talk it over, figure out how to handle this. It's going to take some serious planning. I'll get Mary Ann to drive you over. I'll phone if I need more questions answered." As they were walking together from the room he said, "Have you got cash to pay for the room? If you don't, I'll give it to you. Sign in under a false name. No one will ever find you then. Oh, and tell Mary Ann what it is so she can tell me."

"Please, the file," Fiona said, remembering that it still sat open on his desk.

"It will go into the safe." When she hesitated, he said, looking into her face. "Mrs. Lychenko, you are going to have to trust somebody."

At which, after a split second's hesitation, she nodded. A wave of weakness went through her, her knees nearly collapsing again, for an instant she wasn't sure she could find the strength to put on her coat.

Relief, she realized, that was all, that the file was safe, that she had done the task given her as well as she could, that Zara would at last, after fifty years, receive justice.

Chapter Nineteen

She didn't leave the motel room for the rest of the day. She bathed, washed her hair and wrapped a towel around it, and just as she was considering how she might get some food – it wasn't the sort of place to have room service – her phone rang.

"Steve here," he said. "I'm bringing you over some supper."

When she opened the door to his knock, he was laden with a large take-out food bag, and various other bags and boxes that he emptied carefully onto the sofa and coffee table, before turning to her, and in a celebratory fashion held up a bottle of red wine, a cheap corkscrew and two wine glasses dangling from between his fingers.

"You earned this," he told her so that she had to laugh out loud.

"I did, didn't I? I can't believe it." The take-out boxes contained fried chicken, salad, bread, and there was also a thermos of hot coffee.

"Belongs to Mary Ann," he said. "Her contribution to the cause." One bag left. "Eh, voila!" he said, dumping the contents onto the table. "Books. Don't want you getting bored."

"I need clean clothes," she said tentatively. "I can wash out my underthings tonight and if I'm really lucky, maybe I can get this spot out of my blouse, but…"

"Oh, I forgot." He found another bag on the sofa where he had tossed it and turned it upside down again. A lightweight, pale green pullover slid onto the table. "Mary Ann sent it. She'll bring you fresh undies when she comes back in the morning."

"Mary Ann is a marvel," Fiona said. "You're sure she can be trusted?"

"She wants to be a reporter. She wants that more than she wants anything. She knows if she fucks up she's gone. She gets it right and I'll keep on training her. Anyway," he added, "She's a pretty good person. She won't sell you out. Go ahead, eat, I still have a couple of questions." Fiona set herself up at the round table in the corner, while Steve pulled up the chair on the other side, and opened the wine. He poured her a glass, then a smaller one for himself. "Work to do," he said. "I'll get drunk when I win a National Magazine Award or whatever for this."

They had turned off the overhead light and sat in lamplight. He had a way of grunting when he was thinking as he was now, as if he didn't know he had done so. She liked him; she found him sexy, and was astonished at the realization, and embarrassed as well. He could be my son, she reminded herself; he can't be fifty. But it was the first time since Roman's death that she had felt anything remotely physical for any man. She wasn't sure she wanted such feelings coming back to torment her when there was no hope at all of ever satisfying them again.

"We're going to have to go to Hart City, probably tomorrow," he told her. "Have to talk to some people. Oh, not you! I mean me and the Toronto guy: Doug Hammersmith. He's flying in tonight." She thought then of Connie and Kurt Nordstrom, only yesterday starting out on lonely prairie roads to go back to their farm. She wanted to ask him if he had heard of any car accidents across the border on the way to Ripley, but before she could speak, he continued.

"Oh, I forgot," he said. He produced a pocket-size tape recorder from his pocket and set it on the table between them, pushing the buttons. The tape began to hiss. "It's lousy quality, but the technician did what he could." Startled, Fiona nearly spilled her wine: It was the tape that had been in the file.

Muffled men's voices, two men. Suddenly a loud greeting, a third male voice.

"Recognize the voices?" She shook her head, no. Drinks being poured, one voice close to the recording source, one further away, a third even further away, his voice hardest of all to hear.

"I keep telling you," the third voice, the newcomer, said. "It's packaged up and put away. We're in the clear. We just have to keep our mouths shut."

"Forever," said the middle voice.

"Forever," the other two agreed. The third voice asked, "Anybody question you?"

"Sure," the voice closest to the recorder said. "They asked about you; they got pretty aggressive, but then when a certain person got involved, that was the end of that. Nothing since."

"No matter what happens," the middle voice said, "We have only to keep on denying we know anything about it. We were in different cities that night. What in hell are they talking about."

"They won't be back," the more distant voice said. The voice closest to the receiver asked, "What was that 'missing item' the cops were talking about?"

"I have no idea," the middle voice said, and the farthest voice said, "Oh, cop bullshit, I bet." The voice closest to the receiver was silent. Sound of ice clinking in glasses.

"Okay, this is it," the farthest voice said. "We never meet like this anywhere ever again. That clear? We shouldn't even have risked this. Strictly social stuff from now on."

"We had to meet," the voice closest to the recorder said. "Payoffs."

"I'll take care of that," the distant voice said. "It's done. Forget it."

"How many?" the second voice asked.

"One, so far, or two if you count..." the far-off voice said angrily. There was a long silence. The far-off angry voice said, "I'll leave first," and something about his car, but he was moving away and the sound was too poor to decipher it. The second voice said something about the bathroom. A door shut, a moment passed, then the recorder clicked off.

Steven used his broad thumbnail, to push the 'off' button on the tape recorder. They sat looking at each other.

"That scares me to death," she said.

"But you don't know the voices." She shook her head, no, although the one closest to the recorder had at moments a faintly familiar sound. Could it have been Kirby, before he lost the ability to control his voice? Lots of people would know: secretaries, his children.

"I think you'll be okay here for a couple more days, until we get our ducks in a row."

"I want to go with you to Hart City."

"You'll be safer here."

"I want to go with you."

"Let's talk about it tomorrow," as if they were married, or as if she were a recalcitrant teenager talking to her father. He left then, and she ate her cooling chicken without much relish. Was she really safe? Somehow, she didn't feel safe, would much prefer to be heading out on an airplane, or in Steve's car with him, for familiar territory.

She was in bed drowsing over a movie on television when her phone rang. "Private Caller," it said, no number, no name. She couldn't remember if Vonnie's or Arnie's name and number came up or not when they called. Marian could have had another heart seizure; Vonnie could have news of something or other, or she might need her. But instead, a woman whose voice she didn't recognize spoke crisply into her ear.

"This is Mrs. Edel. Mr. Kirby's housekeeper."

"Yes?" she answered, calmly enough, although once again her heart was speeding up, a sensation that over the last weeks had become all too familiar to her. She reached to the bed table and switched on the light, then put the television on mute.

"Mr. Kirby, I'm sorry to say, has had a bad spell. His condition is grave, I'm afraid. And ..." she paused, as if she weren't sure about what she had to say next. "He has asked me to call you. He wants to talk to you. If he weren't so ill..." She hesitated again. "But one does tend to take seriously what might be a last request. And with Livana...er, gone... and his other two wives not wishing contact..."

"His children?"

"On their way from various corners of the globe," Mrs. Edel replied. This time when she went on a quaver had entered her voice. "I suspect they might not make it in time. Any of them."

Fiona bestirred herself. "I am very sorry, Mrs. Edel. Of course I will come at once. Tell him I'll be there in the morning, or by noon at the latest."

After Fiona had set the receiver gently onto its cradle, she lay back on her pillows trying to sort out the impressions racing through her mind. She felt sure he was one of the killers. Why would she go to him when he called?

The deathbed confession.

A jolt went through her, and she threw off the covers and was standing before she had mentally processed what had just popped into her head. Of course! First the brown envelope, and now, the deathbed confession. She could hardly breathe with excitement. *Is this Zara at work again?* But the thought was gone before she had time to examine it.

I have to tape our meeting, she thought. But, no tape recorder. The one she had used during her reporting days was back in her condo. She could buy a tape recorder once she got to Ripley and hide it in her purse, or tape it onto her abdomen, or something or other. Whatever people did on television shows. Oh yes, they had a van full of the latest recording technology and a raft of agents waiting across the street getting it all on – not tape, but whatever. And hidden television cameras. She paced a bit, drank some water, used the toilet, contemplated leaving at once, decided against it, and finally went back to bed.

She woke at 6:00 a.m. By 6:30 she was showered, coiffed, and dressed in Mary Ann's pale green pullover that actually went rather nicely with her grey pantsuit, not to mention that its looseness would nicely cover a tape recorder. She had decided against checking out; after all, she hoped to be back by late evening, or, if she could get a return flight, maybe even earlier. She was ready to leave when it occurred to her to call her next-door neighbour.

"Carla, sorry to call you so early, but I know you'll be up for work. I'm stuck here in Vancouver and I'm wondering – I've gone without notice to anybody; my sister has had another heart attack – has anybody been looking for me? Or has there been…"

"Break-ins!" Carla interrupted, breathlessly. "I'm so glad you called! Three of the condos were broken into night before last, one on each floor. Yours was one of them. I'm so sorry. They couldn't tell if anything had been taken or not. They left me a number for you to phone so they can… whatever they do." Fiona could hear her fumbling with something, maybe a purse, then she came back on. "A Constable Fairburn. Here's the number." She read it out and Fiona took it down.

"They need a list of what was taken, and you'll have to go to your insurance company although they did tell me the place is mostly just messed up, not really damaged." She paused. "Oh, and they picked the locks – they didn't break the door." Fiona let out a sigh of relief. They were special fire-proof doors that cost a fortune to replace and were a selling point when she'd bought her condo. She tried to think of something normal to say.

"Thank heaven they didn't wreck the place. Do the police have any idea who did it? Did anybody get hurt? Did the police say anything at all about it?"

"Nothing that I know about," Carla told her. "Nobody was home in the other two condos – actually, that one on first? It's empty."

"I'll get right on it, Carla, and thanks very, very much for looking after my place for me. Whoever would have thought…" She could hear herself babbling away on automatic pilot while her real brain, the one that actually thought, was on another track.

Did that mean she could go back home or not? She decided not, at least, not yet. She thanked Carla profusely again and said she would call the police as soon as she got back, which she hoped would be soon, as the medical team had stabilized her sister, and perhaps there wasn't much need for her to stay more than another day or so.

"Oh, and I didn't have any valuables in there. I don't have any valuables," she said, and they both laughed. "TVs and so on – they're replaceable."

Again, she was about to leave when she remembered that she had to get hold of Steve Green to tell him where she was going. She began searching the motel room, trying to find his card, which finally turned up on the floor under the table where they had had supper together. But when she dialed, his phone went straight to voice mail, so she left him her cell number and told him she was going to Ripley and why, and would return as soon as she had seen Evan Kirby.

"And by the way, apparently my condo has been broken into. No worries; you have the only thing that matters. They were wasting their time." As an afterthought, she added, "I'll be careful," even as it occurred to her that she had no idea what being careful might entail. Staying here in the motel, she guessed.

I am being reckless, she told herself, pleased that there was, after all, still room for a seventy-year-old woman to be reckless. She walked out of the room in hopes of finding a cab idling nearby, or failing that, maybe flagging one down on the main road not too far from where she had spent the night. She would go to the airport, get the first available flight to Ripley, and go straight to Kirby's bedside. But first, I will buy a tape recorder.

Indeed, she had thrown caution to the wind, letting this cab take her directly from the Ripley airport to the rest home's massive parking lot, walking boldly in through the front doors, asking for Evan Kirby by name at the desk, telling them, "He asked to see me." The attendant, a young woman this time, petite, blonde, friendly, used an intercom and spoke to someone somewhere in the building.

"Wait here, please." Fiona nodded. Moments passed that she used to look about the very large, hexagonal reception area, with its skylights high above them. It buzzed with people rushing about with trays with medications on them, or carts with pitchers of violently coloured juice and plates of cookies, or pushing wheelchairs with pale, twisted bodies and deep, alert eyes strapped into them, even two hospital beds on wheels with two very pale, gaunt men lolling in them, but she saw nobody she recognized, nobody who looked even faintly dubious. She remembered then that she had forgotten to turn on her cell phone after she'd gotten off the plane, and did so now. At once, it rang. Steve Green hissed into the phone.

"Are you out of your mind? Where the hell are you?"

"In Ripley," she said. "About to go into Kirby's sickroom. Yes, probably."

"I'm sending a friend over to look out for you. Right now."

"Steve," she said, pleading. "You have everything you need to break this whole thing wide open. Nobody would be after me now. It's too late!"

"You're crazy! These are dangerous people! They might just want to teach you a lesson. Have you heard of rage? Have you heard of hate?" Distantly, a chill struck her that she willed away at once. She was calm; she knew what she had to do.

"I'm here to get a deathbed confession," she told him. Her voice sounded firm and clear in her own ears. He made an exasperated sound and hung up. Startled, she closed her cell, and dropped it back into her purse.

"Mrs. Lychenko?" Mrs. Edel had appeared while she'd been preoccupied with her phone.

"This way." The proud Mrs. Edel with her elegant white chignon, her immaculate grooming, her dress that made her look more like the mistress of a big house than its mere housekeeper, was today hard to find under her makeup-less pallor, her coiffure slipping slightly to one side, her dress rumpled, as if she'd slept in it. She walked quickly, her shoes clipping neatly on the hard vinyl floor. Fiona followed her; she didn't think she had ever stood so straight, or moved with such certainty. And best of all, examining herself, she found that she was *not afraid.*

They had moved Kirby to a wing that was suddenly quiet after the steady roar in the main area. Wide doors shut behind them, gowned medical staff wearing masks and with stethoscopes draped around their necks appeared and disappeared. Mrs. Edel pushed open a door, and stood aside for Fiona to enter.

The room was dim, the blinds pulled, only a wall lamp behind the high back of the bed casting some light on the raised figure in the bed. His eyes were closed, his steady tremour had stopped. Tubes came from his nose and from unseen places under the bedcovers and from his arms,

leading to stands holding clear plastic sacks of fluid –
shades of Marian, but Marian was getting better. To her
right a monitor pulsed steadily, its pink and green lines
running ceaselessly across the screen. She turned to Mrs.
Edel, but Mrs. Edel was gone.

"Mr. Kirby," she said. No response. "Mr. Kirby," louder,
touching the hand without the needle in it, and withdraw-
ing again, because it was cold to the touch, and she thought
of Marian and how she had felt as if she'd been in a refrig-
erator. His eyelids flickered, then opened. She was horrified
and fascinated at once by what she saw; as if a malevolent
lizard had been coiled deep inside him all these years and
now, in his final weakness, gazed at her through Kirby's eye
sockets. Black, his eyes were, without light. Inadvertently
she took a short step backwards, tottering, then righted
herself and moved in closer to his bedside again.

"I've come," she said. He laughed, a faint harsh sound,
a whisper.

"You've found that file," he said. "Haven't you." She
didn't answer. "The tape. The earring." She hadn't heard
anyone enter, but a draft touched the back of her neck, her
skin prickled, and she turned quickly.

Blair Fever stood behind her, and in the shadowed room
he seemed about seven feet tall and bulky as a sumo
wrestler. His gleaming too-blonde hair with the light
behind it seemed to give off electricity, and she could feel
her own hair standing up on her head. She put her hand
onto her throat, as if to protect it.

"I knew your husband," he said, his tone conversational.
She waited. "Not the nicest man, was he?" She wanted to
say something breezy and fearless like a tough-talking
dame from forties' films, something such as, *Look who's*

talking, but her vocal chords were frozen. She moistened her lips but no sound came out.

"Is that a threat?" she managed to ask, but her voice sounded so weak that she wished she hadn't spoken. The man on the bed made a strangled sound, and both Fiona and Fever turned their heads toward him.

"He took a bribe," Kirby said. The effort to speak loudly clearly cost him; under the bedclothes his chest was rising and falling too quickly; on the screen the pink line jumped. "You know…what…will…happen if you…"

"If you use the file," Fever said calmly, "No one will pay any attention to you and your findings," his voice dripping with contempt, "Not the slightest bit of attention when it turns out you've been living off dirty money. That maybe you were part of the blackmail scheme. That will be the end of your reputation. You'll probably wind up in court yourself." Was he grinning at her? In the shadows she couldn't quite tell.

"It's too late," she said. "The material has all gone to where it needs to go. It's no use for you to threaten me." Her voice was stronger. He had taken a step toward her; now that he was closer to the bed she could see his face. It was contorted into a sneer, behind which she suddenly saw rage was rising, a rage of such profound depths that she thought she might faint at the realization of what might exist in a human being.

"She was a slut," he said. "She thought I'd marry her. Her! A piece of slime from the backwoods. Cretin parents. Cretin brothers."

"You came from bootleggers!!" Fiona said, too astonished and angry herself to keep quiet. "Why does Zara get murdered and you – scum yourself – marry – what's her name? Rickie the aristocrat."

"Shut your mouth," he said. "It's too late for you, too. It'll be in all the papers in the morning that you've been living off bribe money."

"No," she said, not denying him, but in understanding. "She knew that if your bride-to-be heard about your affair you would lose her, didn't she? That's why she had to be killed. Zara. And you enlisted him," she nodded toward to Kirby panting on the bed like a dog in the sun. "For advice. And Hallett. No wonder he turned into a drunk too. You can't live a normal life with something that terrible on your conscience. I should have started looking at who was wrecked – had every advantage, and still was a drunk, a pill-addicted drunk and a wife-beater. I should have started there."

She put a hand up on each side of her face, while nausea buffeted her so that she fell sideways, her hip resting against Kirby's bed. He made a gurgling sound, but this time neither she nor Fever looked at him.

"You brought them with you to rape her. You brought them so that you would have others from prominent-enough families that if your own father couldn't protect you, the combination of three would do it. You must have threatened the police chief, the prosecutor, who knows who else."

"It was a simpler time," Fever said, his tone reasonable, explanatory. "People respected authority then. Nobody had to bribe a police chief or prosecutor. In those days such men listened to reason. They understood the social order."

Fiona turned to Kirby whose closed eyelids were fluttering as if he were asleep and dreaming, his breath rasping in and out, fast, shallow.

"They didn't know you were going to kill her. But once you'd taken turns raping her, once her skull was broken, it wasn't hard to persuade them what had to be done."

"Why am I standing here listening to this?" Fever asked the figure on the bed, still using the reasonable tone. Kirby muttered something. Fever took a couple of steps and put his ear down to Kirby's face. "What?" he asked.

"The…earring," Kirby said, loudly enough for Fiona to hear. Fever straightened, a sudden movement that made Fiona stand back from the bed and eye the closed door. She could see, even in the dimly lit room, a hard red flush sweeping up Fever's neck and ears. He turned to her.

"He took that earring? He took the earring? He took it?" He turned his head back to Kirby who had opened his eyes wide now, those two black marbles, lightless, in his head, staring at Fever. "You kept it so if you ever needed to you could plant it on me? You could use it to keep me from killing you? You wanted money from me too?" None of this was questioning. His voice was rising.

In one swift movement he struck Kirby with his open palm, hard on the face, but most of the blow seemed to bounce off the tubing coming from his nostrils, and the pillows on which his head lay. Fever, breathing hard now, turned to Fiona. "You have that earring?" She didn't answer, was edging toward the door. He took a step toward her. "You have it." Again, not a question.

She said, "The police have it, or they will by nightfall. I do not have it."

They were standing a few feet apart now, Fiona, too afraid even to try to hide her trembling, Fever calculating, estimating, Kirby rattling and wheezing on the bed, when the door opened carefully. They had expected a nurse or a doctor, but instead a strange man entered.

He was almost as big as Fever, with a dark beard, thick dark hair, wide shoulders under his overcoat, he glanced at Fiona, assessing quickly, then stared at Fever, not even a challenge, not even checking him for danger. This man already knew what Fever was. It appeared that Fever knew what the stranger was too. Without speaking again, Fever lunged past the stranger and out the still-open door.

"Let him go," the stranger said to Fiona in a mild tone. "He has nowhere left to run."

Chapter Twenty

She had been telling Arnie the whole story, it seemed to her for hours, sitting in the hospital waiting room, while across the corridor and behind the double doors her little sister Marian again fought for her life. She had wanted only to distract him while surgeons, cardiologists, kidney specialists, and whoever else consulted and poked and prodded and wheeled in new machines and wheeled out old ones. Arnie had aged over the last weeks and letting this fully register for the first time, she hesitated.

"Arnie," she said. "Arnie. Should I go on?"

"Oh, yes," he said at once, but in a high, soft, un-Arnie-ish tone. "Go on, Fee," and reached out to pat her knee without actually looking at her.

Two days had passed since she had confronted Evan Kirby and Blair Fever in Kirby's hospital room. Shaky as she was, she had insisted to the private investigator, Nasrim Hakim, sent by Steve Green, who had rescued her, that it would be safe now for her to go home to her Calgary condo. He'd driven her to the airport (insisting she wait while he had a private phone conversation, she was sure with Steve Green) and had waited first while she unstrapped the tape recorder she had used in the ward and given it to him, then waited in the restaurant with her, and finally, at the gate, until her flight back to Calgary began to load. She hadn't looked back until she was about to go through the passageway onto the plane, and was in time to see him walk away.

She had wondered if Steve would have another investigator waiting for her at the other end, but when she landed in Calgary, no one approached her, and she didn't see anybody standing around at the luggage carousel who seemed alone and watchful. She had taken a cab to her condo, knocked on Carla's door, picked up all the news about the break-ins, and thanked her for looking out for her, Fiona's, interests.

Carla said, "You were lucky. They picked the lock, I suppose because that's a lot quieter than breaking open the door. You won't have to put on a new door at least." But Fiona gasped when she saw the over-turned chairs, the books on the floor, doors and drawers pulled open in each room and the contents turned every which way. Even the few pictures on the walls hung crookedly, as if the would-be thieves had searched for a hidden safe. Yet nothing seemed to be broken, or otherwise vandalized, and her TV still sat on its console. She could imagine the police officers saying, "They were looking for something," and in the bathroom saw that all her few over-the-counter medications were gone or lay scattered on the counter below. She supposed the police would think the thieves were after the prescription drugs of which most old people had plenty. For the first time, it struck her how deeply fortunate she was at her age to be in such good health.

About 8:00 p.m., as she was sitting trying and failing to read a novel, she heard a knock on her door. She hesitated, her first impulse was to hide, but then, thinking *it is all over now, no point in harming me now,* went to it and without even looking through the peephole, swung the door open to find a strange man standing there, middle-aged, a grey fringe around his shiny scalp, wearing rimless glasses, polished black oxfords, a neat brown tweed overcoat, and carrying a briefcase. He reminded her of an itinerant bible salesman from her childhood.

"Yes?" she said.

"Mrs. Lychenko, I presume?" She nodded. "May I come in?"

"Why? Who are you?"

"I have an urgent message for you," he replied. He spoke slowly, carefully; she felt nothing would dissuade him from entering although he gave off no aura of menace, nor was she exactly afraid of him. She felt in him only a kind of relentlessness, like water dripping evenly on stone, wearing it away, at no visible cost to itself.

"A message from whom?" she asked.

"If I may come inside," he answered and stepped forward so that inadvertently she stepped back. "This will take only a few minutes." As he was already in, Fiona felt she might as well offer him a seat, and she moved in front of him. It occurred to her that perhaps being frightened would be the rational reaction and for an instant she wondered if perhaps he was the television version of a hit man. The kind of person who presented himself as innocuous and mild and would never be suspected, would never even be noticed.

But he had followed her meekly enough to the sofa and sat on it, refusing her offer to take his coat, setting his polished black briefcase on the floor beside him.

"I represent...Let us just say that I represent a number

of high-level officials."

"Officials in what? The government?" He didn't answer her.

"I understand that by this time tomorrow the *National Times* will have broken a story identifying the killers of Zara Stanley, and further, that they will point to a conspiracy of long-standing to keep their identities hidden. That will cause the government to call a Commission of Inquiry, the consequences of which will be destruction of reputations, and most likely, an endless number of people getting in line to sue the government and certain individuals. There will be, at the very least, a scandal of enormous proportions." He spoke quietly, without emotion, as if were explaining the uses to which a donation to the PTA would be put. "An election is expected. This could bring down the government."

"I am sure you are right in all your speculations," Fiona replied politely. She sat across from him in her comfortable armchair with the matching footstool on which the novel she hadn't been reading lay open, face down. He spoke again.

"I am here to dissuade you from doing this."

"It's too late," Fiona told him, then, "Why would you want to do that?"

"Damages might be limited if you were to change your mind."

"There is no reason why I would do that," she told him, faint surprise in her tone.

"Think about it. What good will it do now to ruin the reputations of civil servants and officials who worked their whole lives for the good of the public? Including that of your late husband. It will break hearts, cause scandal after scandal that will surely result in deaths by suicide. Or even a rash of murders, when men who've been incarcerated learn who has kept them in prison wrongly for many years and go after those who were responsible. Families will be torn apart. You can depend on that," he said, as if he thought she was about to argue with him. He cleared his throat gently. Fiona could feel her face and hands, even the skin on her chest heating.

"I'm afraid that none of that matters," she said.

"Do-gooders like yourself always say that. Whistle-blowers." He pronounced the last words in a faintly contemptuous tone, but also as if it amused him to say it. "They have to keep saying it to themselves as they witness the profound damage their self-righteous, pointless revelations have caused. Further," he said, "If you refuse to think of the more personal consequences, think of the taxpayers of the province. These revelations, if pursued, will cost the province many millions of dollars. Litigation will go on for the next twenty or more years. Our courts will be tied up; most of our resources will be spent. Surely there are more pressing matters. All of this happening because of a fifty-year-old murder. Do you really think that all that will follow if you insist on pursuing this course will bring her back to life? Even her parents are dead. Who will be relieved by this?"

Fiona watched him, his patient arguing reaching deep inside her so that she couldn't not listen. Could not help but wonder if he was right, thinking again of Ibsen's play, *Enemy of the People*, and the doctor who was so sure he was right that he didn't care about the costs of his being right. Her visitor went on in the same quiet, patient tone.

"It will take fifty years for the province to recover from

this. Isn't this perhaps taking on more responsibility than you can bear? What about your own future? I am told that you are living on money that your husband extorted – *extorted* – to stop him from doing the very thing you are doing. Because of this, your reputation too will be utterly destroyed. If you are seeking fame and fortune with this revelation, you will not achieve it. You will instead destroy what is left of your life."

He sat quietly; during the whole long speech he hadn't moved his hands once, nor touched the briefcase that sat by his knee. In fact, it seemed to her that nothing but his small mouth had moved, and that only minimally, only enough to form words and send them out across the still air to her half-reluctant, half-fascinated ears.

"And so," she said slowly, "You are offering me, what?"

"Ah," he said, and an amused expression twisted his lips. "I offer you nothing – money being unlikely to per-suade someone of your…type, although if you say so, it is available – only the opportunity to stop this before it becomes unstoppable, a juggernaut that will crush every-thing before it, including, or even especially, you. I offer you the opportunity to save yourself."

She could now see if she did what he asked, what would happen next. Press releases, solemn, sorrowful in tone, would pour out. Names of those long dead would be men-tioned with censure. Forgiveness of those who could not defend themselves would be asked for. The government in the person of certain honourable, trusted men would take care of the matter. The public need not worry; things would be put back on track, and such a long-ago, "bad old days," deviance from the true path would never happen again. Not On My Watch. For a long moment they looked at each other, he with that same air of unflappable agelessness, Fiona listening to his arguments, ticking them off mentally, one by one.

Then she shook her head, slowly, her lips pressed together, not so much to deny him, as to confirm her own decision.

"Sometimes," she told him, "sometimes actions have to be taken in support of the good, in defiance of the muck that creeps everywhere, and always has, that we must keep back at every turn. If we don't sometimes do that, say *this far and no further*, we add more filth to that relentless, creeping tide of muck. We slowly crucify our own humanity." She was breathing heavily.

"Or to be less abstract: People we trusted to work for our good, people who swore to do so lied themselves and supported not only lying, stealing and bribery, but murder. *Do you think we can just let that go?*"

She found she was shaking, but this time with a fury so enormous that it brought her to her feet. It was as if she were swelling, getting taller and wider, altogether more formidable physically; she saw his eyes widen. "You are beyond despicable," she said, meaning all of them, the men who took the oaths of office and the salaries and swore to be honourable, and were not. He did not reply, but rose slowly, keeping his eyes on her face until he turned away, not forgetting to drop a card on her table as he passed it on his way out.

Perhaps fifteen minutes later there had been another knock on her door.

"I strode to the door," she said to Arnie. "I positively strode and I threw open the door as if to invite in an invading army."

"But who was it?" Arnie asked.

"Nasrim Hakim again." She had to laugh, but in delight. "Steve Green had kept him on guard outside my building. Can you believe it? All the time I thought I was safe, that it was over."

"Really, Mrs. Lychenko," he had said to her. "When I saw him come in I honestly didn't realize he would be looking for you. I thought he was a bill collector or something. But a few minutes after he left, it dawned on me who he was. I'm so sorry. Are you okay?"

"Totally," she told him, breaking out in a grin so wide her face felt as if it might split.

She repeated these words to Arnie, or as near a version of them as she could remember, as seemed appropriate under the circumstances, as they sat facing each other in the hard plastic chairs of the waiting room across the hall from the ICU in Vancouver, where drastic measures were being taken once again to save Marian's life, and sheets of rain ran down the one window to the outside. It cast a watery light across all of them seated in small clusters or scattered alone around the dreary room. Far off down the corridor bells dinged and distant voices, faintly heard, carried the ring of urgency.

"Do you think I'm right?" she asked him. If Roman were alive – but Roman was involved. She wouldn't have been able to ask him. He would have done what he could to stop her, without telling her why. It would have ended their marriage. What marriage? she asked, surprising herself with her sudden, new bitterness. And yet, it felt good to be angry at last.

Arnie said, "I can't tell if you're right or not. Her killers should be brought to justice. Of that there is no doubt, but can the one be done without the other? Could the train wreck of a scandal be avoided?" Fiona sat up straight, gave a sound that might have been a laugh or a snort.

"I bet that's what the people involved are pouring over right now. How to do the one without doing the other."

"Who to scapegoat," Arnie said. He moved back, let his head rest on the wall above his chairback. "How to minimize the damages."

"What records to destroy. Armies of lawyers are being hired, I bet."

He sighed loudly, his thick hands lying loose on his lap. He had closed his eyes.

"Probably best not to second guess yourself," he told her. In fact, he seemed less than interested. She thought of Marian, wiped a hand across her face, and sat up straight.

"You phoned within the hour after he left," she told him. "I didn't have time to think about it. I came on the run. I didn't think Marian would still…be here when I got here." She reached with both hands and covered one of his with them.

Chapter Twenty-one

The first night after Marian's death, ensconced in the guest room, surrounded by Marian's knick-knacks, and lying under Marian's flowered quilt, Fiona lay awake thinking of their childhoods together, remembering in detail things such as Marian's fine, thin, pale red hair when she was a child, of how she loved to run, and of Fiona often being sent to chase after her, before she ran giggling out into a street, or lost herself by running too far from home. Her mind shifted to Marian's wedding day. How happy she was, how lovely, so trim and petite, saying her vows in the chapel in front of a hundred guests, the trusting, fully loving way she had looked up at Arnie when he bent down to kiss her in front of everyone. She thought of her own marriage; only their parents and Marian and Arnie present, plus Roman's then best-friend and best man – who had shortly disappeared from their lives, she never knew why – in a judge's office at City Hall. Why was that? Because we weren't kids anymore and a huge expensive wedding obviously made no sense. Her mind shifted to Roman's inexplicable betrayals.

This led her, inevitably, to the fact that the newspaper story would be, by now, in the hands of people from one end of the country to the other, that even now she was being reviled or praised by people she had never met and never would meet. It was an odd feeling, like thinking about a dream, that all over the country people were talking about what had been her life for so long, and that she lay quietly in an anonymous bedroom on the western edge of the country, next to the eternal sea. She shivered at the thought of having to go home soon to face it all, would gladly stay on forever, huddled under her sister's quilt, in the safety of her brother-in-law's house.

First Greg and then Angela had arrived, Angela seeming faintly indignant, her director having given her no choice in the matter, having put her on the plane himself, and sent her home for her mother's funeral, and to be a support to her father. Fiona suspected she wouldn't be much of a support to Arnie, but maybe Greg could do something with her. Arnie walked through the house at all hours, a dazed expression on his face, touching something, moving on, touching something else. Often Fiona or Greg or Angela would find him in the kitchen making himself a cup of instant coffee, or tea, most of which he failed to drink wandering off to walk again through the house, or to stand, his hands in his pockets, gazing out the living room window at nothing in particular. It rained, cleared briefly, rained again, and if they stepped outside, ravens harangued them from the shelter of the massive cedars in the steep backyard.

In the morning Greg said, "I can't leave him like this, but I can't stay either. I'm going to have to bring him with me back to London. Maybe the change will wake him up or something." He was not so much exasperated at his father, Fiona thought, as infinitely pained by the sight of his grief. "I have a lot of friends there; they'll take him out, show him around when I'm working. We can go on outings,

maybe even travel a bit in England or on the continent…"
His voice trailed away, as if the futility of all of this had
struck him, that none of it would bring back Marian or
make his father's life, in the end, any less empty.

Fiona said, "I think you should find him a grief counselor too. I am going to do that for myself when I get back
to Calgary." She hadn't known she was going to do that
until she heard herself say it. She didn't correct herself.

"What's that?" Angela asked. She was leaning against the
door jamb that led down the hall to the bedrooms, barely
in the room with them. For the first time in years Fiona
noticed what a small woman Angela was, small and sort of
chunky, with Marian's fly-away red hair, but curly where
Marian's had been straight. She wore no make-up, was in
faded jeans that appeared to Fiona none too clean, the
rumpled T-shirt she had arrived in, and on her feet some
sort of brightly-embroidered felt boots. She looked, more
than anything, simply lost.

"Just somebody neutral who will listen to anything you
have to say. A safety valve, if nothing else."

"Why are *you* going?" Angela asked. "Uncle Roman has
been dead for over a year now." She sounded belligerent,
faintly contemptuous.

"It doesn't get better," Fiona said, realizing this now,
with some puzzlement. "It doesn't seem to get better until
you…I don't know…figure out the truth about it?" She
hated the sound of the question marks at the end of her
own statements. Angela shrugged, pushed herself from the
wall where she'd been leaning, came into the room, and
threw herself onto the sofa.

Fiona could hear her cell phone ringing down the hall
in the bedroom where she had left it on her bed. Reporter

after reporter calling her; Steven Green and his editor, Ross Williamson; the police wanting to interview her. She wondered, in fact expected, there would also be a call from Vonnie. That one she would return.

From the sofa, not looking at anyone, Angela muttered, "I need to get back to work."

Greg said, "Don't be an idiot. Your director gave you some months off and don't try to tell me he didn't. Why don't you stop trying to save other people and save yourself first?"

Angrily, he turned away to go into the kitchen. Angela blinked rapidly several times. Abruptly, to Fiona, she seemed not the hardened, selfish soul-saver she had been for years, but a small girl trying hard not to cry. Greg could be heard banging the kettle on the stove, opening a cupboard door, slamming it shut. Fiona sighed. This was all too much. Yet she couldn't leave Angela to fend for herself, when her brother had no patience with her and her father was still dazed from the blow he had had.

"Your dad will get over this," she told Angela. "He needs time," and could have kicked herself for the bland clichés that came out of her mouth. Angela stood, one hand covering her eyes, her mouth quivering. Fiona went to her, and as she hadn't in years, decades, put her arms around her niece, pulling her close to her, one palm cupping the back of small Angela's head, the way a mother cups her baby's warm skull, protectively, out of love. "Your father really does need you here, dear," she told her. "You must be here for him; you must help him."

Angela stood quietly for a second before she pulled away, accepting the ever-present tissue Fiona offered her. "Let him comfort you," she told Angela, whether Angela wanted to hear it or not. "You've lost your mother. Think how that must make him suffer, to think that you've lost her too. Let him help you. It will take him out of his own grief for a bit." Angela was blowing her nose, making some other sound too, that might have been agreement. Or not. She wandered away, wiping her face with the tissue.

Cures don't come that easily, Fiona told herself, thinking of her own none-too-successful journey since she had lost Roman. I have had to cope with revelations, she told herself; I have had to deal with the fact that my marriage was nothing of what I thought it was. That I've been a dupe and a fool; that I was married to a liar and a betrayer. There, she had said it, if only to herself.

Satisfaction, though, lasted only a moment, and was followed at once by guilt for having called her dead husband names, and then by confusion, because hadn't they lived together in harmony for many years? Hadn't she willingly let him go his way and wasn't she therefore at least partly to blame for his deceptions? That she had allowed them to happen because she didn't care enough to stop them? Stop them! I didn't even know they were happening. The liar! And round and round she went again, until she was holding her head in her hands, turning this way and then that, trying her best to stop the noise, to find a clear path where no ideas warred, and no stabs of pain shot through her.

She lay awake most of the next night too, aware that down the hall Arnold was almost certainly awake too. She thought back over the years of her adulthood: I shut down after I got fired. I decided not to try to get another job, and then I got that idea to write a book about Zara, and for a few years there, I had an interest in life again, although Roman wanted nothing to do with it, wouldn't even let me talk to him about it. But, no, she thought. Long before that. When?

How lonely she'd been that month while Roman was gone to China, drifting around the house much as Arnie was doing now. Idle, bored, trying to find ways to keep herself busy. Writing her column, visiting Vonnie, helping Vonnie occasionally with paperwork. And I never woke up, she thought. I simply never woke up again. Not really. Roman came back, and a coolness that I didn't recognize or understand seemed to have settled between us, and I could tell he liked me asleep. Not questioning him, not asking him to tell me about his life, what he was up to on his countless trips here and there. Always returning, bringing me a beautiful gift, kissing me, continuing our marital relations, never passionate, and after the China trip, even less so.

We carried on, she thought. I saw no evidence of anything exciting going on in his life that excluded me, and I told him about whatever I was up to. I told him over breakfast while he glanced through the paper, or over dinner on the rare occasions when he was home, and he drank glass after glass of wine, growing steadily more morose and silent, until I grew silent too. And went to get my novel to spend the evening reading while he worked in his office or talked on the phone. I thought it was a good, calm married life. I thought I was lucky.

Then I got fired. I never really got over that blow; I'm still not over it. I'll never get over it.

Oh, stop that, she told herself; stop hoarding that old hurt. It's time to grow up. She threw herself onto her side and pounded her pillow. It's time to wake up. The words floated into her mind, almost as if someone had spoken them in her ear. But she was so drowsy she couldn't think, and then she was in a deep, dreamless sleep, waking hours later to a soft knocking on her door, Angela sent by Arnie to wake her, and behind her, household noises being made, and Greg and Arnie talking to each other in the kitchen. She remembered that today was the day of her little sister's funeral.

Chapter Twenty-two

B y the time she returned to Calgary, she knew that Evan Kirby had died. As nearly as she could tell, not long after Blair Fever, Nasrim Hakim, and Fiona had left him gurgling and gasping on his hospital bed, had left him without a glance back, or a fare-thee-well, as her mother would have said. No one knew for sure, apparently, exactly what killed people with Parkinson's Disease, or there might be this cause or that cause in individual cases. What did it matter? Blair Fever had been arrested; he had at once turned on Andrew Hallett who was also now in custody, had apparently been lurking in the nursing home atrium while Fiona and Fever confronted each other, although Fiona hadn't seen him there, not even when she'd searched the atrium with her eyes.

She saw them both being arrested on television and supposed that the police had told Steve Green or someone in the press that this was going to happen so that the public could see them doing their job, or to humiliate the men who had for so long escaped them, and had first humiliated them. Old men, the two of them. Expensively dressed, not bad-looking, grim-faced and silent. Even Fever's instantly-identifiable, glowing near-pompadour was flattened and looked thin and grey in the photo.

Her voice mail was full: three calls from the Ripley

police asking her to come to the station for an interview; two calls from a national television program asking to interview her; several calls from radio stations around the country wanting to talk to her; a number of calls from strangers either threatening her, or wanting her to call them at once as they had more information that they wanted to give her; a call from an editor at a publishing company in Toronto; and one from a foundation specializing in helping victims of crime asking her to be a guest speaker at a national convention. When she heard the last one, she dropped the phone back on the receiver as if it were hot, and stood, paralyzed, while her mind raced back and forth. This was what she had tried so hard to avoid, had succeeded during the days she was in Vancouver. No more; she would have to act.

She would call a lawyer, and she would call a grief counselor. Lawyer first. But who? She couldn't think of anyone she knew in Calgary who was a lawyer or who had a lawyer relative. Rudy, she thought. Rudy Kovalenko. Best of all, he practiced in Ripley. When at last she had found his office number and dialed, and had persuaded his assistant to let her talk to him, he responded eagerly, at once.

"Fiona! I've been seeing your name in the paper and hearing it on the news! Are you all right? How are you handling all this? I know you were never one for liking a fuss." She told him her situation, that she felt she couldn't go to the police interview without a lawyer, and he was the only one she knew, and that he was located in Ripley was a bonus.

"I may be a suspect in Livana Kirby's murder."

"What? Why on earth do you think that? Did the police say that?"

"I was there visiting her in the hours before her murder." She hesitated. "No, the message the police left on my machine didn't say anything like that."

"Now wait," Rudy said. "The latest news in the paper says Andrew Hallett killed her."

"How do they…" As the news that she wasn't a suspect after all sank in, she was too surprised and puzzled to feel relief.

"The paper says that Mrs. Kirby had a cousin who lived down the hall from her and who kept an eye on her. She reported to the police that you had been there – no, your name isn't mentioned, but I assume it was you – but that Mrs. Welland spoke to Livana after you left. It was within the hour of your visit that a man knocked on her door and apparently when she opened the door a crack with the chain on, he simply shoved the door, broke the chain and was in. Mrs. Welland was vacuuming and heard a noise, or perhaps it was the gunshot she heard, but wasn't sure, then later thought she should check on her cousin and found Mrs. Kirby dead."

"There was someone parked on the street in front of her building when I went in. I thought he was watching me. I couldn't see his face. When I came out and drove away, he followed me."

"And then went back and killed her. No, it had to be Hallett. Maybe Hallett was the man who followed you. Maybe there was only one man."

"How did the police know it was him?"

"Somebody saw him at her door, maybe? The building would have security cameras, of course. But no, here, it says a passer-by saw a small older man with silver hair running out of the building – I bet he got rattled – to his car and burning rubber out of there. The bystander took his license number. Can you believe that!"

"He must have been watching a lot of cop shows on TV," Fiona said, picturing the scene with something halfway between horror and amusement.

A silence followed, judging by the crackle, Rudy still re-reading the newspaper account, and Fiona trying to come to terms with the frightening fact that almost certainly Hallett had been watching her, and how lucky she felt that he had not tried to kill her too. Although why he hadn't she couldn't quite determine. Could it be that they were planning it but just didn't get the chance before everything blew up in their faces?

It struck her that Kirby hadn't called her in order to confess to her; Fever had insisted that he do it. Fever was setting her up so that Hallett could wipe her out on her way to wherever she would go from the nursing home. Steve had warned her, and she had gone anyway.

It occurred to her that people would say she was brave; I was *not* brave. I was afraid, but I was determined not to let a bunch of devious thugs get the better of me. But why? It was something closer to pride – pride, and my anger at what had been done to Zara who had had the world before her, and who could not rest in peace. *I did it for women.* Then, she thought, I will write a book about all this, and a cloud that had been hovering over her lifted off.

"I would be honoured to represent you," Rudy said at once, as if he'd already thought of this possibility and had decided to help her before she'd even called. "I'll familiarize myself with the situation and I'll make an appointment for us both to go the police station. I know some of the boys there," he said. "We went to high school with a couple of them." She gave him the name of the detective who had been calling her. "You'll have to come to Ripley, of course," he said. "What if I make the appointment for next week? That will give you a few days to settle in at home before you have to come here. And we'll need to have a long talk, also. I need to know just what your involvement was in all this. The truth," he added, chuckling. "Not just what the papers say."

Then she called Vonnie and to her surprise Vonnie answered on the second ring.

"Your name is everywhere, in all the papers, on the radio, the TV, nobody knows where you are and everybody wants to talk to you. How are you going to handle this? Fiona, I can't believe this! Why didn't you tell me what you were up to!"

She threw herself into her favourite chair, put up her feet and her head back. "I would have told you if I'd actually known," she said.

"Well, now you know and I want to hear all about it."

"I'm coming to Ripley next week."

"What for?"

"To be interviewed by the Ripley police."

"You better get yourself a lawyer."

"I did," she said, smugly, pleased with herself. "Why don't you come here tonight or tomorrow morning and we can go back to Ripley together next week? I could use a friendly face around here."

"You could probably use a press secretary," Vonnie said. "Or whatever they call them today. Publicist. No, you don't need publicity, you need someone to manage the requests. Am I right?"

"I guess so," Fiona said. "There are a bunch of calls from

the media on my phone."

"I'll be there tomorrow by noon. Don't answer a single one until I get there. I'll manage all of that for you."

Fiona was so relieved she almost cried. "That is so great," she told her friend. "I really do need you." And was surprised, for how often in her life since she had said it to Keith who had dumped her back when she was twenty? She couldn't think of a single time. Yet, always, every single day, she had needed someone.

When she rose the next morning early, refreshed and for once calm, the phone at her bedside was ringing. She thought at once, Marian! But Marian was dead, Marian had died. She was already saying, "Hello," caught between a strange, crackling excitement that had come out of nowhere, and confusion with so much cycling through her head at once, being sorted, discarded, kept.

"Mrs. Lychenko?" a woman's voiced asked. It wasn't a voice she recognized. Now what?

"Yes, this is she," she said, the sound coming out closer to a croak so that she cleared her throat.

"I am… This is Melody Lithgow speaking. I am Livana Kirby's daughter."

"How very nice to hear from you," Fiona said, then, remembering, pulling herself to a sitting position. "I am so sorry about your mother."

"Thank you," Melody said. "I am wondering if I might come to see you."

"Certainly, whenever you're in Calgary, I'd be delighted to see you. Although I didn't know your parents at all well. I had just met them when…"

"I know," Melody said, brusquely. "As it happens, I am in Calgary now. I have come here expressly to see you. Have you any free time today?" Startled, Fiona's first thought was what a mess her hair was, or would be, she was sure, when she looked in the mirror. "My flight out isn't until tonight, so if you could see me later this morning, or in the early afternoon, that would be best." Her manner was firm, brooking no objection, not that Fiona was currently planning to make any. She felt an obligation to see Livana's daughter, although why she was not at all sure.

They settled on eleven, only two hours away. By ten-thirty she had dressed, fixed her hair, put on makeup, tidied the living area, made a pot of coffee, and was waiting impatiently, if somewhat nervously, for her guest to arrive. She had not allowed herself to think what Melody's reason for wanting to see her might be, unless Livana had further material for her that she hadn't given her, or maybe there was a secret memoir, or…she couldn't think what. Just before the phone rang, and she would have to unlock the downstairs door for Melody, she realized that Melody had described herself as Livana's daughter; she had never said she was Evan Kirby's daughter.

Melody Kirby Lithgow was almost as tall as Fiona, and was, not unexpectedly, slim, well-coiffed, and fashionably dressed in a loose coat of soft beige wool tied at the waist, matching knee-high pale suede boots, and a leopard-printed scarf draped around her neck. She was attractive too, although not as attractive as her mother had been. She had her father's pale colouring, but with her mother's delicate chin and pretty mouth.

"You'll be wondering why I want to see you." Fiona nodded, sitting across from her in her favourite armchair, the footstool pushed aside. She had dressed carefully in her new trim black slacks and pale blue cashmere sweater set. Morning sun shone in all along the east wall, striking Melody's light brown hair and making it shine. "It…it's a hard thing to say." She appeared surprised by this discovery, and gave a flummoxed laugh, then sobered. "It's this." Fiona waited. "You knew that my mother had an affair with your husband?"

"How did you know?" Fiona asked, surprised.

"Cousin Olga told me. Olga Welland. She thought it was time I knew and with mother dead and my…erstwhile… father dead and – I can hardly say it – a murderer the whole time I knew him, she thought I should know the whole story."

"The – story," Fiona heard herself say in a low voice, but she knew the answer before Melody spoke it.

"That your husband, Roman, is my birth father." She paused, as if to give Fiona time to collect herself. "That makes you…I mean…If you want to be…You are my step-mother." Fiona was speechless, feeling heat rushing through her body, wanting to say *yes* without consideration; wanting to scream *No* at the same time; all her old fears and wants and memories assailing her at the same time.

"Are you all right?" Melody asked her. "Is it okay that I told you?"

That pounding heart again, that overwhelming desire to burst into tears, that refusal to allow it. "I am…just fine," she told Melody. "I am…thrilled." She was amazed to discover that indeed, of all the competing emotions warring inside her, pleasure at this new young person entering her life, as someone potentially close to her, was the best news she had had in years.

Then she thought of Roman who had betrayed her, that she ought to have nothing to do with this woman, who was no blood relation of hers. Sobering, she and Melody gazed across the sunlit space between them. Out on the street school children's voices could be heard, calling and laughing, and the brakes of school buses droned and squealed.

I cannot undo what Roman has done, she said to herself. I must accept it. And then she took note of the fact that Roman had persuaded Livana to name their child Melody. *In some crazy way*, she thought, *I know he did that; he did it for me. Melody is the child I couldn't have — we couldn't have.*

As soon as they arrived from the airport at Fiona's condo, Vonnie insisted that they go shopping.

"You have to have a decent wardrobe if you're going to be on national television. You have to look crisp and prosperous for your police interview. Who is your lawyer?"

Fiona gave an embarrassed smile. "Rudy Kovalenko. Who says I'm going to be on national television?"

"You dog!" Vonnie shouted. "Good for you!" Ignoring Fiona's remark about television.

"It's nothing like that," Fiona insisted. "He's the only lawyer I know in Ripley, and he knew all of us. He knew Zara, he knows you…"

"Okay," Vonnie said. "We'll just drop that. All right? But that's another reason that the wardrobe of yours will not do. What's your PIN to get into those phone messages? And turn that ringer back on again. I know your tricks." She extracted a notepad and pen from inside her capacious handbag and reached for the phone. Fiona got up and took

Vonnie's bag from the foyer where they had left it, and put it in the guest bedroom. Vonnie called, "And turn on your laptop. There'll be messages there, too."

"There'll be vile messages there," Fiona said.

"Never mind. Don't read them. I'll deal with them," Vonnie commanded. But Fiona's cell was ringing again. This time it was Rudy calling with a date and time for the interview at the police station.

It took them all the next day for Vonnie to be satisfied that Fiona had marginally enough chic clothing for the onslaught ahead of her. As well, a schedule was shaping up under Vonnie's masterful handling, and she and Rudy agreed together, without Fiona's input, who she should talk to and who she shouldn't, and when all of this should happen. No media interviews until after the police interview, he told Vonnie, who relayed this to Fiona. None until I've got the matter in hand. Among other things, though, Vonnie made her say yes to the invitation to be keynote speaker, although Fiona gasped at the suggestion, and resisted for quite a while. It wasn't until Vonnie pointed out that she had months to get an address ready, and furthermore, that she could cancel any time.

Fiona thought, is this what I wanted? Did I want to be famous all along and I was too scared of failing, of making a fool of myself, to even try? But when she thought about it, *the void* seemed to have closed and vanished. She wondered how long it would take her to recover from the past few months, then to get back enough confidence to handle her own affairs. Already she was beginning to feel a faint but undeniable interest in the decisions Vonnie was making for her. I must be getting better, she told herself, with some surprise, at realizing that her very resistance to the facts of her own life now, with Roman gone, was a kind of illness – or so it seemed to her.

But Melody was always in the back of her mind. She had driven her to the airport that evening, studying Melody with rising excitement, listening to her calm way of speaking, so precise and clever, enjoying her quick sense of humour, her sometimes-devastating wit. There was so much to digest, the largest part being the understanding that Roman hadn't pursued adoption, or any medical method of Fiona's becoming pregnant, because he had a child already. Or finally. How she should feel about this still being a quandary to her. No, the biggest thing to digest was that she now had a daughter – yes, a step-daughter – but this girl was parentless and even in her mid-thirties she needed to know there was a parent somewhere, and that is me, Fiona thought. I am now her...her...mother. And the surge of joy that raced through her body from her toes to her fingertips and the crown of her head almost caused her to drive off the road.

Chapter Twenty-three

It had been decided to hold the government Commission of Inquiry in Hart City rather than in Ripley, which meant that Rudy had had to designate a Hart City lawyer to represent Fiona's interests most of the time. He had phoned to tell her when a retired judge, one William Rappaport, was appointed to run the inquiry, and not too long after that, he had emailed her the official list of people who were to appear before the commission: besides her own name, and those of the expected senior police officers from Ripley, representatives of the Attorney-General's office, and the long-retired coroner. Emily Cheng was also on the list, as was Connie Nordstrom and Delphine Chartrand Jellinek, the roommate who had been cold as ice and would say nothing. So was Malcolm Kipp.

There had been a lot of wrangling over the parameters of the commission, called officially *A Commission of Inquiry into the Investigation of the Murder of Zara Jean Stanley*. Rudy explained that such a commission couldn't lay charges of any kind against anyone, nor find people guilty of wrongdoing, such steps being up to the police and the law courts. The commission hoped mainly to discover if, indeed, anyone had attempted to stop the police from doing their job, or to divert them from doing so, or if they had failed of their own accord to do it properly and thoroughly, and whether, if any of this had occurred, there had also been a cover-up of such attempts or failures, a conspiracy at work. Further, if so, who was involved, and why.

He also reported, that the commission's work would be made more difficult in the first place by the fact that so many people in both the police department and the government who might have had relevant information, were dead, including several of the original witnesses at the coroner's inquest. Second, it was being slowly discovered, to everyone's chagrin if not downright horror, at the very least profound regret, a certain number of paper documents had been mislaid or lost, their evident disappearance making it more difficult to find a full paper trail.

Rudy said, dryly, to Fiona, "They can't decide if some of those papers disappeared because there was a flood, or if it was a fire. Depends on who you ask." He gave a long, throaty chuckle, expressing, Fiona guessed, something that wasn't really amusement.

"I can't say I'm surprised," Fiona had responded. "Of course certain relevant documents would have disappeared. Sorry if I sound bitter."

"Cheer up," Rudy told her. "Look at it this way. The killers are finally in jail. Did you really expect more?"

Blair Fever and Andy Hallett had both been arrested, but the prosecutors had decided that DNA would be necessary to make their case against the men unassailable. To that end samples from the still preserved bedsheets, pillow case, and Zara's nightgown, had been sent off to labs, no one knew precisely where, and, according to the police, warrants were being obtained to take DNA samples from the accused. Months had passed.

When there was no result revealed, and messages from the police suggested some sort of unspecified inconclusiveness, Zara's remaining brother had given permission for her remains to be exhumed. More months passed, and then it was revealed that DNA samples from the material in her vaginal area, and from under her fingernails matched the DNA samples of Blair Fever and Andrew Hallett. Case closed, as far as those two were concerned. Evan Kirby's case had already been closed with his death, but his DNA also matched the material.

"I hoped for more," Fiona said. "Such as why it has taken fifty years to solve the crime."

"Well, there still might be more. We can't write the whole Commission off this soon. Rappaport is a good judge and an honest man. He'll do what he can."

Two days before the morning she was to appear herself, more than a year after she had first engaged him, Rudy Kovalenko drove her to Hart City in order to represent her in person, and arranged to have dinner with her at her hotel. Six months into their lawyer-client arrangement he had invited her to his wedding. This hadn't exactly come as a surprise to Fiona, as he had made reference once or twice to 'Belinda' without explaining who she was. It seemed to Fiona that Vonnie was more put out by this news than she was, especially when Belinda turned out to be a tall, slender, attractive woman in her forties, this to Rudy's seventy. Fiona didn't want to admit it herself, but she had felt a faint twinge of jealousy when the invitation came, followed by a – admit it, Fiona – creeping disappointment mixed, once she had had time to absorb this, with a certain surprising, undeniable relief.

The hotel dining room was large, the lighting low, the white tablecloths starched and gleaming, the glassware and silver cutlery polished and glinting light. Roman had liked places like this too, although Fiona preferred cafés she thought of privately as 'funky' bistro-type places. She thought now, I guess I'm too old for funky.

She had said this to Melody when she had spent two weeks with her in New York in the months following their initial meeting, and Melody had thrown herself into the task of helping Fiona become, as she put it, "casually elegant. The perfect style for you, Fiona." Together they had done some shopping, but not much, Fiona being intimidated by the big city stores and styles. Mostly they had gone sightseeing, lunched and gone out to dinner, to Broadway shows, to lectures at the Metropolitan Museum of Art and once, a concert in Carnegie Hall, struggling to become comfortable with each other. Melody told her she had married her college sweetheart; they had divorced after only two years.

"No children, no regrets," Melody told her, but she seemed sad about it.

"Have children," Fiona told her, then, embarrassed, had said, "I mean…"

"For comfort in my old age?"

"And middle age," Fiona answered. "And young middle age." Unexpectedly, she found tears had sprung into her eyes. "I am so glad to have found you."

Fiona had been back one more time after that for a week. This time they had forgone the shopping and city sightseeing in favour of long walks in Central Park, and drives out into the countryside and even to the seaside.

Fiona had spent much time telling Melody about her father, about Roman's family and their history in Canada, as well as the little she knew of their European past. In doing so she had found herself surprisingly recovering much of her feeling for Roman, many memories of their long years together that she had blotted out after his death.

One morning, out of the blue, as she sipped her coffee across from Melody in her New York apartment, she thought, *All those years together; he is part of me forever, like it or not.* He had named her Melody: Fiona was slowly suffused by a fragile warmth, as if he were there beside her, bending to kiss her cheek in love.

As soon as Fiona was free of the Commission, she and Melody planned a trip into the bosom of Roman's family so that Melody might meet her relatives, see where her father had come from, and thus learn more than even Fiona could tell her about who she was. It amazed Fiona how happy Melody made her, how quickly Melody had taken over her heart. I must have been ready for a daughter, she told herself; it took me long enough.

Rudy said, "Fiona, I think we should go to the late showing of Marigold Martin's film."

"What?" Fiona said. "I didn't know it was released."

"Just this week," Rudy told her. "I was driving past that big cinema and there it was, down at the bottom of the list. Wouldn't you like to see it?"

"Marigold couldn't wait to tell me that she had stolen my book to base her film on, and now she doesn't bother to call when the film is finished."

"You've become more famous than she is," Rudy said,

laughing. "She doesn't want you to upstage her. She can't claim to be years younger than you anymore. She can't upstage you with her good looks anymore, either," he added, looking admiringly into Fiona's face. He laughed gently, looked away, then lifted his wineglass.

"I think she didn't let me know because, when she was about to start shooting, she claimed to me over the phone that she'd solved the case. The only problem was that the whole thing – the murder investigation, the cover-up – came to a head before the film was ready to be launched. It may have taken the wind out of her sails."

"And you're assuming she had it right," Rudy pointed out. "My guess is that she went way off the track. It will be interesting to see who she thought committed the murder, or who she thinks needs to be held responsible for the cover-up. Or if she even knew then that there was one."

"Well I have to give her credit for telling me there was a trophy to be found. She did know that."

"What trophy?"

"The earring," she reminded him. He nodded, a little embarrassed at forgetting.

"What a disappointment for her," Fiona said, thinking how triumphant Marigold had been. "Given her real age, this might finally be the end of her career. I mean, to mess up so badly. If she did mess up, and I'm pretty sure she had to have done. There are no second chances, once you get old." Rudy looked surprised.

"I found Belinda," he said.

"You're a man," Fiona told him, patiently. He looked away, but not before she saw him glance quickly at the sagging flesh under her chin. As if women were only flesh, nothing but flesh. How shocked had Belinda been the first time Rudy had taken off his clothes in her presence? Maybe she just closed her eyes. Or did that motherly instinct kick in?

"You can write another book," he told her. "When this commission is all finished, you can write a definitive book about this whole mess."

"Yes," she answered, sharply.

"Give yourself time," he said, and for the first time in all the years she'd known him, she found him annoying as hell.

But the waiter had arrived with their dinner order, re-filling their wineglasses before he went away again. The room was becoming busy, the murmur of contented voices mingling with the tinkle and clink of cutlery and china, and laughter, and sounds from the kitchen, filled the space around them. Fiona thought, I wish Roman were here sitting across from me, and then she thought, no, no, I don't want that. Remembering the long, bored silences, the covert glances at each other to try to figure out what the other was thinking or wanted or wouldn't want once the thinker proposed it. Not just the absolute boredom, but the knowing-the-other-person-much-too-well. I suppose I will never marry again, probably never even have another partner, possibly never even another lover. Such immense sadness she felt at this, her heart aching dully in her chest.

Rudy was watching her, as if he had understood what she was feeling, as if she had spoken aloud to him.

"My daughter-in-law is the same age as my wife," he said, looking back down at his plate. Fiona remained silent for a beat, then said cheerfully, "You men are so dumb." She laughed, and he looked up and laughed with her, but she saw something in his eyes, a flickering of comprehension and then refusal.

Belinda will get older, too, she thought. When you bore her, fail to meet her needs, she will take a lover. She will get over her need for a father, and then you'll become an annoying old beast who has stolen her youth. When you die, your first children, her peers, will hate her for usurping them in your will.

But she said aloud to Rudy, thinking of her own ruined arms, stomach, falling breasts, wryly, "I'm sure there are compensations."

Vonnie had said, so angry her voice shook, "It's not over until I say it's over!" She had paused, calming herself. "I intend to work even harder; I intend to work myself into the grave. I will get every single medal in their arsenal. I will become very powerful. No one will cross me. I will not quit until I lose my marbles or I die!" She breathed through her nose a few times, the redness that had come into her cheeks and forehead dying slowly away, and went on, "We can travel too, Fiona. Together. I've never been to southeast Asia. You haven't either. Why don't we plan a trip? Something exciting to look forward to, eh?"

Fiona had begun to understand then. It was hard, intense grieving for what in the end was the closing down of possibilities, the absolute, irrevocable, no-going-back, closing down of youth. But it was human life: what point in grieving? She had begun to understand that once one stopped yearning for funky bistros, for laughing lovers, for rock 'n roll, and abandon, and magical thinking, and the kind of open-ended richness that life was for the young, something new would begin to dawn.

Ahead of her was life: a deeper, richer, more intensely beautiful grappling with the human condition.

Gazing across the table at her old flame, Rudy, she

thought, I have the better route: I have a step-daughter to live for; I have a book to write about this case, this time with an answer, and a career as a speaker ahead of me; and travelling with Vonnie and Melody, eating up the world.

And as soon as this Inquiry is over, I am going to China.

THE END

Acknowledgements

Many thanks to Roger and Gerald who read the manuscript looking for plot-glitches that I couldn't see myself. Thanks also to others with whom I discussed parts of the manuscript as I tried to figure out what would work and what wouldn't. Thanks to my marvelous editor Lara Hinchberger who kept me on the right path and straightened out my writerly confusion and put up with my occasional obstinacy. Thanks also to Coteau Books who accepted the manuscript with rare speed, surprising the heck out of me. There is also a lawyer I'd like to thank for explaining certain laws to me, and offering wise opinions for which I am immensely grateful. To others who offered advice or read parts of the manuscript, I thank you with all my heart. Any plotting errors or inconsistencies are my fault and nobody else's. And once again, this is a work of fiction, meant to be taken as such.

SHARON BUTALA is an award-winning and bestselling author of both fiction and nonfiction. Her classic book *The Perfection of the Morning* was a #1 bestseller and a finalist for the Governor General's Award. *Fever*, a short story collection, won the 1992 Authors' Award for Paperback Fiction and was shortlisted for the Commonwealth Writers' Prize for best book (Canada and Caribbean region). Her novel, *Wild Rose*, also with Coteau, was published in 2015 and was shortlisted for the W.O. Mitchell Book Prize. Most recently, she published *Where I Live Now* in April 2017. Butala is a recipient of the Marian Engel Award, the Saskatchewan Order of Merit, and the 2012 Cheryl and Henry Kloppenburg Award for Literary Excellence. In 2002 she became an Officer of the Order of Canada. She lives in Calgary, Alberta.